KATIE BIEKSA

Cedar

A Novel

WALTER B
PUBLISHING

Katie Bieksa
Cedar
Walter B Publishing
Copyright © 2022 by Katie Bieksa
First Edition

Softcover ISBN 978-1-7386332-1-0
Hardcover ISBN 978-1-7386332-0-3
Electronic ISBN (Kindle) 978-1-7386332-2-7

Book Design | Petya Tsankova
Editor | Lori Bamber
Publishing Support | TSPA The Self Publishing Agency, Inc.
Cover design based on the photography work by Loren Gu and Cole Keister on Unsplash

WALTER B
PUBLISHING

For my father—
toast with honey and tea

CHAPTER ONE | *Jillian*

In her brief life, my little sister Cedar never said a word.

Yet she and I never stopped talking, about everything, every moment we were awake.

At least that's how I remember it.

When she died, a light went out in me, and in our family. It felt like the only light.

I remember that day in fragments, like a nightmare—shattering, bewildering. Impossible to explain. My parents and the teenagers in the white Pontiac Sunbird that hit her said it was an accident.

Like a lost bird crashing into a window.

Never to get up.

Never to fly again.

I've known from that day that they are all hiding something from me.

Kids can tell. They watch their parents constantly, so they know the little downward pull of an eyelid that says Mom is trying not to laugh—the appearance of a jaw muscle that means that Dad is about to walk out of the house and slam the door.

For one thing, there was no reason for Cedar to be in front of that car. One moment she was beside me on the curb, writing with a stick in the gravel, and the next there was a crash. To be in front of that car, she had to pop up like a Jack-in-the-box and sprint onto the road. Why? For what?

As I screamed and fought to go to her, they took her away. I wasn't allowed to see her, but I was so relieved to see that there was no blood on the road or the sheet my mother had hastily thrown over her. She had to be okay, right?

When my parents came home from the hospital and told me Cedar was dead, I didn't believe them. I've never believed them.

Yet I stopped hearing her voice.

For the first time since she was born, I was always alone in our shared bedroom. I was alone in my head.

As the years went by, I began to accept the silence.

You can imagine my shock when, thirteen lonely years later, about a week before she would have turned twenty-two, I heard Cedar's voice.

It was just loud enough to hear over the traffic. Hustling down Robson on my way to surprise my boyfriend Will for lunch in our apartment, I heard her.

"Jillian, look up."

She sounded older, grown up, but so clearly herself, too—a bit out of breath and mischievous, still. I could hear her excitement about starting one of our games.

I looked up, of course.

It's true that I've never completely stopped looking for her. In bookstores, on magazine covers, on the streets of each new city I traveled to. What if my parents had just sent her away? Given up on trying to teach her to talk? What if she was growing up somewhere with another family, missing me as I did her?

I thought often about what she would look like today. When we were little, we looked so much alike. Even though she was younger, she was somehow the masterpiece and I was the amateur copy. Everyone tells me I was a beautiful child; that I am a beautiful woman. It's never meant anything to me. First, it was inevitable: my parents looked like the model couples in stock images, the kind that come in department store frames and are replaced with less glamorous family photos.

And look what physical beauty has done for my parents.

Cedar was named for the towering tree in our backyard, and she seemed to be born with its other-worldly beauty, too. She was like me with filters—my eyes are hazel, hers were a cat-like green. We both had brown hair, but hers shone like polished mahogany while mine was dull as a sparrow.

Yet I was never jealous. She was mine. We were each other's. It made me happy to watch her grow up and turn heads and charm everyone in her path with a smile.

Even Will, who understands me better than anyone in my life ever has, doesn't get it. There is no way to describe how special my sister was. Is. Was.

"Are you sure you're not just glorifying her memory? It would be understandable if you did," he said when I first told him about her.

Well, sure. Of course, it would be understandable. But with Cedar it is unnecessary.

Now I freeze, stopping dead in the middle of the sidewalk, frustrating the people hurrying by on their short lunch breaks.

"Jilly, look up!"

What?! I make myself take a deep breath, filling my lungs with the moist air off the Pacific, so misty today it feels as if raindrops are materializing around me. Holding my breath in to cradle my pounding heart, I look up.

Above me, pressed against a floor-to-ceiling window, there is a woman who looks like me. She smiles and gives the smallest wave, just one movement of her long fingers against the glass. Then she is gone.

I stand frozen, my eyes darting from the window to the building's front door. I make myself breathe.

Breathe.

Breathe.

I hear nothing else, and the door doesn't open. When a few minutes pass without anything happening, I panic and run to the door of the building, running through the directory and buzzing one number after another. "Cedar? I'm looking for Cedar?"

Nothing.

Is she punishing me?

Does she know that I've stopped thinking about her for hours, even days, at a time?

I finally give up, slumping onto the concrete bench outside the door and giving in to tears. I had seen her for just a few seconds, but I know it was her. Who else could it be? Her smile, small but somehow generous, too, sending me love in the tiny upright curl of her perfect lips. The dress she wore was the kind only Cedar would choose for anywhere but the red carpet: diagonally cut with striking lines and this year's Pantone colors.

I stood up and went back to stand on the sidewalk, looking up at the window for another hour, hoping she would reappear. I knew that anyone I told would tell me I was hallucinating, having one of the "spells" my parents used to tell me I had. But I'm fine—the years of treatment and meds are behind me. Yes, I will always be the girl whose sister and best friend died and whose parents lied to her about it. I will always be the girl who was able to communicate with her mute but telepathic sister and wasn't interested in communicating with anyone else. Yes, telepathic—that's what Dr. X called it, and so that's what I call it.

But I'm doing well now. My success at work, Will—my life has become a real life. That's how I know this is real. It isn't me wanting something to happen so badly I imagine it, because I don't need Cedar that way anymore.

Around me people walk quickly past and the rain continues, running down my neckline with my tears, soaking my blouse and bra.

I finally make my feet move. I can't go back to my office. There is no way I am smiling and making small talk with the mega-millionaire clients who drop in to ask me to pull off today's variety of financial magic.

To see Cedar and then fake-apologize to some landlord for not having transferred an irresponsible athlete's rent on time? Not possible.

I type a quick text to my assistant, trying to steady my still-shaking hands, telling her to cancel my appointments.

My head is spinning so fast, but I just can't walk away. The building I'd seen Cedar in is part of a connected development, so I go to one entryway after another, begging my way in, describing the adult Cedar and explaining that no, I don't have a photo of my sister on my phone.

CHAPTER TWO | *Jillian*

I've tried hypnotherapy and deep meditation.

I've written down all the details I could remember of the dreams: dreams in which the old house is still alive, the color of the drapes and slightly musty smell of the sofa still vivid.

I've tried so hard to make sense of childhood memories that are filled with holes and mixed up with the stories I've been told. I've never looked at a photo of that time without wondering if my memories are just that, memories of photographs.

Childhood amnesia is normal, I'm told. Around age seven, apparently, we start to forget everything that happened before. A grandfather—who pushed us on tire swings, made cars out of old boxes and brought donuts on Sundays—becomes an abstract, flashes that come to us when we walk by Tim Hortons or hear a child laugh in the park.

My only memories of my mother in the years before Cedar was born are of her pregnant, all of us so excited about the baby in her belly. She was so alive then, taking my tiny hand and placing it on her stomach, my father beaming at his two girls, proud and excited to extend our family.

Then the blood, dripping down her legs like the thick sticky barbecue sauce we sometimes had with dinner, staining the butterfly mat in front of the kitchen sink. Mom cried silently, trembling, pretending it wasn't happening, until Dad came in and pushed us toward the car to drive to the hospital.

Afterward, Mom's sparkling eyes went vacant. She'd thank me listlessly for the endless supply of homemade cards I supplied, sticking them to the fridge in a stack when she finally got out of bed. It was as if she was underwater, not really able to see us through the murk.

Not too long after, there would be happiness again. Her tummy swelling, my father, now nervous, looking out of place at the grocery store as he insisted on helping her do everyday things.

And then, once again, my mother would be caught by the riptides of her body, each time staying under longer.

The last time it happened, I remember her screams as they rushed out the door, leaving me alone, shouting to me to run to the neighbor's house. By that time, I hated the "little miracle" tormenting my family.

The way they tell the story and the way I remember it are very different. I remember my father coming home with shaking hands and voice, telling Mrs. Baxter that it had been a "false alarm," before carrying me home across the dark yard, rocking me mechanically as if he was trying to sooth himself.

I can still hear him whispering into the phone after he plunked me into my bed, covering me with my Ewok comforter and placing the quickest kiss on my forehead, avoiding my eyes and my questions.

Aunt Jen arrived in the morning with her largest blue Samsonite suitcase and tried to distract me from my father's coldness. As I made my way downstairs, I heard him close the door quietly and then his steps on the gravel before the car started and he pulled away.

I remember Aunt Jen's visit as long, so long that she quit being a nurse. I wondered if she was my new mom. I remember being angry with her, not wanting to glue popsicle sticks together or poke holes in Styrofoam balls. All I wanted was my mom and my dad, our life before.

When the first day of school came, the yellow bus stopped in front of our home and then carried on without me, my new Jem and the Holograms backpack hanging empty on the back of my door.

"Next year, honey," said Aunt Jen. "You'll go next year."

According to my parents and Aunt Jen, though, this is all nonsense, the wild imagination of a five-year-old about to turn six.

Their version of that time: Mom and Dad bursting through the front door with my new baby sister Cedar in their happy arms. They have the photographic evidence—each step of their story matches a corresponding four-by-six in the family album. Mom in the doorway, with Cedar nestled into her chest; my proud daddy posed with a pink-tipped cigar and a bouquet of flowers.

Cedar and I, as I held her for the first time, braced by pillows, a pair of adult hands hovering in the background. I do remember the scene in this photo—it was the moment I knew I loved her, that she was a miracle as everyone had said.

She was such a good baby. She didn't cry, the way other babies cried. The top of her wooden crib, lined with rose-colored wooden spindles, came just to the tip of my nose. I was barely able to see her inside.

As I peeked over quietly, I could tell she knew I was there and was happy to see me. She'd look toward me with her still slightly unfocused eyes and kick her tiny porcelain-skinned legs. As the weeks passed, she started smiling, and her eyes focused, and she seemed more in control of her body.

Then one day, before I'd even heard a giggle escape from her heart-shaped lips, she said my name as I tiptoed toward her.

I knew I'd only heard it in my head, her voice echoless and contained, but I checked over both shoulders and looked down the hall to be sure Mom or Dad weren't playing a trick on me. It was the voice of a puppy speaking on a Saturday morning cartoon, or the way I imagined my dolly might sound if she talked. It was baby talk, but clear, too: my full name, Jillian, with all the syllables.

Every day after that, I hurried to her crib as soon as I woke up. I couldn't ever catch her asleep. She was always awake, waiting for me, just lying quietly.

"Do it again—say it again!"

She did. As clear and startling as the doorbell ringing on a rainy small-town afternoon.

I knew this was magic. It was the best Christmas morning with all the right gifts; waking up at Disney World. Cedar looked at me like she knew it wasn't normal, like she knew she was magnificent and hoped I could understand.

At first that's all she said, little whispers of my name and an occasional "Up." She was my doll, my baby, my sister. I thanked God for her every night in my bedside prayers.

Before she was a year old, she seemed to know as many words as I did, all spoken within the boundaries of our two minds. My parents moved her into my room, and we sat together in the antique rocker placed between our beds nearly every morning. I read to her, all the marvels of cats and hats, of Wonderland and Fraggle Rock. By the time she was eighteen months, she corrected my stumbles and took over wherever I left off—the two of us silently rocking, flipping the pages.

I'd told them both that first time, so excited. "Cedar said my name—I heard it inside my head!!"

I was so confused and hurt when they were angry instead of excited, as if I was lying. They should have known I never ever lied to them. Lying was wrong. I knew that.

"Jillian, don't be ridiculous," said my mom, turning away from me, the J hard in her mouth.

I tried again when they started to worry aloud about Cedar's silence. Again, I was told not to be silly, not to let my imagination "run away with me."

I didn't know what to do when they started taking her off to the doctor in the city, leaving me with Mrs. Baxter. Cedar told me not to worry, but they never let up on her, first with encouragement and bribes of cookies and popsicles and then with desperate withholding.

"Cedar, if you want a cookie, you have to ask with your words!"

I would have thrown myself down on the floor and howled,

but Cedar just looked serenely at my parents as they first offered and then took away her treats. We both swore off treats, looking at the floor and shaking our heads quietly whenever they were offered.

Around Cedar's third birthday, the house calls started. Dr. X was a friend of Aunt Jen's. He had a long, pointy nose and eyes that were more red than brown. He knocked on the door with hands that seemed strangely small for a grown man. He came nearly every week, and my mother pretended to welcome him, even when he interrupted lunch or nap time. But she didn't fool me. She spoke to Dr. X the way she spoke to Mr. Baxter, a man she told Dad gave her the "heebee jeebees."

Dr. X would take Cedar from my mother's reluctant arms and carry her up the stairs like he owned her. Cedar never cried, but she did call my name, and I learned to quietly stand by the door, peaking in the crack he always left open. I knew something wasn't right about Dr. X. In those first appointments, instead of giving Cedar medicine like a doctor should, he took blood out of her arm with a needle and tubes he then put in his big black doctor bag and took away with him.

Yet Cedar didn't fear him. When he left, she was calm. She was never angry or resentful toward us for not protecting her, as if accepting what our mother kept repeating: "It's going to be okay."

I'd seen the way Dr. X looked at me, not trying to interact with me the way adults usually do with children. No compliments on my purple bow or shiny shoes—instead, it was as if he was inspecting me, measuring me up. Cedar saw too, always stepping in front of me like a shield, distracting him. His visits were usually followed by thinly disguised tension.

During and after these sessions, which continued until Cedar was eight or so, she reassured me the way an older sister would usually reassure a younger one.

"It doesn't hurt. He's helping me be better—I love him."

"Just talk already!" I yelled at her during one of Mom and Dad's long, silent, passive-aggressive fights.

There was nothing wrong with Cedar except her refusal to speak out loud. She was physically perfect, her hair already as long as mine. She ran faster and jumped higher. She was never sick; she never caught my chicken pox even though she crawled into my bed and put her cool hands on my itchy blisters to comfort me.

When you're a child, things just are the way they are. Magic is real. Santa Claus and the Easter Bunny are facts. The threat of Santa watching to see if we're good is not taken lightly, even in the heat of summer.

I guess that is part of the reason it took me until I was a teenager to ask myself what the fuck was going on with my sister. By that time, I'd seen Drew Barrymore in *Firestarter*, further convincing me that people like Cedar are around us even if people say it's fiction.

Science cannot say my sister isn't telepathic any more than it can explain why some people get cancer and some don't. Or why my nine-year-old sister would throw herself in front of a car when seconds before she had been beside me, happily drawing letters in the gravel with a stick.

But I learned that, like my parents, science says that telepathy doesn't exist—or, rather, "has never been proven to exist." As my former best friend Emily Ann Harris also said, loud enough that we stopped being friends even before the "id" in stupid left her lips.

I didn't choose to live my life like Nancy Drew, trying to solve the mysteries of my sister's life and death—and rebirth.

Some children have a parent walk out on them, a father who starts a second family before finishing the one he has. Or a mom who just disappears. They ask questions. They need answers. Until we have those answers, we're not whole. Even when the people you love and trust most tell you to move on, to forget, that some things are better left unknown.

Easier said.

Even before I saw her in that window, Cedar was like that old Willie Nelson song, always on my mind.

Sure, since I'd finished treatment, she was usually in the back of my mind, somewhere behind what to pick up for dinner and what Will meant when he said whatever he said last night.

But always on my mind, always on my mind.

I'm not a child anymore. I don't have to listen when I'm told not to ask questions. I'll always try to respect my parents' grief, but I can't pretend that what happened to my family, to my sister, was a normal kind of tragedy, the accidental death of a child.

I never believed them and I don't believe them now.

And now I have proof—Cedar is in Vancouver.

Cedar is alive.

CHAPTER THREE | *Jillian*

None of the concierges or residents I talk to admit to knowing a woman who looks like the grownup Cedar I saw in the window. I finally give up. Weary and heartbroken and still in shock, I let my legs navigate my way home.

I tell myself that nothing has really changed. I am the same Jillian I was when I left home this morning. Yet as soon as I open the door of our apartment, I feel as if I have a secret, like I've done something wrong. My voice sounds shaky as I call for Will, closing the door behind me and, uncharacteristically, locking it. When he comes around the corner to greet me the way he always does, I want to throw my arms around him and fill in all the blanks I've left in our conversations about my sister. But how? Anyone I've ever told first laughed and then looked at me as if I were certifiable. What do you say when someone tells you they have a mute telepathic sister who died, but that they believe is still alive somewhere?

After Emily Ann Harris, I never took the chance. And the trouble here is that I love Will. His slender body, bordering on scrawny, his chiseled cheekbones. The blue eyes that have yet to see the real me, the *Through the Looking Glass* Jillian.

It wasn't Will's appearance that attracted me, and despite my digs to the contrary, it wasn't the old money he was raised on either. It is that, like me, he tries so hard to be normal. To act as if he was completely unaffected by growing up in a manor with staff, never having a chance to want for anything. I had doctors, betrayal and mourning—he had a family mansion and a trust fund. Yet the outcomes were similar: we both felt alone in the world until we found each other.

We met at work nearly two years ago. We were in a conference room, rain rivulets and mist blurring the view, as is so often the case here. Except for our shared interest in algorithms and complex calculations, I felt very out of place among my peers. Perhaps it was how outnumbered I was by the men in the room: men with the same arrogant airs as their wealthy clients, as if managing wealth somehow made them entitled, too.

For me, and for Will, I was to find out, money had nothing to do with our career paths. Math was safe, "cut and dried," more reliable than anything else in my life. For Will, it was just meeting the expectation that he continue in the family business.

I dressed seriously, a simple, black, fitted skirt long enough to reach my knees while seated, a blouse buttoned up to the collar; flat shoes and an office-appropriate low ponytail. I still had to avoid making eye contact with my co-workers unnecessarily, though. This is not conceit—believe me, I'm not Cedar-level beautiful. But I'm attractive enough for it to be an issue. It's true the world treats good-looking people better, and for that reason I'm grateful to have blessed genes. That day, for example, the men seated around me offered me coffee, opened the door for me and faked interest in my answers to their questions. On the other hand, it also meant that a friendly smile required diplomatically deflecting advances in the coffee room later.

I was used to the attention, never particularly appreciating or enjoying it, almost in the exact way Will explains being inordinately well-to-do. We are well suited to each other that way. We both have something other people want—but neither of us are happier because of it.

It was something in the way Will spoke to me that day that made him stand out, as if he was oblivious to the fact that I otherwise had a hundred percent of the sexual attention of a table full of men. He says it was because he automatically put himself in the friend zone, not wanting to bother competing with the handsome and largely vapid alphas around us. As cliché as it is, this is likely what first attracted me to him. So much that I found myself watching him while a cocksure forty-something executive explained the impact of foreign pension fund moves in the previous week. Will's lips pressed against his water glass as he took a sip and I fixated on the little drop that lingered at the corner of his mouth, wondering how long it would be before he wiped it away. Twenty seconds, it turns out, with the back of his hand.

For the next few weeks, I made a point of claiming the chair next to his in meetings, signing up for the same projects, finding reasons to ask him questions. As if I were just another suit, all of my attempts to make myself noticeable seemed to go unnoticed.

So, I had no choice but to make my feelings known, make one more assault on office policies that were routinely ignored, and ask Will on a date.

I will never forget his eyes, the way they were distracted as I started talking but jetted back to me when I said, "Let's go out sometime."

"Like a date?"

"Yes, a date," I said, with the confidence of a woman who knows she's smart, attractive and in a place where women are out-numbered by about thirty-to-one.

"I'd like to get to know you," I said, with the warmest smile in my repertoire.

What happened next was unexpected, I'll be honest.

"Hmmm," he said, exaggerating the mmm, biting the end of a pen inscribed WXS. "Can I think about it?"

"Sure. Of course. I guess," I managed to get out. I felt both embarrassed and intrigued, not really knowing if he was kidding or not.

"Okay, I'm thinking about it." He touched my arm briefly as he walked past me.

I stood there for a moment before following, giving him a few seconds to round the corner before following him to our communal open office.

Okay, so this is how that feels, I thought, making a note to self to be a bit gentler in the future. Strangely, once I shook off the initial embarrassment, the ordeal felt kind of uplifting. I'd figured he would jump at the chance, if only to climb a notch in the opinions of the alphas. I was happy to learn there was more to Will Sutherby than I'd guessed.

In the following weeks, I did my best to steer clear of him. He still hadn't given me a response one way or another, which not only drove me nuts but also made me feel guilty about all the men

I'd left in limbo in the past. I wasn't in the habit of asking men out; truthfully, I didn't go out on dates. My love life consisted of one-night stands where I took charge, on top, the goal to reach orgasm rather than find romance. You'd be shocked at how much more satisfying this is than the more usual approach of the women I know: letting men selfishly pump away at them in the hope it might turn into a relationship. Dating like a man is very confusing to men. I've often had to explain the concept of a one-nighter to sex partners who didn't realize it could go both ways.

Now, for the first time in a long time, I found myself wanting something more. Sure, it turns me on to watch Will roll up the sleeves of his dress shirts and adjust his collar, loosening it so that I can see his Adam's apple bounce when he swallows. But it is the way he holds doors for everyone (even the assholes) and spends more time talking to the sixty-year-old receptionist than me that fills me with an intense desire to get to know him better.

"What's his story?" I finally ask Paul, a nerdier version of Will who knows everything about everyone in the office, save me.

"You don't know?" he asked, sounding almost as condescending as our bosses any time we underlings ask a question. But his excitement showed too: Paul finally had something I wanted.

"He's Will Sutherby. Sutherby Investments."

Even though I was still quite new to the city, and uninterested in anything but climbing the ladder and paying the rent, I knew something about the Sutherbys and their wildly lucrative international investment firm. But when I said it over in my head, the name made me feel uneasy.

"What's he doing here then?" I asked, watching Will from

the corner of my eye as he typed away at a terminal in the middle of the room.

Then it hit me. I was immediately pissed off as it registered what he must think of me, the conclusion he must have drawn about my interest in him.

"I guess his dad is a dickhead who wants him to earn it the old-fashioned way," said Paul.

"Ha. Dickheads might run in the family."

"What'd you mean?"

"Forget it," I said, smiling as if I already had. "I was just curious."

I have been accused of being many things in my life: a liar, crazy, stupid, a slut (yep, a few jealous girls at college). But a gold digger? That really hit a nerve. Sure, my family didn't have much money and I was drowning in student loans, barely afloat in one of the most expensive cities in the world. But it had never crossed my mind to hook up with a meal ticket. If it had, I'd probably go the trouble-free route—our rich, good-looking clients with indentations on their ring fingers that remind me of my ankles when I take off my gym socks.

Because I'd grown up perfecting detachment, I was able to erase Will from my thoughts and disregard him entirely, knowing that an explanation was both required and not happening.

Of course, it took only a few days for Will to catch onto my new outlook and start finding ways to be around me. In spite of his attempts, however, most of what initially attracted me to him was gone. Now, when he spoke, I heard a pampered, privileged man who thought I wanted his money rather than the humble Will who was oblivious to my superficial charms.

Almost a month later, I was making my way out of the building, annoyed by the rain and the reality of steaming public transit ahead of me, when Will appeared.

He sheepishly opened with, "So, I've thought about it, and I think we should have that date."

"Oh, yeah?" I said, laughing him off, not breaking stride.

"I can't think of any reason not to …" he said, his voice trailing mine as he placed his body square in front of me. His piercing eyes were like a stop sign.

"How about because you're rude, and I'm not into it, or you, anymore?"

"Harsh. Okay, give me a shot to see if I can change that."

"Will," I said, dropping my heavy bag at my feet. "You know, I get it. You're the type of guy that assumes women are in it for your money. But guess what—I had no idea about all that. I just thought you were a sweet guy …"

"So it's settled then, I'm sweet."

"No, Will, I *thought* you were a sweet guy. Now I know you're one more self-entitled jerk who thinks the worst of people, and I couldn't be less interested."

"Come on, Jillian, one date. Just do a guy a favor and I'll never ask again."

"I'll think about it, okay?" I echoed caustically. In fact, it sounded a tad harsher than it had in my head.

I walked away, not waiting for a reaction to appear on his sweetly boyish face.

We continued this charade for another week or so. On my part, it wasn't out of a desire to play games, to reverse the hard-to-get role. The idea of having to prove myself to him, to make gestures that reinforced my disinterest in his money, cheapened any potential romance.

"No, let me buy dinner."

"No, thanks, I'll meet you there—I prefer the bus to your Maserati."

At the same time, I knew I hadn't been telling the whole truth. I still found myself drawn to him. In fact, somehow, I even found myself following him.

It started out accidentally.

I was looking down on the busy sidewalk beneath our office window just to help me think, and there he was, empty-handed and alone. I watched him cross Georgia Street, threading through the crowds of impatient office workers and shoppers. There was something in the way he yielded to people coming toward him, keeping his eyes ahead and not down on his phone, that held my attention. For a few moments I was able to stay with him, to trace my hand along the window, walking the length of the room above him. I felt a moment of panic as he turned the corner and disappeared out of sight, like a favorite TV show had been interrupted for a news report.

The idea that he kept moving, that he continued to live off my screen, sparked my curiosity. For the first time, it occurred to me that Will Sutherby existed outside of our brief interactions.

Who was this guy?

The next afternoon, I waited until he left the office. I watched the elevator door close from my discreet spot in the copy room and then caught the next one, hoping I could catch up without looking obvious. I was careful to stay far enough behind that a crosswalk stop wouldn't blow my cover. I followed him for two blocks, not caring that our final destination would likely be as mundane as a Starbucks. Surprisingly, we didn't stop at all. He kept walking, turning down some streets and up others as if he were ducking a tail, me. It was a peculiar way to spend a lunch break, especially for a man who definitely wasn't walking off calories or trying to satisfy his step quota.

His desire to be alone, to stretch his legs and breathe the fresh air, was so much like me that I decided that if he asked again, I would say yes.

He did, and our first date was the following weekend. He picked me up at eight even though I was starving by six. I understand that no one under sixty goes out for dinner at six anymore—I'm just not one to care. Eat when you're hungry, have sex when you're horny.

Will learned this about me not even three hours after I climbed into his car for the first time.

Back in my apartment, I slipped my dress over my head as he stared, obviously shocked.

We'd only had one glass of very expensive red wine each, so he knew I wasn't drunk. Indifferent to the light I'd flicked on as we came in, I stood in my matching black lace panties and bra, giving him full permission to make his move. I watched as his eyes darted up and down my body, not blaming him for needing a second. Although I'd sprung this on him, I had it planned all along: my apartment tidied, my sheets washed, the toilets flushed. Part of what arouses me about first times is seeing how my date reacts to my boldness. I pegged Will as a gentle, timid lover, someone who might be rattled by my initiative.

I quickly learned that he is none of those things. He casually turned away to place his cell and keys on the entryway table, then took his shoes off one at a time, methodically. Only then did he meet my eyes and move toward me, without hesitation or hurry. He opened one and then another button of his dress shirt, pulled at his collar and swallowed hard. Sweeping my hair off my bare shoulder, he brought his lips to my neck and murmured, "Jillian, you're too beautiful for me."

He kissed me just below my ear with slightly open, full lips. My body responded to him before I did. Urgently, breathing deep to pace myself, I finished unbuttoning his shirt and moved it aside before I pressed my body against his, taking a deep breath that pushed my breasts higher on his chest. I tucked my hands beneath his shirt as he pulled me impossibly close.

Then our mouths took over. I couldn't remember ever being kissed so passionately yet so intimately. Our tongues were completely entangled; it was hard to know where mine stopped and his began.

Driven by hormones and instinct, our bodies made their way toward my bedroom until our legs were against my bed. Will lifted me slightly, just enough for me to lose my balance and relax back onto the duvet.

"Do you have a condom?" he asked, sounding a bit breathless.

"Bathroom, medicine cabinet," I said, pointing.

I shimmied to the top of the bed.

"Don't move, k?" He ran his lips over my collarbone before turning away.

"K."

For the first time in maybe forever, I felt nervous as I waited for him to return. I suppose I was expecting him to slow things down or fumble around, but up to that point there had been no sign of hesitation. He came out still wearing his jeans, now unzipped. His upper body was slight, but he was fit—no hollow-chested Calvin Klein model look here. As he lowered himself on top of me, along the length of my body, I could feel that his lower body quite made up for any shortcomings that might appear later.

It was crystal clear he had the green light, but he still took the time to make sure I was ready, kissing me gently, touching me with soft fingers that moved fast. Kissing me again. I liked it. I wanted it.

This was all an unexpected change from the animals who performed as if I were melting ice cream, forcing me to both take charge *and* slow things down. I was absolutely into it, but his confidence made me wonder if I'd had him completely wrong. I started to feel a bit anxious that maybe Will was less "Ahhh, cute," and more of a sneaky playboy.

"Fuck," he said afterward, rolling onto his back, completely spent.

"Do you want some water?" I swung my legs to the side of the bed and retrieved the silk robe I'd strategically placed within reaching distance.

"Water? I think I need an espresso."

"Really?" I said, underestimating the elapsed time.

"I haven't had sex in like six months," he said, smiling. "And never with anyone who looks like you."

For whatever reason, this declaration re-energized my confidence. I crawled back onto the bed and placed a kiss on his cheek.

"You're adorable," I said.

"No, I'm serious. Do you know how hard that was for me? I was barely able to enjoy it."

"I guess we'll need to practice then," I said, purposely taking my time tying my robe in front of him. "I'd prefer you enjoy it."

So, we were sexually compatible.

I was very interested in Will beyond the bedroom, but hesitant to voice my feelings. After a lifetime of putting up walls, of loss that hurt in my bones, I needed to be sure I was ready. It doesn't take people long to figure out that my direct, cool personality is a screen for some serious issues.

After Cedar, I can't say anyone has ever gotten to know the real me. To be fair, I don't know if I've ever allowed myself to really look inwards, either. Do I know myself?

It took time and a lot of superficial conversations, but eventually Will and I both started to see glimpses of the Jillian neither of us knew. Will taught me that finding joy in little things was okay, even in the absurdity of reality TV and Lifetime movies. Maybe that seems trite, but it was new for me. Sweet. Will says, echoing Andy Warhol, "People need to work at learning how to live, because life is so quick and sometimes it goes away too quickly."

Just as it did for Cedar. Too quick.

So, I'm learning. I've learned that I'm ticklish, and that I actually crave hugs. Physical affection wasn't something I ever saw or experienced at home with my depressed mom and overwhelmed dad—I had no idea what I was missing. I slowly began to see myself as having more to offer than the image in the mirror. That image—a pretty girl without laughter or room for kindness—is one I'm happy to leave behind me. Sure, I'm thankful for the way I look, because who knows if Will would have stuck around when I got prickly otherwise. But looks become unimportant pretty fast in a real relationship.

Slowly, we became a couple. An us.

In the process, as if he had seen me to be brave, truthful and unselfish, ala Pinocchio, I became a real live girl. Someone who laughs with delight at puppies playing and craves pad thai.

Someone who believes in love.

CHAPTER FOUR | *Jillian*

And so here I am, standing with my arms around Will's waist.

Hey, Jude is playing in the living room and a million thoughts are racing through my head. I finger a lone curl at the base of his hairline.

"Take a sad song and make it better," I hum.

I decide I won't tell him about today, watch his expression turn from admiration to alarm. God knows I've seen enough of that look before: fear, worry, confusion.

Yet I feel the words on the tip of my tongue: "I saw my dead sister today."

I saw my dead sister today.

I saw my dead sister today.

I can't think of a single thing to say when he asks why I'm home early, how my day was. I can feel the intrusive thoughts ready to burst free, to destroy my happiness. The way my vision zones out—focused on the wallpaper, tracing the swirl of a flower around and around—feels too familiar. As if it wasn't long ago at all that I'd lived life completely in my head.

Be present, Jillian. Don't ruin this.

Na na na na, na na na na, hey, hey, hey hey Jude …

"Babe?" he asks, peeling me off of him. "What's up?"

I try my best to look strong, but as he tilts my chin up toward his face, I know he's seen right through my clenched smile.

"Have you been crying? Talk to me, love."

I let my bag slide down my arm and onto the tile with a thump as I let out a hard sigh.

"Yeah. I'm fine, Will."

I turn my back to him and hang my jacket in the closet, taking time to straighten out the arm before closing the door and willing myself to find his eyes. I can tell that he isn't going to let this go. He's not going to turn his back on me and go back to his computer, as I've heard other women complain of their partners whenever there is trouble. He's not showing the signs of the frustration and annoyance coffee room banter tells me men tend to have with complicated, emotional women.

My heart says I can trust him, but my head is telling my heart it's wrong. I lie and blame the alders.

"It's just my damn allergies again."

"Allergies?" he echoes, catching my arm as I try to walk past him.

"I wish someone would think about people with allergies when they decide to plant only male trees … I mean who gives a fuck about berries and leaves?"

"What are you talking about, Jill?"

I can hear the strange tension in my voice, so I clear my throat with an exaggerated cough.

"You know, all the fucking trees are male, so there is so much pollen I can't think straight." I rub my eyes, selling it.

"Female trees don't have pollen?" He's off the trail.

"Well, yeah, babe. I don't know, less pollen. But people don't want shit falling on the sidewalk, so they plant male trees."

"Sudafed?"

"What?"

"Can I get you some?" He's already picking up his fob.

"Would you? Thanks so much, Will. I really need something."

"Well, that would be a first. I'll be right back."

I shut the door behind him, happily distracted for a moment.

Then I head to the washroom, my heart beating faster with each step. Even alone in the condo, I lock myself in before turning the faucet on and letting my hands fill with cool water. I plunge my face into it until it seeps through the spaces between my fingers. Hesitantly, I look up at my dripping face, fearing visible grief or evidence of the possibility I'm going crazy. Again.

When I bring my eyes to the mirror, I see my face clearly, but the longer I stare, the more I see Cedar.

Shit.

Karma punishes me for my lie to Will and my head starts to pound. I strip down and hang up my skirt but throw my blouse on the chair, as it's too clean for the hamper but too dirty for the closet. In bed, I stretch out and feel the expensive sheets Will's mom bought us on my skin, like cool milk on a burnt tongue. I pull the comforter over my head and hide, tent-like, the way Cedar and I used to. I hear the game we played in my head like it was happening beside me.

Crack an egg on your head, let the yolk run down, let the yolk run down. People are dying, children are crying.

The song goes quiet.

Now I remember being alone in my tent after she died, pretending to be with her in her little white coffin. Alone in the dark, my ragged breaths are once again the only reminder that I am alive. *Concentrate. Concentrate. Concentrate on what I am saying.*

I can feel the anxiety building as I struggle to resist saying her name out loud. What if she answers? It's fear laced with excitement, like daring yourself to say Candyman three times in front of the mirror. Finally, I blurt her name out like a cough I can't contain. "Cedar!" And then louder. "Cedar, can you hear me?"

I hold my breath and lay perfectly still in the silence, listening…

And then I hear it.

"Jillian?" The covers are abruptly pulled off me.

"Will! What the hell!" I spring up, my heart racing along with my thumping head.

"Sorry, babe," he says, stepping back, his hands in front of him like a shield.

"What are you doing under there?"

"The light," I lie, expertly. "It's making my eyes hurt."

He hands me a tiny red pill and a glass of water. "Can I call work for you?"

"I called on the way home. I really just need to sleep."

"You want company?" he asks, lifting his shirt over his head and throwing it in the corner.

I resist the urge to lecture on tidiness. "Only if you're going to stay on your side."

"I see. Well, I guess I'll finish up this thing for my dad and then join you in a bit. Maybe you'll be feeling better by then?" He raises his eyebrows suggestively and then plants a firm kiss on my forehead. I should be annoyed by his insensitivity, perhaps, but I'm not. I enjoy sex, would probably even benefit from it right now if it weren't for my imploding head, spinning and caving in on me like falling walls.

He leaves the bedroom and I return to my casket beneath the sheets. For the last six months, since Will accepted a position at his father's firm, he's spent a lot of time working from home. There's really no difference—he's working, I'm working. We're both making money and contributing to the new condo, his and mine, that we moved into mere months into our relationship.

It's a happy little place, with ocean and mountain views if you position yourself properly, particularly if you wedge yourself behind the sofa and in front of an intrusive cylindrical support beam. Only there can you take it all in without feeling any eyes on you. Sandwiched between high-rises, we never otherwise really feel alone. Even when Will and I make love I can feel eyes on us. Sometimes it turns me on, I'll admit, and I find myself performing for the would-be cameras or telescopes. But with the support beam at my back, I can stare out into the water, completely alone, watching the cars cross over the Lion's Gate Bridge and into the mountains while I fantasize about who is in their backseats or what's in their trunks. Reusable shopping bags, parcels hidden from controlling husbands, Cheerio-spattered strollers that weigh more than the women who single-handedly pick them up … Cedar kicking, fighting to come back to me. If I were to murder someone, behind the cylinder would be the perfect place.

Will's dad insisted on looking at apartments with us. He'd even set up the appointments, approving only half of the listings we put on our list, sneaking in others. It seemed like little enough to put up with to make Will's family comfortable with me, but I have to admit that Aaron is getting on my nerves more and more. It's the way he watches me, a look in his eyes that says he knows something I don't. At first, I thought it was just a classic case of an aging player who needed to impress his son's girlfriend, but he doesn't really seem to care if I like him or not—he barks at Will and his mom even when I'm in the room.

I'm convinced he blames me for refusing their financial help, but it was Will. We both liked the idea of being grown up, staying within our budget. Although I secretly could have been convinced to accept the keys to a much larger place with un-hindered water views rather than just a sliver, Will yearns for average, for real freedom.

In the darkness of my tent, I roll the small pill through my fingers, feeling its soft edges. I remember the huge pills they used to force me to swallow, dissolving into burning bitterness or scratching my narrow throat. I consider hiding this one under my pillow or the mattress, but it just makes the lie so much heavier, and Will's kind effort useless. Instead, I pop it in my mouth like a Skittle and swallow hard.

I picture the pill on its descent, tumbling, churning around, red within red. I picture Will at his desk, working away, only flashes of profit, pride and sex on his blissfully peaceful mind, completely unaware of what I'm doing.

And what am I doing? Cedar isn't hiding somewhere under

here. This afternoon starts feeling like a dream and doubt creeps in. In the deepest, most shameful parts of my mind, I find myself wishing I hadn't seen her, hatefully hoping it was just some weird kind of daydream.

Somehow, though, I know that everything is about to change even if I never see her again.

I can feel my thoughts getting dense, old questions crawling up my arms and into my ears like little spiders, each carrying another memory.

With every innocent stroke Will makes on his keyboard, he gets further and further away from me, as if he's rowing along with the team of dragon boats below our window.

I already somehow know we won't survive the truth.

CHAPTER FIVE | *Will*

I often pretend that my relationship with Jill is as real as I'd like it to be. As sincere as it felt today when she actually asked me for help. Some days it feels that way, even for hours at a time. But the illusion never lasts through those horrible stretches I go through each night until sleep finally releases me from my self-loathing.

And whenever she does something uncharacteristically cute, or says something brilliant, or pisses me off with her coldness, I remember.

When we make love, I still feel like a rapist. And that makes me physically sick, so much so that I've thrown up more than once afterward. But Jill is almost always the initiator. Before I knew anything about what Aaron was up to, we had already been together. How false could my intentions have been on the first date? Pretty fucking false, if I think about it. But I try not to do that, to think about it.

I swear to God I thought she was on to me. The way she just threw herself at me … I thought there was zero chance she was doing it for real, gearing down in front of me a couple hours into our first date, standing there like my own personal playmate. Almost exactly the way I pictured her looking as I jerked off before I picked her up, as a matter of fact.

Especially after the hoops she made me go through to get that date in the first place, even though she'd asked me first.

She had to be setting me up.

Afterward, I almost couldn't meet her eyes, just waiting for her to be like, "Got ya, you pig!"

But no, she just wanted to have sex. And how cool is that? As hard as I tried not to, and as much as I punished myself, I found myself falling for her—even before I saw her naked.

I also can't stop obsessing about what her parents have on my dad. I mean, he's got his hands into everything, more money than morals, but what kind of connection could he have to her very regular, small-town family? The way Jill makes it sound, they're just a couple of working-class folks who lived through tragedy and revel in insignificance. Not that it is a bad thing—insignificance is my goal, too, actually.

To have a life that doesn't revolve around money even more than it does the sun.

Unfortunately, that idea is something my father holds partic-ular scorn for. In his view, anyone who doesn't make all decisions based on their dollar value is a soft-headed moron.

I did stop cashing his checks—as if that makes it all okay. I haven't gone as far as ripping them up yet, probably because my bullshit idea of being a regular guy may in fact depend on a never-ending supply of his money. I don't know. I've never tried it.

I just stash them in my sock drawer underneath a photo of

my grandparents, and live off my inheritance. They died in a car accident when I was twenty. Who knows, it's possible they were assholes like my parents, but I choose to remember my grandad laughing as he put his hand on my head and the way my grandmother looked as she smiled at me wearing her signature red lipstick. Maybe that's the way little boys define beautiful: loving expressions and pretty colors.

She once told me I could be anything I wanted, that the world was waiting to see what I would do. She was one of the first women to work in finance, to sit at the same boardroom table my father heads now, his version of a cockpit. Sure, it's banal, but when she said it, and maybe even for a couple years after, I believed her.

I knew my grandparents loved me. I know my parents do too, in a more obligatory way, heir of the family and all that. But those two beautiful people whose photo is tucked away with my dress socks? They made me feel loved. So, they guard the checks, the money I receive for the worst kind of disloyalty. If I ever attempt to cash them, I hope Grandma's crooked smile and Grandad's strong hands on her shoulders will be enough to shame me into not doing it.

Perhaps if they were still here, I would've turned out better— probably couldn't be any worse, really. Jill once said that, because I've been raised on old money, snobbery is just a part of me. Like it's okay that I'm a snob because I honestly don't know it.

"It's not like you're trying to be pretentious," she said, laughing after I told her my favorite childhood food was sushi.

"It's a West Coast thing," I argued.

"It's an upper-class thing," she countered. "All I'm saying is most Canadian kids would say noodles. Or pizza."

"And how many of those 'sgetti and meatball' kids turned your head?" I baited, placing my hand on an exposed piece of her thigh as she re-crossed her legs.

"You're absolutely right, Mr. Sutherby, it's your money and obsession with raw fish that does it for me—but you already knew that, didn't you?"

Do you have any idea what it's like being a Sutherby?

It's always been us against everybody else.

He didn't give me a choice, really.

"I need you to do this, son."

A safe distance, he instructed—like a friendly big brother. "Don't get too close."

But with Jill it was all or nothing. I attempted to buy myself some time when she asked me out, and then it was like she fucking hated me. How was I to get close to her without getting close to her?

The first date was a success and an utter failure.

"What the fuck is wrong with you? You have to screw the first pretty girl who talks to you?"

After that, because whatever my dad has going on is always more important than anything else in the world, I had to quit my internship. According to His Lordship Aaron Sutherby—yes, you're right, I'd never call him anything but Dad in his presence—I had to leave the office I shared with Jill.

Suddenly we went from "Don't get too close," to "It's imperative you talk her into moving in with you."

Now, I sit here most days, crunching numbers for Sutherby

International Investments and keeping tabs on Jill, who really doesn't do anything out of the ordinary except when she's sleeping.

Until maybe five minutes ago.

"Cedar!"

She calls out to her most nights, sometimes panicked, like she's falling, springing up with beads of sweat on her otherwise flawless forehead.

Other times, it's different, even more eerie. Sometimes Cedar answers back. I don't know how she does it, but it's like another voice. More than once, I've had my sleep shattered by the sound of two girls giggling together. The first time, I checked my phone and the hallway before realizing it was Jill. For whatever reason, maybe because I've partially convinced myself I'm protecting rather than betraying her, it doesn't scare me the way it probably would most people. Even though I've been told very little, I did prepare myself for … something. It's unsettling, but no more than the teenager with the Dodge Charger who rages into and out of the building most nights, or the slamming of Mrs. Lee's door after her night shift.

Out of love and a sick sense of loyalty, I report half of her nightmares and none of her dreams, the dreams where she lays there smiling, brushing the tiny hairs away from her own face with a hand that seems to belong to someone else.

As soon as she came home today, I could tell something was wrong. She was trying too hard to be calm. She held it together, but I could tell that if I asked one more question or showed any sign of doubt, she would've lost it.

Probably would have broken up with me right on the spot.

That's how it is with Jill. Our relationship always feels one annoyance or small dispute away from over. Part of it is my guilt, sure, but a big part of it—and one of the reasons I can live with what I'm doing—is that Jill always seems ready to run. I see the panic in her eyes, the way they move toward the door, when I so much as ask her what time she plans to be home that night. She softens with me sometimes, often even, these last few months. But her basic nature is trust no one, let no one in. As crazy as I am about her, I would have given up by now, accepted that this is never going to be a real relationship. But "the arrangement" with my father strictly forbids it. And so, I'm sort of a prisoner to all of this, to all of the tiptoeing, lying and treading softly.

Except the sex is fucking amazing and I think I'm in love. It's rare that I don't want to have sex with Jill, even when she's being a cold bitch.

Today's a new thing, though. I have to admit that her talking to Cedar under the covers while wide awake was a turn off, like baby talk and insecurity—erection, gone.

What was she doing under there?

The idea of crawling into the bed beside her, my feet stretched out under those same blankets—it's unsettling.

A third float plane just lifted off from the harbor. Three planes. So, I've been staring out the window for at least thirty minutes. I know I've seen the planes, but I can't recall hearing them. I guess this is what you call zoned out.

In my heart, I believe I'm a good person, just as I know what Jill and I have is real, even if it isn't. And I'm fully aware of how fucked up that is. Do I add this new discovery to my report this week? I need to get out of here, but I shouldn't leave her alone.

She is clearly not herself.

I honestly don't know why I'm an indentured, handsomely paid babysitter. Is my dad protecting Jill out of some obligation to her parents? Is he gathering information on them? I don't know. But until I tell her that my dad pays me to keep tabs on her, we can't have a real relationship. And I can't tell her because she will leave me the moment I do, and I love her.

"Walked into bedroom to find Jill talking to her dead sister, Cedar, under the covers …"

A fourth plane moves across my field of vision, and a bright light dances in the corner of my eye, causing me to turn my head. My neighbors across the street are having one of their perfect family moments, on display behind their glass walls. Their two-year-old is sitting in a highchair with his impossibly chubby legs popping out through the bottom holes. The mom and dad, who we've seen at Urban Fare and even exchanged waves with from our respective condos, appear so happy and entertained by their bundle it's like an advertisement or a message from God himself that this family is the goal.

The cold, quiet home I grew up in didn't leave me with any urge to bring children of my own into the world. Jill and I haven't talked about it, but I'm guessing that losing her sister and her mom's depression didn't inspire a lot of motivation to have a family for her, either.

I can't even imagine looking our children in the eyes, knowing what I'd done to their mother. I'm like one of those Russian spies Americans are suspicious of, playing house with my Canadian bride, collecting intel on her, reporting her secrets back to the motherland. Except I bear no resemblance to Matthew Rhys, nor am I doing it for my country. (Jill could definitely play Keri Russell, though.)

Yet the more I'm with Jill, the more I want to have children with her. This is my other secret. Moving in together was a stretch for Jill. Marriage is not on her radar—the one time I brought it up she laughed it off without any effort at gentleness. I suppose this is a blessing of sorts. How do I marry a woman I am being paid to be with?

This is a whole different level of prostitution. I start to turn my attention away from the family in the next building just as the mother lifts the baby above his feeding tray, the dad brushing bits of food from his round belly.

I pace for a second and then take tentative steps toward my desk. I could just write the report and delete it later. My father's voice is in my head, calling me soft again. Instead of typing, I firmly shut my MacBook and take a deep breath.

"Fucking asshole," I whisper. "Find another puppet."

Jill's probably asleep now, so I decide to just lie in bed beside her. Just before I turn the door handle to step into our room, into her peace and quiet and away from the self-reproach in my head, I stop. I can hear movements, the shuffling of paper, and maybe even the hum of her voice, just above a whisper. Before calling out to her, I consider knocking. My fist hovers just in front of the door as if being fought off by some invisible force. Do I want to know what's on the other side?

It's not as though I'm afraid she will have hurt herself or spewed green vomit onto our linen sheets—but what if what I see or hear puts me in an even tighter spot?

I suspect Jill has some deeper issues than she's let on. Even though I hope my father's involvement is benign, a part of me wonders—what if I'm keeping an eye on her to prevent her from doing something bad?

I flash back to the moment I first saw her. Out of nowhere, I see her sitting across from me in the boardroom again, looking like a professionally edited version of my dream girl—me desperately hoping Aaron's target was the duller woman at the end of the table. The way Jill held herself among those men, owning and dismissing her beauty at the same time. Then I caught her gazing in my direction. Even before she spoke, I already knew there was such a thing as perfect, and she was it.

So how can I open this door?

When I was ten, I walked in on my mother and my father's partner, Richard—Dick, as it were. I still remember the strange pitch of the laughter behind the door to my father's study. It was my mom's, except different. It wasn't the belly laugh she saved for me, or the sarcastic laugh she reserved for my father and grandparents. Something about this new sound caused me to stand frozen as I stand here now, knowing something was not as it should be.

I hadn't figured out the concept of consequences yet, so I pushed through the French doors like our housekeeper did whenever she stormed in to shoo me out.

My mother's legs were draped across Richard's lap and her blouse was undone. A glass of whiskey diluted by melted ice sat on top of my grandfather's favorite book, something by Freud. Go figure. Even now I can't remember another time I've seen my mother like that. Like a woman—like a human, I guess. Not my mother. Not my father's wife.

In the briefest moment, our relationship changed.

I wasn't angry with her. Even then, I knew my father was an asshole. I had no romantic notions of ever developing a real relationship with him.

No, it was the way she looked at me that changed. As our eyes met, neither of us faltered, neither of us apologized by looking down.

That afternoon, I stopped being a child in my mother's eyes, even if I didn't want to. After that, I wasn't her little boy anymore. There was no more childish banter, no more of the babying I still craved.

There isn't much Jill could do that would change the way I look at her. However, if I barge in there and catch her in some humiliating situation, will she look at me differently?

Could she ever know how genuine my feelings are, despite the fact that everything else about my relationship with her is false?

Maybe all women are like my mother: layered, complicated and unable to forget.

I grip the door handle, the metal cool against the stickiness of my palm. Jill deserves this privacy, to be free behind this closed door. But I know that if I don't go in, I'll hear the sound of my mother's laughter that day each time I look at Jill from now on.

I realize the room is suddenly still. For whatever reason, the silence is even more alarming than the strange sounds. I push down the handle with an urgency that surprises me. Maybe I'm not quite as cowardly as everyone who knows me, including me, thinks.

She sits cross-legged in the middle of the room. I blink a few times, perhaps hoping to clear the image, perhaps trying to transport her back to our bed. Her eyes are open, like mine, but she doesn't seem to process my presence. She looks right through me as her hands move in a box I've never seen before. She lifts something up and replaces something else, her eyes steadily on me.

She must have been hiding it. For an instant I have the nerve to feel pissed off.

"Jillian?" I close the door behind me with a force that causes the click to echo. Strangely, the noise causes her to close her eyes. They begin to flicker beneath the lids, tracing thoughts in pace with my heart.

"Jill."

I walk toward her, the wood gripping at my damp feet as if to hold me in place. She slowly rises, as if she is melting in reverse. For a second I hesitate, and my body leans backward, startled.

Even like this, with her body seeming to move without her, she is so beautiful. Her eyes open. They scan the room: the window, the chair covered in her clothes, my shit thrown in the corner, me, and then the wall. I watch as she takes in a huge breath, her belly extending, and turns back to our bed. She pulls back the covers and folds herself neatly under the sheets, one leg at a time.

CHAPTER SIX | *Jillian*

Daylight comes to me and I feel the euphoria of waking up, those brief seconds of consciousness before worry or guilt.

I can't remember the last time I slept so deeply during the day. My eyes are heavy but open, settling on the ceiling. I wait for it—the anxiety, that depressive cloud that washes over me and erases the momentary peace of my sleep-drunk mind.

From here the room looks the same, a little lighter in some spots since the sun has made a rare appearance, but darker in others as it's now late afternoon. My pushy knees bend as if they have a mind of their own and have decided it's time to get up. Begrudgingly, I use my arms to sit up and then wrap them around my legs, resting my chin on my knees.

"I'm up."

At first, I think the sleep was a good idea, but then I see it. The box.

"What the hell," I say aloud, leaping off the end of the bed, taking the comforter with me.

The lid is on, the door is shut firmly, and I am all alone. It took me so long to build up the willpower not to open it every day and even longer not to think of it. But here it is, unmistakable, covered in doodles that span our childhood: our box. Cedar and Jillian—Best Friends Forever, written in what looks like Sharpie but could very well be Black Raspberry Mr. Sketch. Her overly bubbly declaration "Cedar was here!" written complete with her signature loops and finished with a heart; my naive, "Don't worry, be happy!" scribbled nearby.

My first instinct is to put the box away or shove it under the bed, but I can't. My heart pounds against my chest and echoes in my ears. My hands feel shaky and I bite at my lip as if I'm going through withdrawal again.

I am a junkie; this box is my drug. After a bad day, even a good one, I used to devour its contents like a dieter's secret stash of Twinkies or Mom's hidden cigarettes.

Running my hands over the images, trying on her ring, was so satisfying. At first. But then satisfaction was always replaced by the guilt and shame of breaking a promise, the promise I made to give up and forget—to be better.

I realize the box is distracting me from the bigger issue: how did it get here?

I lose my self-control and empty everything out onto the floor in front of me. How have I been so strong to stay away? How have I been so weak to forget?

The first picture I hold up is my favorite. I'm just five and Cedar is still a baby, but the way we're looking at each other is intense. She knew I had her safe in my small arms and I knew I would never let her fall.

I don't notice the first tear until it falls onto a lock of her hair, held together by a pink ribbon. I brush its feathery softness on my cheek, annoyed by the dampness, then carefully blow on it. I catch a glimpse of another picture half hidden by the card Cedar made for my tenth birthday. When I pick it up, the hair falls from my hand. The shaking increases and I run to the washroom, knowing this panicked feeling all too well.

Falling to my knees, I brace myself over the toilet, still gripping the picture.

"No, no, no," I repeat through quivering lips. "This isn't happening, it isn't happening."

I know this picture. I've studied it, memorized every detail: the giant cedar tree, towering over our home; the plaques Mother used as gravestones, attached with Dad's drill to the trunk, to pay tribute to the angels who came before and after me. Me standing proud in the yellow dress Aunt Jen made me—and, of course, Cedar, peaking from behind the enormous trunk, her curls caught in the wind, the expression in her eyes deliciously mischievous.

Except this isn't that picture, it can't be. It bears the same red date stamp, but in this picture, the only thing behind the tree is the field, as barren as our family.

Cedar's been erased from our family discussions, a forbidden topic, removed from the walls and albums. But I hid this picture from them—I kept it safe in this box that holds my memories like a vault.

It's a sign. This must be a message from her, sent to remind me that they're still trying to cover up what happened, to hide what they did. And I'm letting them. My adrenaline surges, providing me with the strength to stand, with the courage I lost along the way, the courage to fight for her. I'm about to make a call that is long overdue when I hear Will's knock and freeze.

"Jillian, you up?" he asks timidly.

Damn.

Our relationship has evolved into something so effortless I don't know if I have the strength to hide this from him. And yet I could never explain everything and allow myself to sound completely insane, either.

I will definitely have to break it off, because he'd never understand this, never be able to forgive me for being such a mess of a person.

Before I can answer, I hear the door opening. My knees feel weak, but I get my shit together in the milliseconds it takes for him to enter. If I give him time, he will figure out that something beyond allergies is going on in here, in this room and in my head. My treasures are still spread on the floor, pushed out and turned upward like puzzle pieces. The comforter is in the middle of the room and I am visibly shaking. I hate myself for putting Will in a category of men who are so easily distracted, but I have no choice. Before he can process the crime scene, I slide my thumbs through the sides of my panties and pull them off.

"I'm up," I say in my best impression of sexy. I free my hair from what must now be a disheveled bun and tousle it about my shoulders.

"So you are," he says, looking less enticed than expected, studying my face instead.

"Come here," I whisper, undoing my bra.

"Wait, Jill …" he says, walking toward me. "What's going on?"

I turn my face away from him, gathering myself. He's a statue, not obeying my very simple request, so I go toward him, except I don't stop. I walk past, brushing one breast against him.

"In here, Will."

I glance up at him as he turns. I open my mouth slightly, pressing my chest against the door frame. He enters the bathroom hesitantly. For a second, I think I'm caught. But he puts his hand to my cheek and then slides it behind my head, tangling his fingers in my hair and pulling my face to his. We back up and I lift myself onto the counter. Every time he pulls away, I kiss him harder, until there is no more pulling away.

Sex has always had a numbing effect for me but with Will there is also emotion, and right now, I feel like I could cry. Suddenly I'm unnerved by his weight on me, the feeling of him pressing between my legs. It's all I can do not to scream. I have the urge to push him off me and run. As if I'm suffocating, the desperation grows until I finally try to push him away, but he pushes back into me. The panic mounts and the nausea returns.

"Will, stop!" I shout as if I had already told him more than once.

"What is wrong with you?" he snaps, backing away.

His question stings. What is wrong with me?

Calm the F down, Jillian.

"I'm going to throw up," I blurt, covering my mouth and rushing to the toilet. He drapes a towel over my naked shoulders and holds my hair up.

"Jill, we need to talk about this."

I throw up a million nerves, wipe the tears from my eyes and say, "I know."

He turns the shower on for me and says he's going to make us tea.

"Thanks, Will," I mumble.

He pauses in the doorway and I hope he'll continue toward the kitchen, but he doesn't. I should stop him, but I'm defeated. I put my hands over my face, still braced over the toilet bowl, and wait for the sound of him going through my stuff, learning all my secrets that are still secret even to me.

When I get the nerve, I turn the shower off, feeling the shock of the water against my arm, and wander into the bedroom. Will is sitting on the floor in the middle of the mess.

"What is all this stuff?" he asks when he senses me behind him.

I exaggerate a sigh, throw on one of his t-shirts and kneel beside him.

"This is everything to me, or it was."

I show him the picture of Cedar and me, tracing my finger around our tiny faces. I shrug.

"Why haven't you shown me this before?" he asks, inspecting the tiny hospital bracelet that I dug out of the trash and kept hidden.

"I guess because I'm not supposed to have any of it. It was too painful for my parents to remember her, so they sort of expunged her from our life," I explain with a wry smile. "I wasn't allowed to talk about her after. It wasn't healthy, they said."

"That's pretty messed up," he says, picking up a picture of me and Dr. X standing outside the hospital where they sent Cedar when she was five.

"That's me and …" I begin but something has changed in

Will's face. The photo in his hand trembles but he tries to hide it from me, putting it down quickly and stretching his fingers. He's avoiding my eyes now, and seems to have lost interest in the rest of my treasures.

I knew this would happen, that the moment I let my guard down, he would see me differently. Why would he want to be involved with a woman whose past is still haunting her? With a family whose parents betrayed both their children?

Then I realize what must have happened.

Aunt Jen—she did this. She promised to keep my secret and allow me these keepsakes. But she lied. I don't know how, or when, but she obviously replaced the only photo I had left of Cedar as a child with this photoshopped one of me in that stupid dress.

In my heart, I wanted to share this part of me with Will. But his reaction now, distant and nervous, proves that my instincts are right. These memories are toxic, as my parents and the doctors said. They are what kept my mother in bed most days, far away from me even when I lay right beside her.

This box belongs in the back of the closet, hidden under the cozy wool sweaters it's never cold enough to wear here.

CHAPTER SEVEN | *Will*

My father is in finance, as was his grandfather. My grandfather, however, was a doctor—a psychiatrist specializing in the treatment of children. He had a calm kindness that my father didn't inherit. I remember the "wasted time," as my father described it, that my grandfather and I spent together walking the property.

"Get your coat, William," he'd say, and I did, even when the warmth of the fire was more appealing than the wet winds outside.

My grandfather always wanted to know what I was thinking, why I was thinking it. He didn't criticize my fears or imagination, my interest in art, my belief that color was interpreted differently by everyone—how maybe someone's blue is someone else's yellow. It was no secret that our home, the home I grew up in, belonged to my grandparents' estate. It was the only reason my father tolerated their unannounced visits. (Perhaps in the same way I tolerate my father.) Often people are better grandparents than they are parents, but I can't imagine my grandad being a bad father. Perhaps he was critical of my dad's drive and coldness, as my father is of my softness. True, there are no pictures or stories of them playing catch or taking family vacations, but what a treat it must have been being raised by a man who was so interested in children, instead of utterly indifferent. In the photos I have seen of my father as a boy, he looks exactly as I would imagine: entitled, spoiled, pouting. I'm guessing he begrudged his father's care for other children, hated not receiving a hundred percent of his attention, a hundred percent of the time—the way he begrudged my mother's care for me.

In many ways, he's still that needy boy, a man I believe borders on sociopathic narcissism.

Other than the awards and degrees on his wall, my grandfather's other children were kept quiet in our house, locked in his files. Only his tape recorder knew their names. He talked into it for hours as he paced in front of the large bay window in his office. I watched him from the tire swing in the yard, wondering what powers these children had to keep him so fascinated. He joked that his hospital was just like the school in X-Men, so that's the way I thought of it. I'm sure he thought that the kids would get a kick out of the idea, especially since his name was also Xavier.

Jill has mentioned Dr. X, but it didn't occur to me that he was my grandfather, Dr. Sutherby.

I recognized him immediately in the photo, though, standing with his gentle arm around Jillian as it had so often been around me.

It was taken in front of his hospital, where I had been a handful of times before I was old enough to avoid it. The smell of antiseptic along with the sounds of screaming children creeped me out—there was no sign of superpowers, just sadness and isolation.

In the seconds it took me to process what I was seeing, I could also see the end of Jillian and me.

Why had my father kept this from me?

Cedar was my grandfather's patient, perhaps even one of the "experimental" patients I'd overheard my parents and grandparents talking about, always quietly and urgently.

Was there any way to explain this connection to Jill without telling her the rest of the story?

Has she spent her entire life trying to recover from something my family had a hand in? And apparently still do?

But why?

What is Aaron's angle?

Overwhelmed by this new information, I handled the situation in the most selfish possible way. I barely gave Jillian's first attempt to be open with me about her past a moment of sincere attention. After seeing the picture, everything else blurred.

What other secrets were in this pile that connected my family to her grief? I got out of the room as fast as I could, blowing any chance I had to be honest.

Funny. I've been told I look a lot like my grandfather. I wonder if Jill knows—if that's why she came on so strong in the beginning.

I'd spent the better part of an hour preparing what I was going to say about her sleep-talking and sleepwalking—how I would be strong for her, but not so forceful I'd scare her off. How

I would put it all out there and be there for her in a way I suspect no one ever has.

When I saw her, my resolve crumbled.

Despite her tear-stained cheeks, the way she looked shattered by something, I let my testosterone pull the strings in the exact way she was hoping I would, and now I feel sick with shame. So, I stand here, outside our bedroom door once again, holding my laptop like a scientist ready to take notes, eavesdropping. I can hear the loneliness and desperation in her voice as she pleads with someone on the phone: "What have you done? What have you done?"

Over and over.

I should be in there, holding her hand, helping her navigate whatever this is.

"Will," she had called to me as I left the room, "did you bring the box in here?"

There was anguish in the way she formed the words. It must have been so hard to ask a question that revealed her confusion, yet she allowed herself to be vulnerable. And I let her down. Why didn't I just tell her I'd seen her sleepwalking, that she was responsible for unearthing Cedar and the box from their hiding place? Instead, I've left her with uncertainty and more unanswered questions.

A long time ago, I loved a girl named Emma—a girl with glossy long hair who was sweet and cruel in random measures. Her parents were friends of my parents; like my parents, they paid very little attention to their only child. Emma didn't like me, really, but she did accept the M&Ms I gave her every year on her birthday. I watched her swallow colorful handfuls and share them with the much cooler boys. She remained oblivious to me, but I thought she was perfect.

All the way through high school, I was content being the friend, taken advantage of on the regular, grateful for any attention. Of course it's pathetic and I eventually got over it. In a way, though, Emma primed me for Jill.

Jill loves me, but she can distance herself as quickly as the second hand on a clock. Hot, tick; cold, tock. There is very little warmth between us, yet she is so delighted with the little there is. She doesn't ever look around the restaurant for a better option—in fact, she grips my hand tighter whenever some guy tries to eye-fuck her in front of me.

I'm a shit.

My dad's a fucking asshole.

This whole ordeal today has confirmed how much I love Jill. For once, my protective instincts kick in and overwhelm my loyalty to my father. I toss my computer on the bench, grab my keys from the tray and storm out of the condo like I'm ready to take on the whole fucking team.

The kettle whistles as the door slams behind me.

It's hard to keep the momentum going when the elevator stops on almost every floor. I'm just not the type of guy who lets his issues make other people uneasy. I suck up the anger and greet my neighbors with the same friendliness as always. Part of this is Canadian politeness, the other part is growing up with a strict, "what goes on in this house stays in this house" policy. It always amazed me how my father could be a complete dick in the car but be so charming once we arrived somewhere, in the same way my mother could disguise her tears with some powder and lipstick.

"Call Father," I command my car as I put my seat belt on.

"Calling Father," it echoes, a British voice Jill aptly named Kate.

"Pick up. Pick up, you prick!" I shout and then slam my fist on my steering wheel. It goes straight to voicemail. There are hateful things in my head while I listen to his cocksucker voice prattle on. But when the beep chimes, I just spit out: "I'm coming over."

I'm about to call my mother when it dawns on me that she's probably two bottles deep. Even sober, she's no help: she survives by being clueless and complacent. In her defense, she used to be different—loving and smart. But he wore her down, and now she's as unhappy as he is.

The family home is in the heart of Point Grey, surrounded by similar century-old mansions with gates installed for pretension rather than protection. The estate was modeled after an English countryside manor by my great-grandfather in the early 1900s. There have always been rumors about the Sutherby Place, much like the locally famous Casa Mia—underground tunnels and basement ballrooms—but neither are true. A voice through the intercom permits me access and I drive down a lane lined with twenty-foot, professionally maintained hedges. As common as old money is in Vancouver, I don't think Jillian understood the magnitude of my family's wealth until I brought her here the first time. There really is no way to prepare someone of Jill's background for this kind of grandness.

About halfway down the drive, you get your first glimpse

of the house set behind an ornate water fountain. That was the moment she gripped my hand and I actually felt proud of this place.

"Wow, Will—this is incredible."

"You're incredible," I answered and gave her a James Bond grin.

When I took her on the tour, I attempted to downplay it all, but I obliviously described the dining room as the hall and the living room as the parlor.

"Snob," she fake-coughed into her hand before pushing me into the hallway that connects the nanny's suite to the rest of the house. She said she felt like she was in a movie, like she was a kept woman having a fling with the butler or gardener. In the hallway I used to ride my tricycle down, we made out until I was hard. Then she walked off and went to dazzle my parents.

I stop the car in front of the main house, a parking spot forbidden to staff and immediate family. This is about as rebellious as it gets for me.

"Mother," I shout, ignoring Mae, the Filipino housekeeper my grandmother was sponsoring before their accident.

"William, so nice to see you," she says, following me. "Where is Jillian?"

"She's not well, Mae. Where's Mother?"

"She's resting now, William. You want tea? I make blueberry scones."

"No, Mae. I don't," I say, heading up a staircase lined with walnut paneling rather than family pictures. Ten stairs up and I already regret being so short with Mae. I fight the urge to apologize in fear of softening my mood, but I'm not my father. As I turn back, she is still standing there, looking uncomfortable.

"I'm sorry," I say, making my way back to the foyer. "How are you, Mae?"

"It's okay, William. I'm fine. But she's not up there. She's in the rotunda."

She points to the area off the kitchen where the roof becomes a dome.

"The kitchen?" I ask, chuckling, pointing in that direction. She shrugs, likely not understanding the difference. I thank her with a nod and muster up a smile before passing through the kitchen to find Mom sprawled out on a lounge chair, dining al fresco on a bottle of pinot. I make my approach known, not tiptoeing around her like Mae does. But even before I step outside, I can see she is asleep.

There's no question my mother is physically beautiful. Even now, well into her fifties and addled by alcohol, she is divine. It's a pity she married my father and produced only one spineless son with below-average looks.

I remember her playful side, chasing me around the large kitchen island, pretending to be a monster; teaching me to dive with patience as my father sat bored on a chaise beside the pool, drink in hand. She used to sneak me into his off-limit office to spin me around in his chair, laughing as the breeze we made scattered his papers.

It's such a shame she had to change. I'm sure it was a matter of survival. The more I started to look like him, the harder it was for her to look at me the same. My instincts are to cover her, to light a fire in the pizza oven to keep her warm, but I have to protect my own happiness now. God knows she learned to put herself first a long time ago.

I sit at her feet.

More gently than planned, I say, "Mom," patting her leg. I watch her stir and bat away an invisible person beside her with a drunken swing.

"I said I was resting."

"Get up, Mom."

"William?" she says, groaning.

"Yeah, Mom. Get up!"

She takes her time gathering herself, dabbing under her eyes and puffing up her flattened curls. "Well, I never …" she says in a southern accent, acting charming as if she knows she's in trouble.

"I'm serious, Helene."

"Helene? My God, Will, you're sounding more and more like your father every day."

She's sitting up now, her legs curled like a cat. "What is it?"

"Where's Dad?"

"Really? Is that what you want?" She pours the remainder of the red wine into her glass. "I haven't the slightest where that man is. Why don't you ask Siri?" She tosses her phone at me.

"Hilarious. How much do you know about Grandfather's patients?"

"About as much as you do." She looks away. "Mae?" she calls into the house, not bothering to move.

Seconds later Mae presents herself and is instructed to get another bottle of wine and a glass for me. I don't bother refusing, as I know the extra glass is just an excuse for Mother to drink more.

"Has Dad said anything to you about Grandfather and Jillian's family?"

"Your Jill? I knew she was too pretty for her own good. Why, what's up, son?" She hands me a generous pour.

"I don't know yet exactly."

She places her glass on the table and wraps her arms tightly around her slim frame. "Why is it every time we talk about that man, I get shivers?"

The wind is picking up now, and it rattles in the nearby doorway like whispers. We both stop and listen.

"The ghosts are at it again," she says, peering over her shoulder.

The sun has nearly set and the idea of Jill alone in the condo is unsettling.

"I need your help, Mom." I rise and wrap a cashmere throw around her shoulders, suddenly seeing her as she was, knowing that, other than Mae, no one really takes care of her. She is my mother, after all.

"Now I'm Mom again?" She thanks me for the blanket with a squeeze of my hand. "What do you need, Will?"

I read somewhere that mothers have an inherent response to being needed by their grown children. As if the words, "I need your help," trigger something in them like the snap of a hypnotist's fingers. Suddenly, she is alert and taking me seriously.

"I need you to keep this between us. Dad can't know. I could lose Jill, and my job."

"Your job? What is it, Will?"

"Promise me, Mom."

"Yes, yes, William. Out with it already!"

I only divulge part of the information. I suspect she knows more than she is letting on. Maybe not about Jill, directly, but there's something she's not telling me.

"I found a picture," I start. I'm not sure which direction to go in and somehow begin at the end.

"Okay?"

"It's of Grandfather and a little girl outside of the hospital."

"And…?"

"And, it's Jill."

She takes a dramatic last swig of her wine and puts it down way too aggressively for crystal.

"I see. How do you know it's even Jillian?"

"Because I found it in her stuff!" I snap. "Because she showed me!"

Helene stands. Something more than the temperature has changed. She's remembering something, or debating with herself about telling me something. She fidgets, rubbing her knuckles like they hurt as she paces two feet in every direction around me.

"Jesus, Mom, what is it?"

She stops abruptly as if she just realized her sudden movements would contrast with her usual lethargy.

"It's nothing," she lies. She manages to calm herself and sits down again. "Your father saved some of your granddad's files after the hospital closed. For insurance reasons."

"Where?" I start toward the house, but she stops me.

"Give me a couple days to look into it."

"Look into what, exactly?"

"It's nothing. It's probably nothing."

CHAPTER EIGHT | *Jillian*

It's not like Will to be so cold. True, my intention was to get him out of the room. But having him turn his back on me was surprisingly hurtful.

Aunt Jen picked up on the second ring, panicked, as if she'd set my personal ringtone as some emergency warning bell. I knew a call from me would shatter her peace, probably disrupting her afternoon tea.

"Jill, sweetheart. It's so nice to hear from you."

I take a deep breath, as right now the kindness in her voice feels like a monster disguised as a friend, or a bully's opening compliment.

"Jillian? Is everything okay?"

"What have you done, Aunt Jen?"

I repeat myself. Louder this time, unable to find new words; there are no words for this betrayal. And finally, "How could you?"

"I don't understand …" I hear her excuse herself to someone, leaving a pleasant situation for yet another Jillian crisis.

"You couldn't just let me have it? The only picture I had left of her!?"

"Okay, slow down," she says, her voice bouncing with her steps. "What picture?"

"I know you all choose to forget her, but why can't you leave me with my memories?" I'm close to hysterics now.

"Take a breath. Which picture, darling?" She tries to calm me, but it's patronizing.

"The only fucking picture I had, as you well know. The one of me in that dress, the one with Cedar!!!"

"I know you don't believe me, but Jilly, I didn't take your picture. How could I have?"

I slam my fist down on the night table, releasing enough frustration to allow me to continue with this bullshit.

"You switched it!"

"Have you been going through those old things again?"

"You know what? Fuck you!"

"Jill! Watch your mouth, young lady!"

"Please," I manage to whisper, clenching my jaw to hold back the tears. "Just tell me what you did. Where is the original photo with Cedar in it?"

I give up trying to stand on my trembling legs, lean back against the wall and let my body slide downward until I'm sitting on the floor.

You know when sisters look so much alike people sometimes mistake one for the other?

After Aunt Jen came to help, she never really left. She was so much like my mom, except happier. She sang while she did the dishes. She tapped her toes to the radio.

Mom was quiet. She sat so still I used to convince myself

she was asleep with her eyes open. It was easier when she was asleep, because she was never really awake—never really present. Then I didn't have to feel guilty for pretending Aunt Jen was my mother. Aunt Jen always made excuses for Mom, encouraging me to interact with her even though she rarely responded.

It wasn't my mom's fault; it was the medicine, she said.

The medicine stopped her from crying all the time and screaming at us, but it caused a kind of deadness, too. Except on the worst days, when it was replaced by constant rocking.

Even without makeup or her hair done, Mom was prettier than Aunt Jen. When she was well, she was the prettiest woman in any room. She sparkled for a while and then she faded, more and more, until one day she was just the background in our sad house.

Aunt Jen is not as beautiful as Mom, but she is alive and vibrant. And she was in love with my father. After a while, people lose their patience for depression. I'm told Mom had bouts even before I was born. I think pregnancy helped her but also caused her to slip further and further away each time the loss came.

Cedar wasn't even two when Mom once again fell away from all of us. And while Aunt Jen was a constant for my mother, her caregiver more than ours, I think she stayed because of my father. She left her job at the hospital for us, but she gained a family— two children and a husband.

I don't think their affair started right away; my best guess is that it happened when Cedar was about five or so. Whispers were a large part of our childhood: concerns about Mom's mental stability and Cedar's development. But Dad and Aunt Jen's night whispers were happy. And if I knew, at ten, I'm sure my mother did, too. She may even have been grateful to her sister for keeping her husband happy enough to stay. Not that he would have left.

The mornings afterward were the closest we ever came to what people describe as "one big happy family." Father was more affectionate to Mother; Mother was more affectionate to everyone and Aunt Jen was more affectionate to me. My father loved Aunt Jen and appreciated all that she did for our family, but we all knew he was in love with my mother. I once heard him tell a doctor it was like watching her drown right in front of him, with nothing he could do but watch her go under.

"Are you still there, honey?" Aunt Jen asks gently, the love in her voice still there after all these years. Even after what my parents did to her.

"Look, Jillian, why don't I fly down and help you find what you're looking for?"

"No," I snap. "I'm fine."

"Okay, Jill, but I could be there tomorrow morning—the twins would be fine on their own for a bit."

"I'm good, Aunt Jen. Just forget it."

"Jill?" There is a pause. "Are you taking your medicine?"

The year following Cedar's death was the darkest. Not only did I lose my sister and best friend, but my parents and Aunt Jen wouldn't stop lying to me about what happened. I didn't know what they were lying about, or why, but I knew that they were. I lost Cedar and my trust for them at the same time, the time I needed them most.

Yes, it happened in front of me. The memories are clear. Time has not altered them, and yet I still don't really know what happened at all. It was like losing all the thoughts in my head at once, as if they were sucked out by a vacuum.

Our voices were silenced, Cedar's voice and mine.

I was stuck in my mind all alone. There is no escaping the thoughts you speak silently to yourself. Without Cedar, my internal dialogue was sadness, depression and disappointment.

Cedar was my champion. Without her, my thoughts were riddled with self-loathing. She was the one who said, "You can do this, Jillian!" She constantly complimented qualities in me even though they paled next to hers.

Without Cedar, my thoughts became an enemy I couldn't hide from.

Strangely, as devastating as losing Cedar was for me, it seemed to reawaken my mom. Not long after Cedar's funeral, my mother became a mother again. For the first time, it seemed, she was content to have only one child; it was as if all the losses she'd suffered and mourned so deeply were finally enough. She became desperate to hold onto her living child, me.

Dr. X seemed to take Cedar's loss the hardest. He somehow expressed more grief than my parents. As he did not care for me the way he did for her, he wasn't distracted from his grief the way my parents seemed to be by their suddenly despondent living daughter.

The day they brought me to him, he embraced me for the first time, dropping to his knees and throwing his arms around me.

"A great loss, a great, great loss."

The way he shook his head and rubbed his forehead, looking sideways at my parents, somehow seemed rehearsed. But rehearsed or not, it was a relief to share my sadness with someone.

"Remember the pills Cedar used to take?" he asked as he gave me some water. I nodded as a montage of memories raced through my mind, Cedar at all ages, taking her medicine, her fingers slowly growing from chubby to long and delicate.

"Well, we think they may help you, too."

"I don't need any medicine. I don't think Cedar did either." Against my will, I began to cry, overwhelmed by sadness and confusion.

Dr. X placed his hand on my knee as he passed me the tissues on his desk.

"Why would she do that?" I yelled at him suddenly, pushing his hand away. "It was the medicine! She was happy. She wouldn't have just run out in front of that car if …"

I heard my mother rushing to my side and suddenly she was holding me.

"Shhhh," she soothed, brushing the wet hair off my cheek.

"We've been over this, Jillian," said my dad. "It was an accident. She didn't try to kill herself. She must have seen something she wanted on the road."

He sat beside my mother and she rested her head on his shoulder. For a moment it was so nice to be a family, to see my parents respond to each other in such a loving way.

But it was just that, a moment. Because they now had each other, but I felt entirely alone.

Cedar said she felt more loved by Dr. X than she did by our

parents. I tried to tell her how our much our parents loved her, how happy they were the day they brought her home from the hospital. It was the happiest I'd ever seen my mother.

"I want to be his daughter," Cedar would say to me. "I want to stay there," she whispered when we brought her home for weekend visits.

It was shameful that my parents weren't able to show her the love they had showed me when I was younger. How wonderful it would have been for her to be accepted by them the way she was, which was perfect.

Mom especially treated Cedar as if there was something terribly wrong with her. The fact that Cedar did not speak troubled our mother so much that she put up a wall between them. And because I was so close to Cedar, that wall stood between my mother and me as well.

"Why, why is this happening to us?!" Mom would shriek at Dad. "Just make her stop, goddammit!"

Dad would tell her not to be so ugly, that Cedar was their daughter, that they loved her.

"We never should have had children. There is something wrong with us!" Mom yelled more than once, twisting her fingers as if packing an invisible snowball.

Dad said Mom was just frustrated, just worried.

Dr. X, however, treated Cedar as if she were a miracle. And she was. My guess is that he hoped she would attempt to communicate with him the way she did with me, but she never did. They used clipboards, chalkboards and colorful magnetic letters when she was younger. It didn't take them long to develop a secret language, one that aggravated my dad as much as the silence did my mom. I suppose that if Dr. X had been a woman, Mom might've been jealous of their bond, too.

Dad bought Cedar a bright purple clipboard and a brand-new package of Crayola markers. He wrote DAD LOVES YOU in Dolphin Grey and passed her the clipboard.

She was hesitant, but after a minute she chose Hot Magenta and wrote, I KNOW, and then smiled. He said that he liked her writing, he liked the heart she drew underneath.

He passed me the board next and asked me if I would like to write something.

"Why, Dad?" I questioned, not realizing he was just trying to include me. To be funny, I grabbed the board anyway and wrote, WHY DAD? in Basic Brown.

"Hmmm," he said, looking at the paper, likely noticing how messy my printing was in contrast to Cedar's. "Because I love you too."

This game was short-lived. Mother put a stop to it, saying it was "just encouraging her." The clipboard and markers ended up in the junk drawer with the tape, scissors and old pieces of mail.

Dad went on talking to both of us, but only one of us continued to answer.

"Yes, I'm taking my medicine," I finally answer Aunt Jen's question reluctantly, lying. "That's not what this is about."

She releases a sigh of relief and tells me she thinks this is good news. It took me forever to realize these types of comments weren't made to hurt me but out of complete ignorance. Is it good news someone tampered with my things, or good news that I'm medicated enough not to completely lose it?

The truth is that I stopped taking my medication years ago, right after I graduated from university.

I'm not like my mom. The darkness that followed her around like a truculent shadow was not exactly contagious. As much as our parents' behavior can be hereditary, depression never came naturally to me. Sure, I'm reserved with people, but these traits developed after Cedar died, after I started taking the pills Dr. X gave me.

I often aligned myself more with Aunt Jen—I was happy even when it made more sense not to be.

After Cedar's death, we drove off to my first appointment with Aunt Jen in the rear-view mirror. She had her brave face on, smiling so hard her eyes squinted into upside-down smiley faces.

When Cedar died, Aunt Jen lost more than just one of her nieces. She lost her whole family, her identity for half a decade. With Mom in remission, Dad began to treat his lover like an inconvenient houseguest. Before the dust settled, before ashes were ashes, Aunt Jen was invited to leave. They suggested she go back to work, as if relieving her of her role in our family was a helpful gesture and not a tragedy.

I know her heart broke, but Aunt Jen continued to love me and visit me often. If she ever wished that my mom had died instead of Cedar, she never showed it.

I would have done almost anything to stop the pain of losing Cedar, but I choked down the pills Dr. X handed me because of the way my mother was looking at me: like I was a baby about to take my first steps. As I brought them to my mouth, the three of them seemed to be watching for magic to unfold. I'd seen my mother and Cedar take pills all my life—surely they must've known there is no magic involved. But they did help. I was able to carry on. The nausea seemed a fair tradeoff for the mornings I'd woken to find myself outdoors, curled beneath the cedar tree.

So, I started operating just above autopilot. I occasionally smiled, but mainly for their benefit. Mostly, I stuck close to my room, where my memories were still alive even though Cedar was not.

By the time I hung up with Aunt Jen, her goodbye thick with disguised hurt, I knew how the box had gotten out of the closet. It was reassuring, then troubling. I have no idea when it started again.

Did I somehow switch the photos? Why? That would mean sleepwalking through whole days, something I haven't done since I stopped taking the meds.

Had Will seen me? Is this what he wanted to talk about— that I've been sleepwalking?

Oh, God. Right now, I can't worry about Will. If I'm sleep-walking again, it could mean that I imagined the whole scenario this morning.

But it could also mean Cedar is sending me a message.

Why would I start thinking about her all the time again now?

Dr. X died six or so years back, a car accident. After his funeral, which my parents of course tried to make me attend, I held my breath hoping that Cedar would finally be free to come back to me. But she didn't.

I couldn't bring myself to attend his service. It made the news, the way funerals always do when very rich people die.

Cedar would have wanted me there. Yet, regardless of the kindness he showed us, I still held him responsible for her disappearance.

From the way my parents talked to him, I knew he was in on whatever it was they weren't telling me. I suspected that, after Cedar was hit by the car, Dr. X helped my parents send her away to whatever institution adults send children who don't talk.

Well, I could lie too. In my appointments with him, I was always pleasant and cooperative, but I spent my time looking for clues in his office, unspoken words between him and the staff.

My parents went to the funeral. They spoke of it as if it were the state funeral of a member of the royal family; everyone who was anyone was there. Some people they recognized from the hospital, others from television. And the parents of the many children Dr. X had treated were all there.

Eventually, his death helped me finally deal with the idea that Cedar was gone. Whatever had happened, I knew that if she didn't come back to me then, she wasn't coming back.

A few months later, I stopped taking the medication. At first, it felt like I was dying. My whole body turned on me, my muscles convulsing until exhaustion set in. My nerves were on fire, shaking me until I was clammy and cold all over. Emotionally, the penalties were worse. For nearly a week, I swung between irritable and excited, restless and lethargic. The images in my head were heinous: the knife that my roommate placed on the dish drainer could slice across my wrist or plunge into my stomach, I could drink the can of motor oil at the gas station before the attendant returned. The matches, the scissors, my freshly sharpened pencil were all weapons of self-destruction, and my mind played each scenario through till the very end.

I would breathe through these visions like awakening from a nightmare and settle myself until the thoughts drifted away.

Managing withdrawal is especially hard when you're afraid that the real you is the panicked, destructive, mentally ill one. I'd started the medicine so soon after Cedar's death that I really hadn't been alone inside my head since I was five years old.

Then one day, after about a week off the meds, I went to my regular coffeeshop, filled with the usual students having the usual conversations and typing on the usual laptops. I ordered the usual coffee and poured in the usual milk. This time, I watched the milk dance and swirl, folding under and then rushing up again, a kaleidoscope of images.

A beautiful everyday occurrence I had never noticed before. So, I persevered. I locked myself away in my dorm room, filled my prescription and pretended to take it every day. Every morning, I removed one pill from the bottle. Instead of swallowing it, I placed it in a sock. At the end of every prescription cycle, I'd filled a new sock. After four years, I had a small suitcase full of lumpy socks, always within reaching distance should it ever got to be too much.

Away at school, I didn't live under the microscope I did at home, but I was regularly reminded that it was conditional: I had to take my meds. I knew it didn't matter where I hid them, though, because my parents checked in with the pharmacist more than they did with me.

The urge to kill myself never really faded, but it became more of a fantasy than a force. I kept imagining new ways to do it. I've gotten close. But, there's one thought that always stops me: what if Cedar is still out there? The idea of leaving her alone, of her finally finding her way back to me only to discover I'm gone … It always stops me in my tracks, makes me get up and try again.

Now the urge to dig my university suitcase out of our storage locker from beneath my rollerblades and old CDs is intense. I've worked so hard to close off the part of me that puts people off, that scares them away. To lose control now, to know I've been stumbling around revealing my secrets—is there anywhere to go from here except back into the darkness?

Except. I saw Cedar today.

And if I saw her once, I have to believe I will see her again.

CHAPTER NINE | *Will*

I'm irrelevant. I get this.

In the big picture I'm as immaterial to Jillian's past as any other creep she might have hooked up with.

Except, I'm not. My family is not just in the business of keeping Jill safe. This is not some weird Sutherby International client favor, as I'd hoped.

Whatever the reason I've been designated Jillian's keeper, her guardian, it's becoming harder to convince myself this is all for Jill's benefit.

My grandfather had a secret.

My father has a secret.

I have a secret. I just don't know what it is yet.

Flowers. That's what I came up with. I'll be happy if she hasn't changed the locks—or if the kettle I left on hasn't burned the place down.

I texted her to see if she wants me to pick up dinner, if she needed a coffee. I haven't heard back in over an hour. So, I bring home flowers.

I pull into the garage, relieved to see there are no fire trucks.

Jill doesn't have a car, so I'll have to wait to see if she is still up there. I consider stopping by the concierge to ask if he saw her leave, as if he too is keeping tabs on her, but think better of it.

When the elevator door opens onto the lobby I step back instead of forward; it seems half of me hopes she isn't here. If she went to cool off, or for her usual late afternoon run on the seawall, it would buy me some time to collect my thoughts. And if she's gone, then we both left the scene. We both freaked out and therefore no one really walked out. We both just went for a walk to cool off. Right?

These thoughts, these games, really, are my father's. He never fights fair. It didn't matter what my mom did, what she said or refrained from saying. He always manipulated any issue into something that was her fault, or, at the very worst, a mutual misunderstanding.

Yet the truth was that it was always his fault. Always. Even when it was hers.

I consider knocking. It's our condo, but right now I can't shake the feeling that we are strangers to each other. I'm not sure what's going on with her, and she certainly doesn't know what I'm doing, what I have been doing. Bringing attention to this feeling by playing awkward is likely not the smoothest move, but maybe knocking would be romantic, given that I'm standing here with flowers? Probably not the time for romance, though, or for forcing Jill to answer the door when she is so distraught that she is physically ill.

The door is locked. I pull my keys out of my pocket, hyper-aware of the sound they make, clanking against each other and scraping on the wood. I used to dread this sound growing up, the opposite of the way I imagined loved children looked forward to their dad's key in the lock.

I hope Jill isn't having that feeling now.

The lock resounds like a bullet. The door is even louder as I push it open against some paper left on the floor. I pull it away with the sole of my shoe and then close the door as quietly as possible.

The condo is still.

Jill is always quiet. She walks like she's floating; she eats, drinks and even chews gum in the least obnoxious ways possible. After growing up with my father's noise sensitivity, I appreciate that. My own light-footedness is as practiced as my posture and annunciation.

Ignoring my inner self-ridicule, I carry the flowers down the hall to our room. Before I turn the corner, I can hear the shower. She's home.

It's not too late to rethink the flowers. It's not too late to sneak back out and save this encounter for when I have more information.

Mind you, being a man, being her man, is my main priority. This is so clear to me suddenly. Whatever she decides to do with me, love me forever or have me arrested, it will be her choice. Despite her limitations, I realize this woman is everything to me.

"Jill," I call into the bathroom to avoid startling her.

She's been through the "You don't know what it's like to be a woman" speech more than once; how I don't worry in parking lots or avoid taking a shower when I'm alone. I'm not a huge guy, but she's right. Those aren't fears I have. I do worry when we're out late and have to pass a bunch of guys leering at her, but I'm happy to have those worries. I worry because I love her, because I want to protect her.

"Jillian," I say again, stepping into the bathroom.

She turns her face toward me behind the glass of the shower, drenched in what looks like a million tears. She doesn't cover up; it's less instinctual for her than me. Why would she? Her body is a gift, as if God wanted to give her one less thing to worry about.

She presses her palm against the glass. I watch the tiny beads of water move away from her hand as if she's somehow repelled them. From the steam, I gather she's been in there for quite some time; I can't make out the expression on her face. I mirror her hand with mine and hold it there until she lets hers slip down.

For a moment I catch the sadness in her eyes and it's as if the knife I've placed in her back stabs me through the heart.

She turns the water off and opens the shower door. Her nipples harden and tiny goosebumps rise on her arms. She says something, but it's lost on me. I just take her in, the way her waist gives way to the curve of her hips. The water trickling past her belly button, sliding steadily down, down, hypnotizes me. I'm like a thirteen-year-old seeing a naked woman for the first time. Fuck me, she's beautiful.

"Will?" she interrupts.

"What?" I almost snap, caught completely lost in teenage wonder.

"A towel, babe?" She giggles, holding her chest to warm rather than cover herself.

"I'm sorry. You bewitch me." I toss her a towel and crinkle my nose in disgust as she covers up.

"You okay now?" she asks me, sitting on the edge of the tub, her hair soaking the floor.

"Me?"

"Will, you ran out of here!"

She's composed now. The fragile Jill I left here is gone. She's put the wall up again. Can I blame her?

"No way!" I lie. "I went to make you tea and my mom called. She ah … she fell."

"What? You're so full of shit, Will." She stands and wraps the towel around her hair. "Don't do that."

"Do what?"

"Don't lie to me. Just admit it, you freaked out."

"Why would I freak out?" I shift my body and try to look like I'm not full of shit.

"My mom, she…"

"Stop!" She puts her hands on my shoulders and I do my best to be mature about the way her breasts feel against my arm.

"I was sleepwalking, wasn't I?"

"What do you mean?" I ask awkwardly, failing at eye contact while I quickly process the out she's just given me.

"Will?"

"Okay, yeah, so maybe you went a little Emily Rose this afternoon."

"Emily? What?"

I give her a second and then watch it register.

"That possessed girl from the movie?" She slugs my arm.

"You're an ass!"

"Honestly, it didn't freak me out. You were fine. You looked a bit odd, I guess." I hand her the flowers. "Maybe a little creepy."

"Yeah. I used to do it all the time, especially after Cedar died."

She smells the flowers and puts them on the counter before slipping on her silk robe. She tightens the tie with a sharp tug as if she is trying to further compress her tiny waist and looks me in the eye.

"I'll try not to do it again." She steps out of the bathroom and adds, "Cause you're such a pussy."

And now I feel foolish. She's always had the ability to swing the mood. If she's happy, I'm happy. If she's distant, I'm worried. If she's sleepwalking and disturbed, I run to Mommy. I literally shake my head at myself in the mirror. She's fine. So she releases her troubles in her sleep? Perhaps that's better than being stressed all day, or drinking, or cheating. In the grand scheme of things, I've got it real good.

I pull my phone out of my back pocket. A text from Mother says to call her ASAP, but the urgency and panic that I felt just minutes ago has calmed to the point that I put the phone back in my jeans and focus on the girl I left high and dry. I know I owe her an honest apology, at least. We both know my behavior was poor and definitely out of character, but only I know why.

She's pulling her old UBC sweatshirt over her head as she stands with her back to me, her jeans hugging her body perfectly. I place my hands on her hips and turn her around to face me. Her hair sprays water on me when she pulls it out of her shirt. I sneak my hands into her back pockets and pull her toward me.

"I love you, Jillian."

"You don't have to say that," she whispers, unexpectedly resting her head on my shoulder. The weight reminds me that everything isn't great, not with her, not with us. The simple gesture reminds me I may need to carry her through this for us to survive. Superficial banter and her pretending she's fine is not going to do it.

"Jill? I love you," I repeat. "I'm here for you."

She lets me hold her for another minute.

"I'm sorry," I say. "I'm really sorry." And even though I may sound like a "pussy," apologizing makes me feel more like a man than my father has ever been.

She clears her throat, calling cut on the scene. Her voice is steady when she says she's starving but her eyes can't turn the fear off as quickly. She's been crying, I'm certain of that now, but I remind her to take an allergy pill as she walks out of the room. I stand still for a moment to give her space. I know she is more comfortable being cool, so I play along. We've had enough emotions for today.

When I grab my sweater, I see that the box has disappeared again. Part of me feels relieved that Grandfather won't be within reaching distance. Another part feels guilty that I've shamed her into hiding her past.

I'm not far behind her but when I catch up to her in the foyer, she's completely focused on something on the floor. It's as if she's just randomly, suddenly dropped to her knees. I know she can hear me approach her. She's not asleep, I hope, and yet she seems almost as she did earlier, completely out of it. She doesn't move when I come up behind her.

"What are you doing now?" I joke, casually reaching for my shoe beside her, secretly holding my breath.

"It's Cedar," she whispers.

Shit.

"What?" I manage, now even more afraid that the love of my life is losing her fucking mind.

"She's back."

CHAPTER TEN | *Jillian*

After I hung up with Aunt Jen it dawned on me that, as much as she loves me, as much as my parents may love me, they will never understand my need to know the truth.

Truth is simple even if telling it is hard. Even if it hurts. Even if they've done something unimaginable.

If I'm going to keep this from Will, I need to accept that I'm on my own. Again. Part of me hoped that Will might be able to help, to handle the impossible. Now I have to accept that, like my parents and Aunt Jen, Will's love for me isn't up to this. Even if he could accept the truth, how do I know he'll believe I'm strong enough to handle it? No, this is up to me. And there is no point dragging him into something even my family—Cedar's family—can't handle.

I put my big girl face on. I held it together long enough to share a moment with Will. The normalcy of my wanting to grab food seemed to appease his worry and fear. Determined to wash away this afternoon's shit storm with a glass of wine, I left him in our room and propelled myself toward the kitchen. But as I pass the front door, I see a piece of paper on the floor. Somehow,

I know it is more than a dropped receipt or condo board notice.

I can't recall the moments between seeing the paper from thirty feet away and sitting here now, staring up at Will.

I hear myself saying the words, "She's back," with eerie certainty. Yet my hands are trembling so hard that I'm barely able to hold onto the note Cedar has somehow left for me.

The writing is identical. It is definitely her childish handwriting, and the words are familiar too.

Jillian, I need you to be strong. I know how hard this must be, but I need you. Help me leave this place for good. I don't belong here.

I got lost at the mall once. Mom was in one of her spells, walking beside me, oblivious, until she wasn't. Even as a small child I knew it was my job to stay with her. My frantic search for her made everything around me a blur. Holding my breath and spinning around to look in all directions made me dizzy, and when I saw her standing at the sunglass kiosk and knew I was safe, everything went black.

Now Will is standing over me. He's yelling something but I can't hear what he's saying. It's like that day in the mall all over again. With nowhere to go, my adrenaline overwhelms me.

Now I hear a voice. It's mine. I'm saying her name over and over. My sister is alive, and I finally have proof. But more than that, I have Will to witness it.

I slowly become aware of the cold, the pain in my elbows pressed against the tile, Will's hand behind my head, my hair tangled in his grip.

"Jillian!" He pleads. Each time I shout "Cedar!" Will responds, "Jillian!" as if we're playing a game of Marco Polo.

"She's really alive," I say, meeting his eyes for the first time.

"Jill, love, you need a doctor," he says, pulling me into a sitting position.

"I'm okay," I manage, then realize I'm shaking wildly. I clench my hands into fists and tuck them away from his view.

"Cedar wrote this—it's her writing." I wave the letter at him again and try to stand.

"Look, babe, you have to take it easy. Stay here, I'll get you some water."

This is too much to ask of Will, too much to ask of anyone. As soon as I hear the faucet turn on, the urge to run overcomes me. I grab my keys and jacket, knocking the hanger to the floor with a reverberating clunk.

"Jill?"

Shit. I want to scream at him to leave me alone, slam the door in his face and never look back, but instead I freeze.

"Where are you going?" He looks frustrated. Angry even.

"Look, Will, listen …" I sit on the bench across from the door. "There's just too much to explain, I think maybe …"

He leans back against the wall heavily, as if his whole body is a sigh.

"You think maybe what, Jillian?" Instead of passing it to me, he places the water down on the table and crosses his arms. "I think I deserve a real explanation, don't I?"

I listen to his words and really consider the question. Deserve? Yeah, maybe he does deserve to know, but how can I tell him what I don't know? Do I deserve this? Cedar certainly didn't, and yet her whole childhood was taken from her. I don't even want to think about what kind of institution they stuck her in.

I can feel the adrenaline surging again. Why am I sitting here when I should be looking for her? I'm suddenly furious with Will for getting in my way.

"What's your problem?" I bark. "This has nothing to do with you!"

"So, you're just going to leave?"

"You did!"

I'm almost crying with frustration. There are so many other things I should be doing right now. But truthfully, I have no idea where to go, where to start. I do know that, besides Will, I have no one else in the world to turn to.

He senses my hesitation and comes to sit beside me. His touch, the warmth of his shoulder, seems to discharge some of the tension in my body. It's a comfort I desperately want. I bury my face into my hands and Will runs his fingers down my back.

"I saw her today."

"Cedar?" His hand falls away.

"Yes. Of course, I wasn't sure if it was really her or if I was going crazy."

"But Cedar is dead, Jill. Are you saying you saw a ghost? Or …?

"Fuck, Will! I know," I snap, springing to my feet.

"Relax, I'm sorry—I'm just trying to…"

"Relax? Relax?" I start biting at my nails, pacing like I'm mad. "My dead sister is alive, my parents are… fucking evil…"

"Breathe. We're going to find out what's going on." He

anchors me, his hands firm on my shoulders. "I'm going to help you."

I stop moving. "So, you believe me?"

My eyes are so focused on him they start to burn.

"Give me the note." He gestures at my hand and I realize I have scrunched it up between my fingers. I'm clutching it so hard that pain rushes in as I try to loosen my grip.

"Geez, Jill, you have to relax." He rests the note beside him, takes my hand and blows into my palm. "I'm worried about you."

"I'm worried about me, too."

After some convincing, Will and I are headed down Alberni Street toward my office.

"You've had a death in the family," he's saying, not acknowledging the irony.

Before today, taking time off was non-negotiable for me. Last spring I worked with a fever that made me feel like I'd been hit by a bus. I took Tylenol, sipped herbal tea and crunched numbers, ignoring everyone who said I should go home.

Now I'm not entirely sure what I'll say when I walk in there, or who will even be there to say it to, but I'm a hundred percent certain I can't be at work when Cedar needs me. I nod as Will continues to unnecessarily convince me why it's important that I take some time off.

"To rest, to see a doctor …" He finishes whatever bit of advice he was mansplaining just as we arrive outside the building.

There is another voice in my head now, my own, telling me not to fuck this up, reminding me of what it took to get here and how many other people are waiting like understudies for me to fail.

Shut up, Jill.

That part of my life just can't be important now, and maybe it never was. Maybe it was only something that filled the void of loneliness, offered a sliver of normal. It has only been hours since I was last here, yet I feel the awkwardness of stepping into somewhere new. Even the steel door feels heavier. I glance back at Will, waiting in the rain, so eager for me to get help.

He nods encouragement, and for whatever reason, it irks me.

Henry Bourbon, my boss, is sitting in his office for once. I'd hoped to leave a note with less detail than my personal explanation and distressed face will provide, but no luck.

Still, the sight of him calms me down quickly, returns me to the here and now. Henry has made many inappropriate advances toward me over the past two years. And perhaps I've played with him a bit, too, not stepping away when he unapologetically pressed into me in the copy room. I know I may have led him to believe we were on the same page, but my lack of protest was really just my way of handing him more rope to hang himself with. I've seen the faces of other women as they left his office—shaken, awkward. Not me. I play it where it lies.

Henry is tall and attractive, with confidence and a butt that fills out his dress pants nicely. It's peculiar how a man's extreme confidence can confuse a woman. Even if we know better, the fact that a guy truly believes he is alpha makes us take notice—a hunter to our gatherer.

Could he be that good in bed? If it weren't for Will, I likely would have hooked up with Henry by now. His personality is far less becoming than his physical presence, however. In fact, it borders on revolting, the type not even a third shot of tequila could mask.

"Henry," I say, knocking on the half-opened door.

He drops the paper in his hand and leans back in his chair. His fingers clutch his belt, perhaps subconsciously, but more likely on purpose.

"Come in," he says, like a man twice his age.

"Hey," I say, forcing eye contact and cutting to the chase. "I need some time off."

I have his attention now. I'm asking for a favor and he's wondering what he will get in return.

"What's up?" he asks, sitting up straight, asserting his power while playing professional.

"It's a personal matter."

"What'd Sutherby do? That family …" He shakes his head, somehow conveying condescension that almost makes me cringe openly.

"It's not Will." I shut the door and sit across from him.

I lean in like I'm going to tell him a secret.

"It's my sister." I hadn't planned on being honest, but even if I'd told him about my sister in the past, there is a very little chance he cared enough to remember.

"Younger or older?"

"Younger." Skeeve.

"She look like you?"

"Seriously?" I stand and fake shock even though I expected nothing less.

"Settle down," he says, laughing, pleased about getting a rise out of me.

"She okay?"

"She's … missing."

"Shit," he says, with an expression I don't recognize that may actually be concern. "How much time do you need?"

"Not much. A few days. Maybe a week?"

"Can you pass on your accounts…temporarily?" He straightens a photo of himself and his mother before standing to walk over and sit in the leather club chair next to mine. He places his hand on my knee and I pretend to appreciate it.

"I think so," I answer, in my best impression of a damsel. I return the inappropriateness and put my hand on his leg to help pull myself up.

"Thanks, Henry. I'll let you know what's going on."

"You have my cell, right?"

"I do." I fake a grateful smile and leave his office while he's still talking. I vaguely hear, "If you want to grab dinner … or a drink …?" from two offices down but keep walking.

I pop into my office to organize some files for whoever will take over and notice how impersonal it must seem. No plants or art, no family pictures. Until Will, this office was a fair representation of my life. It's a lonely room. One you can walk away from, lock the door and keep moving—forward or backward. I make a mental note to improve this situation once everything is settled.

I pass Erin, the firm's personal Alexa. We're as opposite as two women in the same male-dominated field could be. She's bubbly, apologetic—she's sincere. The type of person you feel

guilty asking anything of because you know she'll say yes; generous to a fault. As I approach her, I watch as she prepares for me.
She finishes a call, opens her tablet and tucks her hair behind
her shoulder. When I get to the desk, she's alert but I can see a
look of concern on her face. This is a skill very thoughtful people
have. She's learned my expressions, put in the effort. As much as
I try to mask my conflict, she reads it straightaway.

"Jillian, everything okay?"

"Ummm … no, actually."

I tap my fingers on her desk in rhythm with the thoughts
in my head. I lower my voice and lean in toward her. "I have a
personal matter and will be out of the office for the next week."

"Oh, Jill. Is there anything I can do?"

For a second, I consider confiding in her. In terms of work
friends, heck, friends in general, she's about as close as it gets
for me. I quickly weigh the benefits and risks of getting Erin
involved. I have a list of leads I've agonized over in the years
since Cedar died: hospital records, background checks, police
reports. I imagine she could work her magic on them as she
does last-minute reservations and uncovering the private lives of
shady clients. But I realize this is not what she's asking. And this
type of research will only lead to questions I can't answer. Not
to mention that, despite being the best person I know for the
job, this is not within Erin's pay grade. It's also not within the
boundaries of our friendship. I don't even know her birthday, I
realize—I'm not going to tell her I think my parents faked my
sister's death.

I get a forced smile past her, assuring her I'm fine. As I turn
to leave, she calls out for me not to worry.

On my way to the elevator, I glance back and realize all of the people around me seem as trapped as birds in cages, longing for the world outside the glass windows.

It's only free will, I suppose, that separates them from Cedar, forced to live under a microscope, who only yesterday was enclosed much like this.

I can't get out of here fast enough. The air is so thick I swallow it in gulps; the everyday voices are sirens. I push the down button over and over, frantically, like I'm being chased.

"Jillian," someone whispers behind me.

CHAPTER ELEVEN | *Will*

My father always warned me about getting involved with women with baggage, but I am beginning to think a couple kids and asshole ex-husband might be easier than this. I'm trying to keep my shit together. I'm trying to find the right words, but I suspect there are no Hallmark cards that say, "Congratulations on reconnecting with your dead sister."

The best I can do is to minimize the amount of batshit crazy she puts out there.

I know she could hear me tell her to tread softly, but I also know she wasn't listening. Hours after falling apart in my arms, she walked into her office building dripping confidence. It baffles me. She baffles me.

She dropped my hand, stopped abruptly twenty feet from the door and cut me off mid-spiel. It was as if she stepped out onto a stage from behind a curtain after a total costume change. When she glanced back at me, her smile seemed more of a smirk. For a split second, it was like she knew my secrets.

But of course she doesn't know. She has no idea how I eagerly waited for her to turn the corner so I could pull my cell out of my pocket. To anyone watching the scene unfold, I'd just identified myself as a cheater, a liar. Or is that just in my head? The thought of being part of some kind of child abduction has been on fire in me, and my hand shakes as I try to dial my mother.

Over the last couple of years, I've been witness to a steady parade of the many sides of Jillian, despite her attempts to keep her softer sides hidden. It's alluring, really. I learned from my mother that the really beautiful ones are never "normal." But Jillian is a different type of complicated than my mother. I've seen no stunts for attention, no intense waves of neediness followed by silent treatments or spending tantrums from Jill. There is something captivating about how she reinvents herself, walking into a restaurant restroom with brisk, unyielding steps, and moments later, returning hesitantly, gracefully pardoning herself to the people at the table for interrupting them with her return. But this is different than mere personality shifts—either my family is involved in something terrible that shattered her life, or the woman I love is unhinged and in deep need of help.

The phone is ringing, twice, now three times. I picture Helene sprawled out drunk, her face pressed into the pillow, oblivious to the vibrations of her phone, the needs of her son. I'm not sure she ever had the instincts other mothers talk about having, the premonitions of danger to their offspring. Certainly not the times I spent waiting for her to show up after school or the afternoon I spent alone in the ER with a broken arm. She never "just knew something was wrong."

I wonder if wealth minimizes those senses. In my circle of friends, family sitcoms like "Growing Pains" and "Full House" were fantasy. Our family lives were closer to the ones portrayed in "90210": Kelly Taylor's mom snorting a line at a school function; David Silver's dad, the serial cheater.

When her voicemail clicks in, I want to throw my phone.

"Fuck, Helene, get it together." I can feel my breath hard in my throat, my lips twisted, wishing for a door to slam. But then my hand vibrates. The screen lights up with her name and I realize that, as much as she is a cliche, I'm a spoiled brat. Entitled every step of the way. Our relationship is a give and take of who needs what from who, when.

I'm a fucking asshole to two of the three women in my life that ever cared about me, and one is dead.

"Mom!" I answer, smiling a guilty, appreciative smile. "Thank God."

She doesn't say anything straightaway and I realize she's talking to someone in the background. I practice patience this time, giving her a second before I shout her name into the phone. "Mom!"

The inevitable fumble comes next. I hear the phone being jostled about and her voice gets quieter. She's walked away. Fuck, Mother. I call her back but get her voicemail. She probably didn't even hang up. I feel the frustration mount and I'm about to punch something but the phone twitches again.

"Jesus, Helene!"

But it's not my mother. The sound of his voice startles me and I straightened my back like I learned to the hard way as a boy. I instantly regret not looking at the phone before answering, and both blame my mother and acknowledge she is the lesser of two evils. I roll my cowardly eyes instead of sighing and brace myself.

"William," he barks, "who the hell do you think you are, answering the phone like that? What kind of person talks to their mother …?"

"Dad …" I try to interrupt, to no avail.

"Trust me, I know how your mother can irritate …"

"Phone tag, Dad. I just lost it …"

"What the hell is this I hear about your mother in your grandfather's things?"

Fuck. Really stealth, Mom.

"What are you talking about?"

"Don't bullshit me, Will. Mae …"

"You've got Mae reporting on Mom?" I automatically blame Mae, thinking about her disloyalty to my mother. How Helene's heart would break if she realized Mae, her only confidant, is working against her, working for the enemy—and then I see the glaringly obvious parallel. Although, in Mae's defense, she is an employee, not a partner.

"Someone has to watch that woman. Your mother, Will …"

"Why are you calling, Dad? We're out doing some errands. Jill just stopped by her office to pick something up and she'll be back any second."

"Ha! Let's not pretend to be the perfect boyfriend, son."

"And what choice have you given me?"

"No one put a gun to your head. Cut the crap. I know you've sent your mother looking through your grandfather's shit. Those files have nothing to do with you."

"Dad …" I attempt to reason, but he continues.

"I don't need you stirring things up and upsetting your mother. She's fragile."

"Don't pretend to care about Mother."

"Oh, shut your mouth. You can't begin to appreciate a thirty-year marriage. Of course I care about her—just keep out of things that don't concern you."

"Don't concern me?"

"That's right, Will. It's a job, after all, and you can be replaced."

I can hear that he is getting winded, frustrated beyond his usual cocky composure.

"What the fuck does that mean?" I've touched a nerve.

"You don't want to find out." He sighs heavily. "Do you need any money? I think you should take Jill somewhere for the weekend, maybe four or five days."

"For what?" I ask, taking the bait and forgetting about his threat.

"You two seem stressed."

"What the fu—" I stop myself. "What are you talking about?"

How does he know? What has Mother told him? Is there someone watching me as I watch Jillian?

"Look, son, this is part of the job. I need you to get her out of town."

"Okay. But I need you to tell me what the hell is going on!"

"Will, don't let me down here, not over some silly flirtation."

"Flirtation, Dad? We live together. I love …"

"Well, no one asked you to do that. She's not for you—she'll wise up eventually." He's chuckling. "Have you seen her?"

"Thanks for that, Dad."

I take a deep breath, the way my therapist told me to.

"Is that everything, then?" he asks, as if he is talking to his personal assistant.

What is the point of arguing? He's impossible. He's the definition of narcissist, with every fucking clinical characteristic: vain, pompous, smug, self-important, self-righteous, self-contented, conceited, self-referential—fuck him.

And fuck me. Will the Coward: chicken, craven, cur, dastard, cream puff, poltroon, sissy, weakling …

As if I don't have enough to worry about, now I need to figure out a way to drag Jillian out of the city, the city where she absurdly believes her dead sister is being held. Or is it absurd? There is something my father is hiding—among all the questions I have, that is one thing I know for sure. I should've demanded to know more, stuck my neck out for her. He's my father, for God's sake. He's not Putin. I could've threatened to go to the police, the friggin RCMP. But that comes at a risk, an enormous and unknowable price. It's beyond pissing off my father, having him destroy me financially—it's about Jill now. Whatever I do now, I risk losing her. And for the first time, I understand what that means. I love her, and I do not want to go back to a life without her.

I think about all those afternoons my mom spent dancing around the living room with her glass of pinot, belting out the lyrics to the "Glory of Love" along with her Peter Sedara CD, shaming my father with every verse.

Jill is probably on her way down by now and I am further away from having a plan than when she went in. Worse, I have another job to do, one more way to betray her and pull her away from what she wants more than anything else in life: answers.

As I tuck my phone into my pocket, trying to slow my breathing, I get an email notification. Normally, I would ignore it—it isn't as though I'm receiving updates from important clients these days. Jill is my only job and I am failing miserably at it, at her. But now I welcome a distraction and click open my inbox. There are a bunch of new emails, mostly junk, but at the top is one from my mother, the subject line: WTF? I glance at the door of Jill's office tower, hoping I have a few more minutes. With no sign of her, I open the email.

Will, thank you for coming to see me. We don't see you enough. I was able to get into Dad's office, but I think he's stuck Mae on me. There were actually a few strange things about Jill right on top of the desk, dated a couple months back. I know there is probably a file on her sister in the case, but it was locked. I will get in, just give me some time. It's pretty bizarre, I admit. I've attached photos of the stuff I found … I hope it worked. Let me know if you can access them. I miss you, son. Please come over again soon.

Lots of Love, Mom

Jesus. I don't know if I have the patience to wait but I also can't get caught with whatever this is. I can feel my heart quicken with dread about what's on the other side of this email. Bizarre, as my mother put it, is not the word I want associated with Jill, but at this point I can't think of a better way to describe the current situation, either. She's been in there close to twenty minutes. I consider texting her, but I don't want to come across as impatient. Fuck. Against my better judgment my finger goes ahead and double clicks on the first attachment. Of course it can't pop up right away the way it does when it's a coupon or porn ad; the phone is thinking, as Jill describes it, the spinning icon amping my adrenaline with each rotation.

"Hurry up," I whisper, my knees flexing in and out. I feel myself starting to blink incessantly, a tick I thought I outgrew as a child. Suddenly I have to pee urgently. Physiologically, I don't handle stress well. I am, in fact, a pussy. The icon disappears and the attachment finally reveals itself.

At the top, JILLIAN GANNON is written in red sharpie across an email correspondence with a woman named Heather Andersen. It's dated August 18. And it's still on my father's desk months later? Who the hell is Heather? The name is familiar, but I can't quite place it.

Mr. Sutherby,

As I mentioned previously, Jillian was extremely private. I have not spoken to her in at least two years. Just as I told your assistant last year, I am POSITIVE I only met Cedar once in college.

I read the sentence over and over. How could this Heather person have met Cedar? My panic surges even higher.

Is it possible that my father and my beloved grandfather could really be involved, scratch that—orchestrate—something as sinister as institutionalizing a child and telling her sister that she was dead?

And if Cedar is alive, where is she now? Has she escaped wherever it was they've kept her? If she was institutionalized, how did this Heather meet her? If Heather met her, how could Jillian not know for sure that Cedar is alive and where she is?

What the fuck is happening?

Is this why I have to get Jillian out of town?

My head is swirling and then I see Jillian—and she's running toward me, flat out, like she's being chased.

CHAPTER TWELVE | *Jillian*

The elevator finally arrives but I don't move. My eyes are glued to the far window, beneath an exit sign pointing to the stairwell, where my sister stood a moment ago. I don't care that I'm in the way as two executives maneuver around me.

"Jillian?" the younger of them says, as if asking for an explanation for my frozen state.

I don't respond, don't offer a smile or explanation, and her name escapes my lips.

"Cedar," I whisper. Then, louder, "Cedar!"

I feel my bag slide off my shoulder as I run toward the stairs. If they weren't before, I'm certain everyone is staring at me now. From the corner of my eye, I see Erin stand at her desk. She's calling out to me, but I'm focused, weaving through the office, scanning faces.

"Did you see that woman?" I plead, finally making eye contact with Mark, one of the trio of interns in the back cubicle.

"What woman?" he asks, his hands an upturned question. He looks over both shoulders, frazzled as always.

I bump into a mail guy I don't recognize and he drops

everything in his hands. I realize I'm a spectacle.

"There was a woman there," I point crazily to the space behind him. "Right there—did you see her?"

"I'm sorry, I didn't," he says, not looking up from the floor, where he is re-sorting his envelopes.

"Did anyone see her?" I can hear the desperation in my voice as I shout. I know I'm about to cry. No one here has ever so much as heard me stutter before, and now this.

Suddenly Erin is beside me, my bag in her hand. The huge room is silent.

"Everything is fine," she calls out, smiling in a way that instantly lightens the tension.

"Which woman are you talking about, Jill? Maybe she signed in with me?" She puts her hand on my arm and gently tries to steer me away.

"Umm," I look around, hoping to find someone with an expression of recognition. "She's tall, beautiful—someone must have seen her?"

"Come, let's get you some water and you can check the list at my desk."

Suddenly I feel like my mother must have waking up from each of her episodes. Everyone looking at me like I'm unhinged, pretending to understand, with their small, sympathetic smiles. It's been years since I've felt this humiliation, since Emily Ann, who I thought was my best friend and the only person who understood, turned out to be the cruel Regina George of our school.

In all fairness, the more Em tried to make me feel better, and she gave it a good go, the more I'd resisted her. Troubled teens aren't exactly fun, which is why I never blamed her for ultimately pulling away. But I'll never forgive her for what she did to me after.

I didn't go to parties, I didn't add my name to the prom queen ballot, but by the time I was seventeen, boys were starting to notice me. Perhaps this is why Em thought a little humiliation was warranted.

At first, I thought it was in my head—which I now know was the punchline.

"Cedar," came the first whisper from behind me in third-period English. I turned around to nothing but blank faces and buried heads. Later, in the hallway, I heard it again. Then again in math, which drove me to storm out of class as I realized what was going on.

Alone in the washroom, I cried hysterically in spite of myself. It wasn't enough for them to break me, to make me cry—when I opened the stall door, someone had written CEDAR in blood red lipstick on the mirror. As I ran from the bathroom, I was greeted by the school's mean girls, moaning, dancing about list-lessly, saying her name over and over.

"Cedarrrrrrrr, Ceeeeedarrrrr."

I left school that day knowing that everyone was looking at me like I was the mentally ill one, like there was something wrong with me and not the classmates who thought it was hilari-ous to torment me with my family's grief.

Later I found out that Em had told everyone that my dead sister Cedar was also my imaginary friend. I didn't have the strength to defend myself. School was over in a few weeks, so I kept my head down, ignored the taunts, left school and never spoke to Emily Ann or anyone else in that town again.

But this is infinitely higher stakes. Falling apart at work after you hit twenty-five is associated with instability rather than immaturity. If it were anyone else behaving this way at work, I too would've rolled my eyes and checked the crazy box.

On the flip side, who the fuck cares what they think?

"Cedar?" Erin asks, looking at me as though I've spaced out.

"What?" I ask, confused.

"You were calling Cedar? What an interesting name …" She's looking hard at a list with only a few names on it, not wanting to give up. "I don't see it—could she have signed in under another name?"

"It's fine," I snap. I take a deep breath and try to pull myself together. "I'm fine," I add.

I don't have time to chat with Erin, and anything I add at this point will only make the situation more troubling.

"I was probably seeing things," I give her a weak smile. "There's a lot going on."

She tells me not to worry, that it was no big D. To my surprise, and totally outside of my comfort zone, she throws her arms around me while needlessly narrating: "Let me give you a big hug!"

I think I've minimized the damage, but then she asks me if there is anyone she can call to come and get me.

She's worried. I laugh to brush it off and tell her Will is downstairs.

"Oh, good," she sighs a little too dramatically before back-pedaling with, "I mean I hate being alone when I'm upset."

"I'm not upset," I lie, almost tantrum-like, instantly undoing my attempt at calm.

Paul is walking toward us now and I'm not sure I can handle another sentimental ambush. Trying my best to ignore his presence, I turn and say goodbye to Erin, but he puts his hand on my shoulder. Ugh. I take a deep breath, shake off his hand and offer my most casual smile.

"Yes?" I ask, tranquil.

"Trevor and the guys over there," he points toward the water cooler, "said there was a really good-looking girl taking the stairs?"

I grab my bag and race for the stairwell, abandoning my attempt at composure, oblivious to anyone or anything in my path. I'm saying her name again. It's been too long, but maybe she is hiding there, waiting for me to find her. Why else would she be playing this game with me? I take the stairs two at a time. They're hypnotizing, becoming a blur. I know that I'd fall hard with one false step. I can't care. I keep running and yelling to her.

But the closer I get to the bottom, the further my heart sinks. Shit. Shit. Shit.

The last floor landing is empty. I kick the cinderblock wall, pull open the heavy steel door and gasp. I'm shattered; I probably held my breath for most of the nine floors. I don't understand.

Why is Cedar doing this to me?

It's raining harder now, and I see Will still standing on the sidewalk, waiting.

I'm drawn to him. In spite of my need to stay strong there is something about him that comforts me. Will has always felt so familiar, his eyes, his uneven smile. His quiet strength. I don't know why, but even when I don't want to trust him, he feels like home, home when Cedar and I were together.

I run to him, desperate to throw my arms around his neck, desperate for him to hold me together and keep me from breaking into a million pieces right here.

His face is white. How certifiable I must look to him, running from the fire exit like somebody is after me.

"Babe," he calls out, running to meet me. "What happened?"

I make it to him, almost crashing into his body, unsure of my next move.

"Did you see her?" I say, still winded.

"Who?" He looks around, following my gaze as it darts up and down the street.

"Cedar? You saw her?"

"She was there, Will. Watching me—then she disappeared."

I bend over, brace my hands on my knees, try and steady myself.

"Why is she watching me? Why does she keep running away?"

I stand and pull him tighter to me, resting my head on his shoulder. "I think I should call the police."

"No," he says flatly. He pushes me back and looks into my eyes. "You can't do that."

I'm not sure Will has ever looked at me so sternly. It's unsettling, but a bit of a relief at the same time. It's been a long time since I've allowed someone else to be in charge, if ever.

"Why not? Something has happened to her, Will."

"Yeah, Jill. She died."

His words sting. I realize he's frustrated—annoyed, even. I want to explain to him in a way he can understand. A quiet voice in my head is pleading with me to tell him everything, to tell him

I heard her this morning on the street; how I heard her just now in the office and how I heard her every day of our childhood—even though she was mute.

"It's crazy, Will, I get it."

I'm trying to be the Jill he knows, but it's harder now. He's seen how desperate I am and in so many ways I want him to be strong for me. I realize I'm tired of being strong. I don't know if it's the emotions of the day, the headache that still seems to be peeling parts of my skull away, or just the consequence of my useless race down the stairs moments ago, but I feel an immense wave of defeat.

"I'm sorry," I say. "I love you."

And I do.

CHAPTER THIRTEEN | *Will*

Since we've been together, Jill hasn't responded to any romantic gestures. Whenever she's had the opportunity to let go, to be intimate—she's backed away.

Today, after confirmation of my worst fear, that my family is somehow responsible for all of this, she is more tender and loving than ever before.

I said the cruelest thing she could have heard in that moment, a moment she needed my support. "She died."

I could hear the ice in my tone. This was the time she should have run, should've said something completely Jill-like: I need to do this on my own; I need some space; FU, Will Sutherby.

Instead, she apologizes and tells me she loves me as if she really means it.

She loves me.

I manage to get us back to the apartment, order sushi and settle Jill on the couch before sneaking into the bathroom to open the second attachment on Mom's email.

I tuck her under a blanket, drape the silly Magic Bag snuggly around her shoulders and kiss her forehead. This is what it's like to take care of someone, someone you love who isn't just drunk. I don't know if it's the contrast to her usual nature that's unsettling or if it's just the degree of vulnerability she's displaying, but it scares the shit out of me. She's present, wide awake, and following me around with her eyes as if she's completely dependent on me.

The toilet seat is down and I'm sitting here avoiding the mirror. Maybe Jill can't see the blatant betrayal on my face, but I know I'll see it right away. I flex my hands and stare at my phone on the counter like I'm gearing up to take a shot. Whatever is in this attachment, good or bad, it's information. Maybe it'll help Jillian—or maybe it will further incriminate me (if that's even possible). I know I have to decide soon what kind of man I am, what kind of son I am.

How could I let her call the police on my father?

How could I stop her from saving her sister?

Either way, I can't sit on this. I have to face it and deal with the consequences alone—or, I hope, with Jill. I click on Mom's email, feeling grateful to have her on my side, like maybe she is my only ally, the only other person who knows both sides. My eyes focus on her final sentiment, *Lots of Love, Mom*, while the attachment loads.

Property of Sutherby Investments
Private and Confidential
Transcribed conversation with Heather Andersen
April 7th, 2018

Davis: Can you please state your name and relationship with Jillian Gannon?

Andersen: My name is Heather Andersen and I was Jill's roommate at the University of British Columbia from September 2008 to around April 2012.

Davis: And how would you describe your relationship with Jillian?

Andersen: It was fine. We weren't BFFs the way I'd hoped but it was fine. We respected each other's privacy and she was very neat.

Davis: How would you describe Jillian's mental state at the time?

Andersen: Her mental state? What is this about? I thought you were just checking references …

Davis: Standard question, Ms. Andersen.

Andersen: She was normal. [laughs] I mean she kept to herself, but she was very stable, if that's what you're asking.

Davis: How would you describe her relationship with her family?

Andersen: What family? [sighs] Jill's parents are strange—cold and uneasy around her—or maybe it was me. They didn't visit often, and Jill didn't talk about them much.

Davis: And what about her sister?

Andersen: Her twin?

Davis: Is that what she told you?

Andersen: Well, no … but I met her once and I think they might be twins.

Davis: So you saw her sister?

Andersen: Yes, just once. At a bar. She looked just like Jill, but so much more confident. Like she liked the attention she got. Jill was never like that. Maybe a little taller? And lighter eyes.

Davis: And how did they interact with each other?

Andersen: I don't see what this has to do with a background check … does Jill know you're talking to me?

Davis: If you could please answer the question … we're almost done.

Andersen: I never saw them together. Jillian had mentioned her sister Cedar, but she hadn't even told me she was in town when I ran into her. She was way more approachable than Jill—really warm and outgoing compared to the rest of their family.

Davis: Why do you think Jillian didn't tell you about her sister?

Andersen: I mean, Jill didn't really get personal, she basically just slept in our place. She was gone all the time. I'm pretty sure she didn't have the easiest childhood.

Davis: So she didn't have any relationships?

Andersen: I didn't say that. [laughs]I mean, I respected that about her. Pretty cool. She's her own person, Jill.

Davis: What do you mean?

Andersen: She had goals for herself. She wasn't interested in settling down but that didn't mean she …

Written in red pen at the bottom of the report was: *Ms. Andersen could be mistaken or lying—no other evidence of lapses documented in 2012.*

The screen turns black from inactivity. I knew I recognized her name. Jill mentioned her roommate once or twice, but I got the feeling they were closer than Heather made it sound. More importantly, WHAT THE FUCK?

I put the phone down and pause. Likely because I'm an

over-privileged asshole, I leave the washroom almost pissed off. It's clear Jill is not being honest with me, which makes me feel less guilty. When I turn the corner into the living room, Jill is still sitting up—not looking at her phone, out the window or at the TV. She's thinking. She meets my eyes as soon as I enter the room, like she's only been waiting for me to come back.

"Hi," she says, looking like a Victoria Secret angel.

How is it possible to love a human being this much? I didn't know her eyes could be so innocent, her smile so sweet.

"Hi," I echo, my edge disappearing. "You wanna talk?"

I sit down on the couch, lift her feet and place them on my lap. I squeeze her foot and bring it to my lips. "I think we should, babe."

"I know," she says, with an endearing shrug of her shoulders. "I'm just so confused."

"I know you are. But you know I love you, right? You're not confused about that?"

The moment is interrupted by the house phone. The sushi. The phone is connected to our buzzer downstairs; I'm not even sure it has a number.

"Saved by the bell," I say with a wink, and head to the kitchen.

"I know you love me," she calls to me unexpectedly.

Despite everything, the sincerity in her voice warms every part of me. I'm part relieved, part turned on. This amazingly beautiful, complex woman is mine. I can't blow this.

I catch the phone on the fourth ring.

"Come on up," I say, my finger already pressing the pound key. Beneath the extended buzz, I hear the faintest "hello?"

"Come up," I repeat without much consideration for the delivery person.

"Jillian?" The voice shakes. It's a woman, and she sounds scared.

"Hello? Who is this?" I demand, trying to keep my cool. There's no response. Shit. My pulse starts racing. I'm torn between yelling to Jill or holding my breath and hoping whoever it is just goes away.

I get the plates down, grab some chopsticks and try to make enough noise to cover up the explosion of thoughts in my head: Cedar is here.

"Do you need some help?" Jill calls.

For whatever reason, I want to keep her as far away from the phone as possible. Of course I should buzz this person up. I should dart down to the foyer and greet her—she may have all the answers we're both looking for and bring Jillian everything that's keeping her from complete happiness. And yet I don't. Something about this whole situation is beginning to really scare me.

Like maybe Cedar is not what Jillian needs, maybe Cedar is the problem. There's a knock on the door and it startles me to the point that I drop the glass of water I'm filling into the sink.

"I got the door, clumsy," Jill teases, completely unaware of who might be on the other side.

"Jill, wait!" I yell after her. "Don't!"

I'm too late.

She gets to the door as I enter the foyer. I watch her open it in slow motion. I should run to her, but I don't. What can I do, really? I stand there, her back and the open door blocking my view.

"What the hell, Will?" she finally says.

The door closes and she turns, holding two bags of sushi. "How hungry are you?!"

She makes her way into the kitchen as I run over and glance into the hallway. But whoever it was is gone and the elevator door is already closed. I close our door behind me. Then I lock it.

I realize I need to get some answers before I can possibly be of any help to Jill. I can't imagine how she must feel if a simple utterance of her name from a stranger throws me into a complete tailspin. But how do I get answers while being secretive at the same time?

Jill dishes out our sushi as I gather the broken glass from the sink into a cardboard box. I haven't made eye contact with her since I picked up the house phone.

Somehow, she overlooked the urgency in my voice when I shouted at her not to answer the door. I keep the phone in the corner of my eye, prepared for it to sound again so I can silence it like a game of Whack-a-mole.

"Have you ever thought you saw Cedar before?" I ask, sheepishly keeping my head in the sink. She pauses, her hands frozen mid-motion.

"Like, before today?"

"Umm yeah, like, while you were in university?" I hold my breath.

"No. Not like this anyway ..." She gets back to work, preparing our plates with wasabi and ginger.

"I bet there were lots of girls there that looked like they might be her, though, right?"

"People always remind me of her, but Cedar is incredibly

beautiful—was beautiful—or would be." She's flustered. "You know what I mean."

"But Heather saw her?" I instantly regret saying it. Fuck.

"Heather?" She puts down the soy sauce packet she was struggling to tear open. "How do you know about Heather?" She's deadpan, completely emotionless again.

Keep moving, idiot. Don't look guilty.

"Your roommate, right?"

"Yeah, but how do you know about Heather?"

"I don't," I say frankly.

She turns and walks out of the kitchen.

CHAPTER FOURTEEN | *Jillian*

I'm suspicious. So much so that I can't stand the sight of his sneakers when I pass them on the way to our room. Our room. Suddenly the idea that I share a room with him makes me uneasy. This is what I get for trusting him, for asking for help.

Only hours ago, running toward him from the stairs, I realized how much I love him. For just a second, even with shaking legs, gasping for air, feeling the sting of humiliation, I thought that if I could just make it into his arms everything else would wash away with the rain.

But how does he know about Heather? It can't possibly be a coincidence that he asks about the one adult I ever mentioned my sister to. Even then, I hadn't given her any details; not about Cedar's accident, nothing—just, I had a sister named Cedar. How could Will know that?

I'm exhausted to the point of delirium. The idea of Will lying to me, of him snooping behind my back like one of my parents minions, brings a tightness to my throat that almost gags me. I'm sitting at the foot of our bed, listening for the footsteps that will come down the hall any minute. My adrenaline is killing me. If I don't move or scream, I'll explode. I throw the clothes off the chair in the corner and sit down with a huff. My arms are crossed firmly around my body, my feet tucked under my legs, my eyes staring straight ahead. With each passing second, I fluctuate between wanting to believe whatever he says so I can go back to how I felt twenty minutes ago and wanting to tie him up and dump water over his head until he tells me how he knows about Heather.

I hadn't considered a third option, that he wouldn't come at all.

CHAPTER FIFTEEN | *Will*

Today has been turbulent. It wasn't what I expected when I woke up this morning, to rise only to fall, to rise again and then avalanche. In addition to my own emotional shifts, Jill has been more emotionally variable in the last eight hours than she has in our entire relationship: wrecked, strong, heartbroken; in love and dependent on me, then hostile and suspicious.

The latter I didn't prepare for. Sure, bringing up Heather must have surprised her. But the look in her eye wasn't surprise. I realize I haven't asked specific questions about Cedar's death, but I was under the impression she died when she was a little kid.

At this point, I have zero idea who is lying, other than me. Perhaps if Cedar is still alive and frequenting school pubs, I don't have to worry about my family's involvement? As much? Fuck.

I didn't think it was possible get this angry with Jill while she is so obviously tormented, but when she stormed out of the kitchen, it rattled me.

My father is a liar. And when we didn't believe his lies, he got angry and stormed out, banged things, cancelled Christmas. My mother usually ran after him to sooth his ego, defusing the situation, giving him incentive to do it again. I wasn't having it.

I need to know what's going on before I will allow myself to hash it out with Jill while she is so vulnerable. I was absolutely sure that she'd mentioned her university roommate Heather to me, but I will not risk confronting her with more information I received behind her back until I'm certain it's legit.

So, I prepared a tray of food for her, tiptoed down the hall to our room and spinelessly left it behind the door she'd just slammed in my face.

My father is expecting us on the next plane out of here to God knows where, for God knows what reason.

Twenty minutes later, I'm in my car in front of my family's house for the second time today, waiting for him to get home so I can finally have it out with him like a man. I've attempted man-to-man conversations with my father before, but they always end the same way, bully-to-pansy. Years of failed patriarchal revolts have taught me how to manipulate my old man. In order to get what I want I need to keep the peace, kiss his ass and play the game by his rules.

I'll tell him I'm taking Jill to the Okanagan, then ask him what I need to know to keep the plan on track and hope he gives me something I can go on. Next, I'll ask him for some type of remittance for my participation. To a man like my father, this will seem reasonable and should throw him off the track of my loyalty to Jill. Nothing money can't buy, right, Dad?

It has been at least twenty minutes, maybe more. I'm sitting in silence, on edge, the way my father has conditioned me to be. The automatic wipers on my Range Rover are on and I have no idea when they started. I hadn't even noticed the rain, the drop in temperature, or that it's now completely dark. If he's not home yet, he's probably not coming home.

What an enormous waste of my time.

He would kill me if he found me in his office. The thought hadn't even crossed my mind until now. Forbidden territory.

Jill is waiting for me to come explain myself, the possible betrayals festering in her head the longer I'm away. And I'm sitting here doing less than nothing, focusing my energy on a plan that will likely implode. I can feel the adrenaline rising in my chest. I remember standing on the high dive waiting to jump—edging forward, and then backing up.

My hand is on the door handle, waiting for the surge to reach my fingers. One last breath and I'm going to do it, plunge into the house and not resurface until I have what I need.

One. Two. Three.

Fuuuuuuuuuuck.

Okay, I'm outside of the car. The cool air drives me forward. My senses interpret each drop of rain as a warning but too bad, this is what needs to be done—toughen up, buttercup. I put my key in the lock and turn slowly, hoping it will be quieter that way. It isn't. The click cuts through the night as I push the door inward. It's close to 7 pm now. Mae is likely tucked away in her quarters, exhausted from a long day of cleaning and espionage. Helene is harder to predict. Some nights she turns in after dinner, taking her nightcap to the privacy of her room; on others, she'll pull everything from the kitchen cabinets and reorganize, or set herself up in front of a Suzanne Somers' exercise video doing jumping jacks into the wee hours.

Inside, the house is oddly alive. A television is on somewhere; I can hear Lieutenant Olivia Benson's voice. The rain is coming down harder now, as if it was holding off until I got into the house—now it's holding me in here until I get shit done.

I slip my shoes off and make my way towards Father's office. There is no sign of movement in any direction. My steps are confident as I move through the foyer and down the long back hallway lined with ornate light fixtures. I stop short six or so feet from the French doors ahead.

I'm less confident now. There is a light on in the office, seeping into the hallway. I freeze, holding my breath, and try to figure out how to proceed. I tell myself I'm being ridiculous. This is the home I grew up in.

Paper is being moved, shuffled, scattered. The movements are angry; a drawer is slammed. Is it possible I missed my father's car? Did he park in the garage? Maybe he does that now. I try to find the original plan in my head, but it's lost. The more desperate I am to get my thoughts right, the more muddled they are. I'm a hundred percent tempted to retreat.

Pull back, Will.

As much as I hate my father's selfishness, it is his choleric moods that unnerve me most.

I'm an adult—I don't have to feel like this anymore. But I do have to be able to sacrifice for Jill, to find the truth. And if I survived my father as a boy, I can handle him now. Still, I approach the door timidly—not a good idea to poke the bear right out of the gate. After my grandfather's passing, my father inherited his office and his rules: no one else goes into the office. This includes visits or tea deliveries, as Mae learned the hard way. The intercom is there to use.

My fist rises to the door in slow motion. I inhale a deep breath through my nose and hold it in; I feel the oxygen recharge me the way it does on long runs.

It's the hand of a man, but the knock of a child, two tiny taps that echo through the cold hall.

Everything in the office stops. I imagine my father frozen, his vexed eyes fixed on the door like an enemy.

"Mae?"

It's Mother. Thank God. My body relaxes and I feel my shoulders drop two inches. Her voice warms me and I want to be in the forbidden office with her, out of this hallway where I stand exposed. I turn the handle, but it's locked.

"Mom?" I call out, trying the door again. She's probably as nervous in there as I would be, bravely doing my dirty work.

"Will?"

I hear fumbling and quick steps. She swings open the door and greets me with mascara streaming down her cheeks. She's drunk.

"You okay?" I ask, gently pushing past her into the room.

Not only has my mother broken the cardinal rule and entered my father's office, she has trashed it. Files are scattered as if she threw them; there's a broken picture frame, a ridiculous name plate thrust up against the wainscoted wall. His monogrammed pens are haphazardly spewed all over the rug.

She's standing strong, wearing a self-assured smirk on her face like a mask.

"What the hell, Mom?"

"We're broke! That bastard took it all. All our money, Will!"

She walks over to a pile of papers and selects one with a gesture so casual it seems random, but it what's she looking for.

"Look—look at this!!!" She forces the paper on me. "Look!"

It's a current account statement and it's definitely in the negative.

"How do you know he didn't just move the money? Maybe this isn't even the right account."

When I look up, I don't recognize the look on her face. It's a combination of distress and disgust.

"You think I'm an idiot, Will? Your father does. He doesn't have the power to just move our money. I know our account numbers."

She snatches the paper back and points like a lunatic to the number at the top.

"My money, Will! My family's money! Gone!"

"I'm sure there is an explanation."

I lead her to a well-worn leather chair that I've only sat in once.

"Come sit. I'll see if Mae can make us some coffee and we'll take a look. Have you eaten?"

"I fired her."

"What?"

"I fired that snooping … bitch." She's sobbing now.

"Jeez, Mom." I can't recall the last time I heard my mother curse.

"Does Dad know?"

"No, your father doesn't know. Ha! Well, he probably knows … let's be serious, it's for her own good." She's slurring but it's clear she means what she says. "He knows everything I do, literally has me followed, but he can ruin us and I haven't the slightest." She bursts into hysterical laughter. It's as if she's performing now, pacing back and forth, uttering a stream of consciousness to no one in particular. "Really, he keeps me drunk and I don't ask questions …"

She's interrupted by the sound of the front door. Shit. We both stand at attention: Dad's home. What a sight this will be—maybe we'll get lucky and it'll shock him into a heart attack. Helene starts laughing again, but it's nervous laughter now.

His footsteps halt and it dawns on me that my mother has just blown any chance I had at helping Jill.

"Mom," I whisper, "go to your room. I got this."

I shoo her away, swallowing past the lump in my throat. "Hurry."

Instead, she comes up behind me and takes my hand in hers.

"No, it's about time we start getting some answers."

The two of us united against my father, armed with proof of potential bankruptcy we can perhaps use as leverage. The footsteps are coming fast, like he's running toward us. There is nowhere to hide, and I refuse to allow my mother to take the fall for this. After all, she only made this discovery because I asked her to spy for me. The lights in the hallway come on. My mother tightens her grip on my hand.

Unexpectedly, there is a knock. "Mrs. Sutherby?"

"Holyyyyyy," my mother says through clenched teeth, throwing her hands in the air, "shit!" She holds her hands over her heart and releases a huge breath. Her laughter returns as I open the door to Mae, who seems even smaller than normal. She's soaked, her dark hair stuck to the side of her face. Like Mom, she's been crying.

"Oh, no, Helene!" Mae covers her mouth with her hand, her eyes wide with alarm. "What you do?"

"I lost it!" Mom cries. "I'm sorry, Mae."

"No, Ms. I'm sorry." Mae tiptoes around the mess toward my mother, who has dropped into the chair behind the desk. "I don't work for your husband no more; I won't tell him anything …"

"He's a bully, Mae! I know it's hard to say no to him."

They're hugging.

I'm still recovering from our close encounter.

We make a plan: Mom gets some food, Mae puts on the kettle and I tackle the office. I believe what Mae says about her renewed loyalty, but I can't risk telling her what I'm doing in here. Once I'm alone in the office I do my best to make sense of the mess, organizing the papers as logically as possible into folders and stacks, and asking myself where I would put the stapler if I were an anal, obsessive asshole.

After Mom and Mae bring me tea and force feed me a chocolate croissant, they retire to the front room to stand guard, giggling like children. They come up with plans to warn me of the enemy's approach: Mom will smash a glass (ha ha ha), Mae will knock over all of the chairs (chuckle, chuckle).

Helene seems to have temporarily forgotten about the bank statements. Chalk it up to intemperate memory loss, I guess. For now, it works for me. Better they're not here to witness whatever

I uncover in case it somehow incriminates Jill. I'm alone, surrounded by his secrets.

I take a few fuck-you spins in Father's chair, keeping the
filing cabinet in sight. What I wouldn't give to have some Kanye
in my ear right now, a little, "They say that people in your life are
seasons, and everything that happens is for a reason …"

Even I can't figure out why I'm attacking this war like a peace-
keeper. I've had ample time to dig in and yet here I am, stalling,
afraid to make a move.

Screw it. Armed with a letter opener I stand in front of the
cabinet. Of course, there are no obvious tells (no post-its reading
"shit on Cedar in this drawer") so I have no choice but to start
at the top. Unexpectedly, the drawer flies open so easily it forces
me to jump back out of the way. Smooth. I look over my shoulders once more and then begin. I leaf through files that all seem
ordinary, some investments and other financial stuff that Mother
would be interested in. The second drawer holds insurance, deeds
and last wills and testaments. I slam it shut and crouch lower to
pull open the third.

Something is different here, even the smell, the bleach I
remember from the hallways of Grandfather's hospital. The files
are older, a mildewed yellow. There are names on the top of
each file written in his pristine handwriting. Richards, Veronica/
Extreme Savant," with a photo of a red-headed preteen. "Kefner,
Tania/Childhood Agoraphobia." I start flipping quicker: Leung,
Lilly; Zuzek, Jennifer; Taylor, Jackie, et cetera, et cetera. I can't
begin to understand why my father held onto these files or what
implications it might have, but I also don't have time right now
to investigate.

I do a quick double check. Still no files on Jill or her sister.

I take a knee and pull the final drawer, but it's stuck. Once more I give it a good tug, preparing this time for it to come at me, but it's definitely locked. It has to be in here. I thread my trusty letter opener through the gap just above the lock, point it downwards and give it a good smack on the end. The lock clangs in defeat and gives way. Of course, there is no one here to witness what must be my most brawny moment.

Before I've even pulled it all the way open, my stomach drops. The lock isn't the only thing different. The fucking drawer is empty.

"Mother," I yell, leaving the now tidied office. Unless he misses the glass in the photo frame or I've left files out of place, my dad might not even guess someone has been in here.

Hearing no response, I find them in the kitchen, eating what looks like cold chicken.

"Can I talk to you a moment, Mom?"

She looks up. Suddenly she's exhausted and her age shows right through her fillers.

"Is the office okay?" Her eyes drift away from me, in embarrassment, maybe.

"Yes, it's as stuffy and intimidating as usual." I gesture to help her up, but I can tell she is done for the evening.

"You think you could come back tomorrow, darling?" She wipes at her forehead. Mae hops off her chair to help Helene to her room.

"Do you mind, son?" she asks, already on her way.

I tell her to sleep well and make my way to the door, disappointed. Like I feel most times I leave this house.

The rain is still on my side, though, as I make it to my car without being hit by a single drop. Even in the car, with the door shut behind me, it's dark, damp and creepy as hell surrounded by all these trees, no neighbors in sight. I'm glad Mother has Mae. I'm sure she's better company than my father.

I let the car warm up and pull out my phone. Three missed calls from my dad, two texts from Jill. I ignore my father altogether, delete, and hit Jill's name. The first one is a predictable, *where are you?*

As always with texts, it's hard to pinpoint the tone. I assume it to be hostile. But the second text reads, *I overreacted, come home* [sad face].

It's the second time today I feel like I've dodged a bullet. I mean, I can't say I disagree with her. We are both to blame, sort of. I shouldn't have mentioned Heather—and Jill is definitely hiding something.

I just really hoped I would be returning home with something more to go on. It's way too soon for me to divulge my source. I don't know where her mind is, but I'm fairly sure she hasn't jumped to the conclusion that my father has set her up and that my deceased grandfather was her MIA sister's psychiatrist.

I throw the car in reverse. My head is completely scrambled, and thoughts of just taking off alone run through my mind: stopping at an ATM and draining my accounts before my father cuts off my credit cards, flying somewhere with some fucking Vitamin D. I'm mid-fantasy when I see Mae run out of the house, waving her short arms in the air. What now? The devil on my shoulder tells me to burn rubber, but I stop abruptly. I don't get out, however, just roll my window down like a dick and make her walk over to me.

She comes to the window and unzips her jacket, revealing a thick manila envelope.

"Here, take this." She glances in every direction. "Don't show anyone. I make you copies."

"What is this?" I ask, hoping I already know.

"Your father tell me to move these files, not to let your mother get them. I make copies." She holds herself in a tight embrace against the cold night. "I try to give them to you at your apartment right after Mrs. Sutherby fire me, but I couldn't hear you on the …"

"Did you ask for Jill?" I put it all together, instantly relieved it wasn't the ghost-sister after all.

"Yeah, I ask is Jill home?" She lowers her voice, and, on her toes, she sticks her head in the window. "These files, Will—I think they have something to do with Ms. Jillian."

She turns and scurries into the house like a frightened child. A silly sense of triumph washes over me—I've somehow beaten my father at his own dirty game. I've gone from empty handed to knowing Cedar did not call on her sister earlier, and I have an envelope full of answers on my lap.

The car is warm now, but this isn't the ideal place to delve into the file. I make a quick call to Jillian, but it goes right to voicemail. I send her a text: *Almost home … sorry Mom needed me. For real this time. Love you.*

Not complete bullshit.

Ten minutes later, I park curbside in front of Indigo on South Granville. Self-indulgently, I prepare for my reading like

I'm going to a movie, replacing the popcorn with a coffee. The place is buzzing the way Starbucks usually are, particularly in wet cities, but I find an empty chair tucked in the corner.

I stopped drinking cappuccinos when Jill made a face early on in our relationship. Understandable, I get it. Currently, it's all about the Grande Americanos, black. They're playing some new artist I don't recognize but my head bobs to the rhythm anyway. Strangely (pathetically), I'm more at peace here than I am in my family home and, because of my father's games, even in the condo I share with Jill.

I pull the contents of the envelope out and stack the pages neatly together like a deck of cards. Holding them in both hands, I gently tap the bottom, so all the sheets fall into place. Mae must have hidden the originals per my father's instructions, because these are clearly copies, especially the photos that I shuffle to the bottom of the pile for later.

I fan through the documents. They are all stamped Sutherby Investments and labelled Cedar Gannon, Classified. (What is this, the FBI? Please, Father). Toward the middle of the pile is Cedar's original file from the hospital. At the very top, Grandfather has very legibly written DECEASED with two red underlines. I continue flipping, scanning over transcribed appointments and medical jargon until I come across another name, highlighted within her file: Jillian Gannon, Complications related to Childhood Bereavement. I've been toying with the idea that perhaps Grandfather's estate is being sued for something to do with the Gannons. Maybe this is why Dad's kept her file, why he keeps all those other files.

Fuck. I can't wait for my next assignment.

It's getting late and the baristas are hinting it's time to close up, one cleaning out the pastry shelf with her eye on me, the other sweeping around my feet. The only thing I've really uncovered is confirmation of what I'd already believed to be true: Cedar is dead. She did not call up on the intercom today; she didn't show up at Jill's office or slip a note under the door.

Heather's statements don't make any sense, but maybe she was just mistaken. It happens. Everyone has a doppelganger, they say.

Clearly, Jill is just traumatized by her little sister's death and is sleepwalking again.

My phone rings. It's Jill. Seeing her name and her beautiful photo light up my screen, I realize I'm incredibly relieved that this is only extreme mourning. We can deal with that. There has to be some sort of support group or doctor who could help. If there is some sort of lawsuit, I'm confident I'll be able to help defuse that situation, too.

"Hi babe, on my way," I say, juggling my phone and coffee, knocking some of the papers to the floor.

"Will?" she whispers, her voice shaky.

"Babe? What is it? You okay?" I kneel down and pick everything up, but stop as soon as I realize what's in my hand.

These photos are not what I expected. As in Grandfather's other files, there are intake photos of Cedar around five or six years old and one of Jill, I'm assuming, as a teen.

Then there is another photo. It's of a woman who looks a lot like Jill. Beautiful, but not Jill—a firmer jawline and higher forehead. It's dated last week, labeled Cedar Gannon, Age 22.

My eyes squint hard. Who the hell is this?

"Jillian? What is it?" I ask, swallowing hard.

"Will," she repeats, almost pleading.

I can barely hear her.

"Are you in the kitchen?"

CHAPTER SIXTEEN | *Aaron*

The thing about self-righteous people, the ones who "follow their dreams" and "live their passion"? They leave all the other shit for someone else to deal with.

My father chose his work and his patients over me. Sure, he didn't miss birthdays or Christmas mornings like I have, he never passed up on an opportunity to bring Mother flowers, and he posed for all the right photos. That's the type of man Dr. Xavier Sutherby was. But as a kid, I knew he was there only in body. His mind and heart were with his patients. People loved him, worshiped him. Regardless of the failed cases, the kids who got worse in his care, my parents' funeral was a spectacle. They were adored for their commitment to the hospital and the patients everyone else had given up on. I guess you can't blame him for trading my emotional neglect for their love.

Worse, my mother's support of my father's passion was endless. She was a blind follower.

But that all ended when someone ran them off the road. Or maybe it was just an accident, two senior citizens driving under the influence of a single glass of wine on a dark, slick night. It wouldn't surprise me, though, if some distraught parents had taken their revenge. It always seemed suspicious to me: his extreme attachment, his desperation in his office late at night, flipping through reports, bracing his head in his hands with frustration. He cared too much about them. About what happened to Cedar, especially.

You don't forget a name like Cedar or a case like hers.

My grandfather helped me to see the Good Doctor for the hopeless romantic he was. Sure, Xavier was a scientist, but he was soft. Just like Will. I see so much of my father in my son. Their hearts are big, foolishly so. Yet they put their focus, their loyalty, on strangers before blood.

Protect the family, my grandfather preached—the money, the privacy, the legacy. He encouraged me to stay away from medicine, to follow in his footsteps instead. My father's face fell when I told him I was not interested in continuing his work at the hospital, that I would be joining *his* father at the investment firm instead. It was baffling how surprised he was. I showed no interest in medicine to that point, so it clarified how little he knew me. In fact, I found all his work stories annoying.

Having my own work to focus on, to succeed in, helped me forgive my father for his emotional abandonment, for his obsession with other people's children over his own son. Making money filled a void.

My wife was chosen like a smart business merger, as Grandfather coached. She was so beautiful, tall and strong. Independently wealthy, also raised on old money.

My father loved her. He seemed proud of me for landing a

woman like Helene. For a while, I began to appreciate my father; I honestly believed he was starting to love me.

Helene got pregnant only a few months after we were married; a boy, no less. Grandfather brought cigars to the hospital and an expensive bottle of champagne. Father and Mother were there, really there. Like our wedding, it was a good moment for the Sutherbys. My father wept; my grandfather shook my hand, hard.

As a boy, my father's insistence on talking his theories to death while tuning out my interests was maddening. However, as a grandfather, he bothered me less. My parents got on the floor with Will, lined up toys and watched to see what he would choose. They brought him gifts and took him to brunch on Sunday mornings.

Then Cedar came along. Father's attention shifted again. He became obsessed with her: "They don't appreciate her; they're not fit to be her parents …"

Mother started coming to visit Will alone, making excuses for Father the way she had when I was a child. When he did show up, he spoke only about her: how her family didn't even try to understand how brilliant she was.

My Will was elected captain of his hockey team; *his* Cedar could read an entire book at six. It was like reliving my childhood all over. But this time my protective instincts came out. Will was my son, his grandson—he was a remarkable kid, but that wasn't enough for my old man. We would never be enough for him: textbook daddy issues.

Somehow the realization caused me to drift away, not just from my father, but also from my wife and child.

I buried myself in work. Every time Will failed at something, it was like my father's disinterest was warranted.

I was a shit father to him, I know it in my soul. But at least I didn't choose another kid over him.

Helene kept up the relationship with my parents. She brought Will over to the house a couple times a week. They both felt at home there. Everyone loved Xavier. Will wanted to be just like him. It unnerved me. Could he not see his grandfather did not value him as much as he should have been valued?

My grandfather died when Will was nine. I dove into work even more, determined to preserve what Grandfather had built.

In the process, I destroyed Helene. The light she carried started to fade. The smile she'd saved just for me stopped appearing. She filled the void I left with booze, just as Will had replaced me with my father.

Then my parents died. After the car crash, Will had no choice but to gradually turn back toward me. I helped navigate his financial education and got him the best summer internships. He did well and had a natural talent for reading trends. I watched how he held himself around important people and it made me proud, like he had been paying attention after all.

I also saw how he treated his mother, gentle and patient despite her often embarrassing behavior—that came from my father. Maybe it was having my son in my life again, maybe it was no longer having to compete, but I started to appreciate, even miss, my father. In Will, I could see everything that was good about him.

The hospital had a lot of secrets. There were times my father would lock himself away in the office, whispering into his tape recorder.

We were forbidden to go in, ever—it was Father's only rule. Now he was dead, too early, without an opportunity to clean up any of his messes.

What have you done, Father?

The secrets in that cabinet would destroy us. He left me no choice but to take extreme measures to protect everything my grandfather and I built.

I've been staying one step ahead of my father's failures.

Then Will falls in love with the girl.

It's a complication, but that's all it can be. Involving him was a mistake, I'll give you that. But when this all comes to light, which it will at some point, I have to be prepared to discredit Jillian, to undo the impact of my father's brilliant madness.

It's for Will's good too.

CHAPTER SEVENTEEN | *Jillian*

Fear has no logic.

I'm on the twelfth floor of a building with a twenty-four-hour concierge, each floor locked. Yet here I am, hiding behind the column in our living room, trembling in a way I didn't know was possible.

It's not logical that someone is in the apartment with me, but that doesn't mean I'm alone.

After our argument, it took me the better part of an hour to realize Will wasn't coming in to grovel. I waited, sitting up straight in my chair, pouting. Any minute. He'll be right in.

The forced solitude forced me to be reasonable, to really think about what happened.

How would he know anything about Heather and Cedar? He wouldn't; it's just not possible. I may have mentioned Heather to him—that's possible. It wouldn't be difficult for him to remember the name of my one college friend.

God, I must have sounded insane. What exactly was I accusing him of, anyway?

It's been an emotionally devastating day. Obviously Will is confused, in some ways maybe more than I am. Of course he wasn't about to come in here looking for more aggravation. Not even saintly Will would subject himself to that.

I slowly came to my senses, felt ridiculous and then realized I'm starving. I pictured Will sitting in our spot on the couch eating his spicy tuna roll, discarding the edamame peels, sipping a pinot. My mouth waters and I regret my tantrum. I will apologize and we will have a good night.

With a contrite new attitude, I hop off the chair and practically run to the door. When I open it, there is a tray of food on the floor. How had I not heard him bring it to me? I wonder how long it's been sitting there. I pick it up and carry it down the pitch-black hallway, through the foyer and into the kitchen.

He isn't here. I'm certain he must have left right away because there is no way he left me here alone in the dark—he knows how I feel about the dark. I also know how lazy he is about turning off lights.

My disappointment makes my stomach turn. Or that may be hunger. Either way, I won't enjoy the very thoughtful tray of food until I know Will is alright, that we're alright. I call him twice and text him a lame apology before adding a glass of wine to my dinner and making my way to the living room.

Our condo is open concept. After the hallway from the foyer, the space opens up to unhindered sightlines from the kitchen, nearly fifty feet across to the living room, with a sitting room and office in between. There are two bedrooms, one on each side of the foyer. Originally two condos, it was renovated before we moved in to have two large bedrooms with en suites; floor to ceiling mirrors were installed along the back wall.

As guilty as I feel about my behavior, I realize I am now quite relaxed. I know Will loves me. Even though I'm unhappy he isn't with me (worse, that I'd driven him out of here on a rainy night), I'm not afraid he won't be back. He'll be back.

Obviously, I need something light, so I start an episode of Friends. After only a few pieces of sushi and maybe half a glass of wine, my eyes get heavy, like I've been drugged. I force a few more bites and then bury my head into the pillow. Knowing my body really needs the rest, I close my eyes.

I don't remember dreaming. I slept hard, comfortably, not feeling uneasy in the dark room, just heavy all over. I don't know what time it was when I fell asleep, nor do I have any idea what time it is when I wake up.

Then the front door opens. In this apartment, it's a distinct sound, no way to miss it.

I sit up slowly—Will's home. That's good. I rub my eyes, trying to wake up, feeling the disorientation of interrupted deep sleep, but then I hear footsteps.

Will is a heavy walker; the woman underneath us has complained more than once. These steps are different. Almost sticky, as if they were purposely quiet, peeling themselves off the floor like tiptoeing through wet paint. Will is probably trying not to startle me. He's thoughtful, he's romantic—he's a good one.

It feels like a minute or so passes before I realize I am holding my breath, waiting for him to appear out of the dark hallway. When he doesn't, I call out to him.

"Will?" My voice sounds a bit fearful, but there is no reason to be scared, right?

I repeat his name, feeling equal parts frightened and irritated at him for not answering. I'm not brave enough to venture from my spot—instead I remain still and silently pray he'll knock it off.

But I realize that Will wouldn't do this to me, especially not after today. Practical jokes are not his thing even on a normal day.

The only thing I'm sure of is that *someone* came in. After another minute of sitting in silence, the footsteps start again.

My phone is in the kitchen. I called Will from there.

So stupid, Jill. I think about screaming and stomping wildly on the floor to get someone's attention, but I am frozen. The sound of my breath is so loud, like a wheezing, elderly smoker—I know that if I hide in this otherwise silent apartment, it will give me away.

The footsteps stop again, taunting me. That's when I hear muffled talking—maybe Ms. Lee across the hall? At first, the end of the eerie silence is comforting; someone is within yelling distance. Then it dawns on me that the voices are coming from our bedroom TV.

Damn it, Will. Had he come home angry and left me here on the couch to sleep?

The good news is I've never heard of a burglar taking a minute to watch television during a theft. I stand up and make my way toward the foyer. I'm still scared, but, logically, it has to be Will.

Okay, this makes total sense. He's ignoring me because I was so awful earlier.

It is nearly pitch black in the hallway so it's easy to see that the front door has been left open. Light bleeds in from the elevator area, casting lines of shadows. Why wouldn't Will close the door? I turn in the direction of our room and then I see it—a person moving incredibly fast, almost leaping from our en suite into our closet.

I can't be sure what I'm seeing, but I am certain it is not Will.

Stupidly, I run past the foyer instead of out the door to the safety of my neighbor's, or down the elevator to Alan, the night concierge. Before I have time to think about it, I am back in the kitchen, where I grab my phone before sprinting across the condo to hide behind the pillar. I can see people in their condos across the street watching TV, chatting with wine glasses in their hands, oblivious to mzy danger in plain sight.

"Help me," slips from my lips, the only words I remember right now. I open my phone, shielding the light with my body.

Will texted me thirty minutes ago that he was at his mother's. My hand is shaking as I click on his number. Pick up, Will. Please, pick up!

It feels like it takes forever for the first ring. I look back to the happy people across from me, keeping the fear at my back. But before the second ring, in the reflection of the window, I see someone go into our kitchen.

So here I am, scared to death—I haven't taken a real breath since Will said he was ten minutes away. Not in the kitchen, the parking lot or the elevator.

"Stay on the phone, Jill," he says. "I'll be right there."

But I don't want to stay on the phone. I want to call the police or for him to call the police, to call Alan—anyone who isn't ten minutes away. But I'm too scared to speak. I don't want to give away my location. Will asks me if I was sleeping—is it possible I've been sleepwalking? His questions anger me, but for a second, I consider it. I was asleep, sound asleep, the state in which all my past night terrors have occurred. Could my own sleepwalking have woken me? Had I imagined everything?

I listen to Will get in his car, to the sound of the engine starting. To his breathing, now nearly as ragged as mine. I'm about to make my way out of hiding to make a dash for the front door when I hear my name.

"Jilllllllllian."

It's coming from the kitchen. My shaking stops abruptly. I'm frozen into stillness. It's a woman's voice, but there is no warmth or kindness in the way she has exaggerated my name. Whoever is in there is trying to scare me.

I hadn't considered what Cedar might sound like outside of my mind, but this voice couldn't be hers. Could it?

"Babe," my voice trembles, "someone is in the kitchen. A woman."

"I'm nearly there." He's panicked now too.

I just don't know if he believes me or if he thinks I'm really unwell.

You would think I'd be less afraid of a woman intruder—women don't typically break into houses to assault other women. But I am terrified for so many reasons: that this woman is here to harm me, that I'm still sleeping and this is all an extremely vivid dream, that I'm really losing it and having a psychotic break, or, worst of all, that this woman who is tormenting me is Cedar.

It certainly felt that way at the office when she ran from me. She must know I never truly gave up hope. I was barely a teen when she was taken; what could I have done? Maybe she's been brainwashed? I think of Patty Hearst.

But if it is Cedar in the kitchen, why wouldn't she communicate with me telepathically? The thought gives me a second's comfort, then I realize it could be someone trying to find Cedar through me.

I drop the phone and cover my ears firmly with both hands, like a child who refuses to hear, and wait for it, for her to say my name again.

It is alarmingly quiet. I hear the buzz of pressure in my head but nothing else.

This is stupid. I grab the phone again. Will is saying my name over and over. I whisper that I'm back.

Then I hear the voice again.

"Jillybeaaaaaan."

Cedar's nickname for me. No one has called me that in more than a decade. There is the faintest echo as it bounces off the walls and windows.

"Why are you doing this?" I yell, not moving.

Silence, and it kills me.

This is like losing Cedar all over again. I call out to her, over and over, begging her to talk to me. There is no response.

The front door slams shut, and I jump.

"I'm here, babe, I'm here!"

I can hear Will simultaneously in my phone and in the foyer.

"I'm in the living room," I breathe into the phone, still frozen.

"Jill?" he says loudly, flipping the lights on. He's in the room, I can see him in the window. He's right behind me, but I can't move. I finally slump down to the floor, exhausted, and shout, "She's in the kitchen!"

I slide around the pillar, keeping my back pressed firmly against it, and watch as he pivots and strides across the condo. He grabs his laptop off the desk on the way, to use as some sort of weapon, maybe.

"Hello?" he shouts aggressively, a toughness in his voice I hadn't expected. He dips around the wall. I can't see him now. I hold my breath waiting for her to come running out, but she doesn't. Instead, Will reemerges, his hands on his hips. He doesn't say anything, just continues his search of the house. I track his steps, down the back hallway toward the guest room, back through the foyer, the powder room, and then down the hallway toward our room.

She must be hiding.

What if she attacks him—what if she's not alone? I force myself up and arm myself with a heavy brass bookend. I creep toward the sound of Will's footsteps. I call out to him, my voice soft.

"In here," he says. I find him standing in our room, looking completely calm.

"No one is here, Jill. I checked everywhere."

"You couldn't have checked everywhere." I'm still whispering, my pulse still racing. He takes my hand and leads me toward the front door.

"I locked it behind me, babe. See?" He gestures toward the bolt.

"Then she's still in here."

"But she isn't. It's just us. I've checked everywhere."

I'm not convinced, so he gets me a blanket and plunks me down in front of the door.

"Stay here, babe."

He disappears around the corner again, but the foyer is bright, and his footsteps are casual.

My heart is slowing but it's confusing how peaceful and safe it all seems now. With the lights on and Will here, the condo isn't scary anymore. What is scary is the thought that I really might be losing my grip.

"What the hell is all this?" Will yells from the kitchen.

His voice is accusatory, like he's scolding a pet who had an accident.

CHAPTER EIGHTEEN | *Will*

The drive home may be the closest I've ever come to out of control: the rain obscuring the windshield, my lazy wipers doing a half-ass job, oncoming headlights piercing my eyes like lasers.

Worst of all, Jill alone and scared for her life. What could I do? If I called the police the ramifications could be bad on so many levels, to so many people.

Not to mention if the intruder turns out to be Jillian's sister—the police barging in would undeniably put a damper on their reunion, especially if she has escaped from an institution. So, completely helpless, I sped through the city, willing to kill myself or someone else in order to protect our secrets.

If I'm being honest, seeing a photo of the adult Cedar was a relief. Yes, it implies that my grandfather has done something unforgivable, but it also means my girlfriend is not a psycho.

Walking into our apartment, I felt more creeped out than threatened—more concerned for Jill than for my bodily safety. I may be emotionally fragile, but I'm pretty confident I can hold my own with most girls, physically at least.

There was no evidence anyone besides Jill had ever been

there. She was completely shaken up, though, and since I'm not a complete ass I knew not to treat her fears lightly. I searched each room top to bottom, more than once.

What I eventually found was way more troubling than a long-lost sister.

I don't know how I missed it the first time I checked the kitchen. Probably because I was looking for a person. Where would someone even get this many pills?

What has she done?

"How many did you take?" I yell before she comes into the kitchen. I pick up handfuls and watch them fall through my fingers. At least thirty empty pill bottles are scattered on the counter. She comes up behind me, the blanket still draped over her shoulders.

"I didn't do this!" She looks around and seems as dumbfounded as I am.

I pick up a bottle. Jillian Gannon. Olanzapine.

"Your name is right here, Jill." I pick up two more. "It's on all of the bottles."

She just stares at me blankly. It's enraging. I put my hands firmly on her shoulders and lead her over to a dining room chair, away from the pills. I'm scared now. I can hear it in my voice. Her head is down but I lift up her chin gently so I can see her eyes. A tear runs down her cheek, but I repeat, as sternly as I can, "How many did you take?"

"I don't know what's going on."

She tries to push past me. I can't let her.

"I know you are a bit out of it right now …" I attempt, but she pushes me roughly.

"Calm down, Jill. What I mean is that I know you're confused, but you have to explain this! Where did these come from?"

"I don't fucking know."

"Well, I don't believe you. You're telling me you've never seen these pills before?"

She pauses in a way that immediately tells me she is lying. Why would she do this? Then again, why was she sitting in terror behind a pillar in our living room?

Interrogating her isn't going to work if she doesn't remember doing it. She walks over to the counter and starts pushing the pills into a pile almost like she's trying to cover them up, like she can't bear to look at them. In a way, it seems so unfair for her to be exposing all of her secrets in her sleep.

"They're obviously mine. But they're from a long time ago." She tosses a bottle at me and she's telling the truth: it's dated four years ago.

"Were you saving them for something?" I ask, thinking the worst.

"My parents couldn't know if I took them, only that I filled the prescriptions," she says quietly before walking toward the window and looking out at the night.

"I don't know why I didn't just throw them away. I didn't want them going into landfill, and I felt like I couldn't take them back to the pharmacy without my parents potentially finding out. They were in our storage unit. And I do know I didn't sleep-walk down there and dig them out of the suitcase they were in."

"Babe, I think you may have."

"Someone was in here. Someone is trying to scare me," she says to the darkness outside more than to me.

I come up behind her, and when I touch her shoulder she jumps.

"It's not possible," I whisper. "She didn't just vanish."

"She did before …" Her quiet voice trails off completely.

"So you think it was Cedar? Why would she do this? How would she even know about the pills?"

"I don't know what to think."

She turns to me and wraps her arms around my neck, holds me so tightly her bracelet scratches my neck.

"But I need to find out what's going on," she whispers.

Less than an hour later we are in bed. Jill is curled up beside me. Her breathing has slowed and her head has grown heavy on my shoulder, so I think she's finally asleep.

I, however, am staring into the dull city sky outside our window, aware of nothing but my thoughts. My mind is swirling. I'm afraid to sleep in case she wakes. On top of everything, I'm trying to come up with a plan to get her out of town as various awful parts of the day bounce in and out of my consciousness. It feels like being caught in a nightmare. Yesterday I was an asshole, my father's bought and paid for quisling. Jill was my miraculous girlfriend, stunning and brilliant and somehow mine. Tonight, nothing is clear. Who is this woman beside me?

I drift off at some point and dream of my grandfather at the hospital. He's wearing his white coat and his round glasses, sitting with crossed legs. He watches two young girls, patients, interacting; he takes notes and speaks into his tape recorder. His voice is hushed so I can't make out what he's saying. He smiles as he talks. He's very fond of them. They don't seem to notice his presence; they carry on, their backs to him.

Someone else is in the room now—a young boy in a polo shirt. I see the boy is me. A young Will, pale and small for his age. The realization sends the room spinning and I now see everything from his viewpoint. My grandfather, dressed for work, stands and moves quickly, too quickly, until he is looming above the girls. He holds up something that looks like a needle, a large, frightening needle. I try to look away, not wanting to watch any more, but I can't. He grabs one of the girls by the arm, hurting her. The other whips around, faceless, and yells, "Help me, Will!"

Awake, it takes a minute for my eyes to adjust to the dark. Jill is still pressed up against me, the door to our room is still shut tight. I get up slowly so I don't wake her and go into the bathroom to splash water on my face. The cool water brings me further from the dream but when I look into the mirror, I remember what scared me awake.

The girl's voice was Jill's, but she had no face.

It's a little after three. I probably only had a couple hours of sleep, but yesterday's events and the dream have reenergized me more than a full night's rest. I make a quick coffee and grab a blueberry muffin that Jill picked up from JJ Bean two days ago, when everything was so much simpler.

I make my way back to the bedroom, not wanting to leave her alone and not really wanting to be alone. On the way, I pass through the foyer. Purely out of habit, I glance at the door. I freeze, my breathing and logic halted.

It's unlocked.

I hope I'm still dreaming. But the coffee on my tongue is bold, it's awake, and so am I. Could Jill have done this? Why? For validation—evidence to support her fears? I lock the door. Then I unlock it and lock it again.

She is still sound asleep when I get back into bed, and a relieved sigh escapes me. The comforter has fallen off the edge of the bed somehow and the room is cold. I cover her and see that her eyes are twitching quickly beneath her lids. I can't imagine her dream is any more comforting than mine was; I just hope she is a little less tortured in her sleep than she was awake today.

I give her a "shhhhhh," my best attempt at white noise, and hope it's enough to scare the monsters away. Wanting to be close to her, I make my way over to my side of the bed.

I do my best to settle, I take a big bite of the muffin. It's stale, but because I skipped dinner, I eat it. I never had the appetite other boys did growing up, often ordering two burgers just to save face. Right now, however, I'm near ravenous. I take a large gulp of the scalding coffee and shove the rest of the muffin in my mouth. Wiping my hands on the sheet, I grab my laptop from the night table and type olanzapine.

I'm expecting it to be an antidepressant, but instead words like schizophrenia, manic depression, bipolar disorder and anti-psychotic pop up. What the— ?

Jill is exhibiting some unusual behavior, sure—but I wouldn't classify her as even minimally depressed, never mind manic. I shield the screen from Jill's side of the bed and click on a Harvard. edu article on the possible usages and interactions. Just reading words like psychotic makes me feel like I'm double-crossing her.

I wouldn't appreciate her jumping to far-reaching assumptions about my mental health or my past.

Yet I read on. Jill could have been anorexic—maybe bulimic? Obsessive compulsive? I keep skimming but think back to the picture I found in Dad's office. If Cedar is still alive and gets some sort of kick out of tormenting her sister, might it explain Jill's need for such a serious drug?

The doubt and questions alone would drive me crazy. Someone did move those pills into the kitchen, and Jill was alone. Which means her subconscious must be asking for help, finally letting me in even if she doesn't consciously trust me.

I'm starting to think my father is protecting Jill from her sister and maybe from herself. I can't allow myself to think about the danger she was in, sleepwalking with all those pills in reach. If she had taken them, she could have died before I made it home. And it would undoubtedly have been ruled a suicide.

If we are protecting her, I bet my grandfather's will has something to do with it—funds to my father in exchange for her safety. Aaron doesn't do anything without a return. The thought motivates me to plan our getaway. It makes sense. Reduce the stress.

My father didn't give me any specifics so I suppose we can go anywhere. Without giving it a lot of thought, I book flights to the Okanagan Valley. Jill grew up in a small town south of Kelowna called Ravenscliff. Even now the population is only a little over thirteen thousand; fifteen years ago, it was probably only half that. I used to love the drive up there, the winding danger of the Coquihalla Highway, the odd bear drinking at the side of some stream. Any time we spent more than a couple days there, though, I got a claustrophobic itch to get back to the city, as if the mountains could somehow hold me captive.

I really don't know where my head is: she might hate the idea of confronting her past, or she might welcome the chance. Small towns are known for gossip, everyone knowing everyone's business. Someone is sure to know more than I do, probably more than Jill seems to.

Grandfather's hospital isn't too far from there. I haven't been up there since he died. Truth is I can't think of any other place that made me so uncomfortable, not even the galas and charity events my father dragged me to, a little kid in a tux trying to make small talk. But if Jill wants to go, I'll take her.

The woman who took over the hospital turned it into a private addiction treatment center. Rumor has it they're opening a separate wing for gaming addiction. No joke.

Just being on the property might spark her memories, and I highly doubt anyone there will recognize me after all these years.

Or I'm a complete fool and this will all backfire and I'll get what I have coming. My eyes are stinging, the caffeine standing no chance against my emotional exhaustion. If anything, the warmth of the cup in my hand is more soothing than stimulating.

I would rather not stay in the Super 8 or the RV parks in Lake Country because I'm a hotel snob as well as an accused all-round snob, so I book a suite at a resort on Lake Okanagan before closing the computer.

CHAPTER NINETEEN | *Jillian*

Even though less than twenty percent of the world's population has ever flown, the fact that I've only been on a plane once before is, according to Will, "adorable."

It was a short trip, the same as this one in fact, but in reverse order.

Dr. X and I were off on a trip for some tests and "happy time" in the city, away from my shared bedroom and the lingering sounds of sisterly banter. I remember being frightened by the turbulence, the way the small plane bounced and shook, the sound of the engine screaming. It wasn't the fear of dying, or even of falling from the sky, but rather of not having any control over what would happen, having to sit and wait until it stopped. Or didn't.

The day of my sister's accident was sort of like that. Even though I wasn't strapped down by a seatbelt, I was stuck, frozen, watching a nightmare-like scene unfold, with no power to stop it.

Nothing about that accident seemed natural. But maybe no tragedies do.

I'm not afraid of the turbulence today. In fact, I welcome the uncertainty of takeoff—it is energizing to be afraid of something as colloquial as a crash. Will is watching me; I can feel his eyes questioning my every expression, his analysis of my behavior. He sprung this trip on me and every fiber of my being hates him for it right now, for forcing me to confront my past, for not giving me the option of saying no. How could I? I need help and I'm teetering on mentally unstable. I can see that. How irrational my behavior must seem to him. I figured it was pack my bag or have Will suggest I see a doctor and insist on calling my parents.

A few days ago, I was a different woman. Strong, independent, secure. Now, somehow, Will is in charge and I'm in a position where I can't say no. Not because I trust him but because I don't trust myself.

I'm starting to feel Cedar again, as if an invisible umbilical cord is reattaching us somehow. I have not heard her in two days, nor have I physically seen her, but my dreams are so alive they carry over into the day. I find myself zoning out, drifting into myself to find her, to hear her voice.

I'm almost sure she's not on the plane. Since the moment Will pulled up to the valet service door at Vancouver International, my eyes have been scanning, my palms sweating like I'm a smuggler or terrorist. I'm watching my back while trying to seem normal. One woman at the baggage check, another in the security line and three more at our gate could've been her but weren't. I estimate there are two-hundred passengers on this flight, and more than half are women. I've been doing a mental inventory, counting and scrutinizing as Will talks and talks, but he is getting suspicious now. He turns his head whenever I look around, looking over his shoulders to the beat.

"Turbulence makes me uneasy," I tell him, as if I'm a frequent flyer.

He buys it and squeezes my leg.

There are at least three rows at the very back of the plane I haven't processed. I'd hoped to have the aisle seat but Will, ever the gentleman, paused and gestured for me to sit first. Anyone who boarded the plane after us is accounted for. I'm patiently waiting for the seatbelt sign to turn off so I can use the restroom and get away from Will's watchful eyes. On the other hand, I might be safer if I stay seated. I don't know what they've done to her. Is the Cedar I love still in there? Or have they reprogrammed her into someone I should fear?

I'm assuming takeoff was reasonably smooth; everyone around me seems oblivious. We're safely in the air but the pilot has yet to free us from our belts. I'm watching for the sign to go off; Will is watching me. My anxiety is building, as if Jack is going to spring out from the box at any second. My knee desperately wants to shake just as my fingers want to fidget, but if I can't move, neither can they.

Unintentionally, my hand gravitates to the belt, hovering just above it, waiting. Any second now. Instead, the attendant comes on and makes an announcement about the refreshment service. I let my eyes drift out the window to clouds that look like animation. Up here, it's impossible to fathom everything not being perfect. We are literally flying away, floating above the clouds, momentarily looking down on all our problems. Yet I have this sneaking suspicion someone on this plane is not right. Somehow my problems are right here beside me. I pull my eyes away from the window and look up to the seatbelt sign. When I do, I hear a click at the exact moment it turns off. For a second, I think my reaction time is uncanny but then realize it was Will. He's beaten me to it. He stands and looks around at everyone, as if he too is anxious, like he's expecting someone. He catches my eyes for a second before he looks away, then excuses himself to go to the bathroom.

The thing about Will is that he doesn't drink from fountains, he doesn't use handrails, and he absolutely does not use public restrooms unless it's an emergency. This flight is just shy of an hour—he really is off his game. Then again, could he be checking out the other passengers? Does he know more than he is letting on? Why this trip to the Okanagan? Why now?

The last thing I need is another person to be wary of, but with my past, I can't even blame myself for questioning Will's faith in me.

With the little I've told him, there is no way that Will could be prepared for this sudden drama in our lives. But I do expect him to call the police if I'm in danger. I've been replaying that moment on the phone over and over again, the moment in which I told him to call the cops and he said no.

How could he have been so certain I was safe?

Unless … I can't go there right now. I only have a few minutes alone. The bathrooms are in use. A small line is forming. I'm hesitant but I shimmy out of my seat and make my way toward the back of the plane. Before I've taken a proper look, I lock eyes with the baby two rows behind me. As I walk toward her, she smiles a toothless grin and reaches out to me. I'm desperate to hold her, as if this small creature's acceptance and offering of love could somehow heal me. Her innocence brings me back to my

Cedar, my baby sister who so often wanted me to carry her, her chubby hands pressed up against my cheek.

"Hi, sweetheart," I coo, my softness surprising me.

"Up," she says, stretching her arms out to their fullest extent. I feel it before I realize what is happening. The mother stands and uses herself as a shield between her child and me.

"I'm so sorry," she is saying, bouncing her baby, whose attention has now moved on to someone else.

I realize that tears are rolling off my chin.

She thinks I've lost a baby, that I can't get pregnant—or some other reasonable explanation for my tears.

I've seen the look in her eyes before. It's the way people looked at my mother, despite me clinging to her legs. I still don't fully understand why everyone felt so sad for her losses even though I was right there.

"Hormones," I say, patting my stomach and offering her a sizable smile. The idea that I am expecting a healthy baby puts her at ease and she looks delighted. She tells me she totally gets it, though I suspect she does not. I turn back to my seat. I buckle myself in quickly, like I'm trying to contain myself before I detonate. I want to rock, to tuck my legs into my body and bury my face—I want it all to go away.

Strangely, my mind goes to Dr. X. I'm yearning for him the way even adults sometimes long for their parents, for their mothers' arms to shield them from life's cruelties. Something about that baby has rattled me, but I can't place the reason. I hear Dr. X's voice telling me to breathe. In and out, in and out. I picture his heavy, furry-knuckled hand on my knee, telling me I'm getting better, stronger every day, without her. At the time his words cut, but now I hear them differently. A wave of calm washes over me.

The plane will land soon, and I haven't decided what I want to see or do on this peculiar getaway. The world we are entering is not a happy place for me. On top of having to re-live the pain of losing Cedar, I now feel sharp grief for someone else, and it's unexpected.

I miss Dr. X.

Surprisingly, I'm starting to grasp the usefulness of the many meds I was prescribed after Cedar's death. I feel a shiver run up my spine as I crave the foggy haze of barbiturates.

On one hand, I've seen what these pills can do to you, what they did to my mother. And because of the pills they gave me, I've lost so many memories of the years after Cedar died. Since Will told me about this trip, I've been trying to picture myself in the town I grew up in, but it's all a blur, like I was never really there.

I have a sharp recollection of carrying boxes to my car, along with a reluctantly accepted gift from Dr. X. It's the day I left for school, the same day my parents left this place to start over on the island. After Cedar's accident and before that day, there is an unexplainable void, like someone erased the years.

On the other hand, here I am.

Will is back, sipping a ginger ale and working through a cross-word puzzle. He sees me look at him and without a pause asks me the name of Garfield's nemesis.

I laugh at the contrast of our minds.

"Odie," I answer out of a vast pool of useless knowledge.

Later, in the rental car, I tell Will I want to see the hospital. I don't tell him that it is no longer in operation. It's not like he would say no, but it's a bit of a drive in the opposite direction from where I grew up.

The windows are down, my hair is tousled, and the voices on the radio are singing happily. For the moment, this is the best welcome home I could've hoped for. Will says that British Columbia air is like no other: unprocessed, garden-fresh, somehow carrying more oxygen. But here in the Okanagan? It takes all the self-control I have not to stick my head out the window like a dog and inhale it in huge gulps.

"It's your trip, babe," he answers with a smile. But instead of asking for directions, he does a U-turn.

Like he already knew.

I bite my tongue and wait to see how long he will continue on before asking. I can feel myself tensing, my tone hardening even as we make small talk about the view.

I don't talk much about my past so the chances of me having told him specifics about the hospital are slim. We're close to the highway now. If he takes the 97C West to Merritt, I'll know that he somehow knows way more than he is letting on.

Has Will been talking to my parents? Would he do that?

He turns the radio up and Carrie Underwood masks the sound of my racing heart. We pass by the onramp to Highway 5 which means there's only one more choice and I want to jump out of the car. There is too much pretending going on between us. It's clear he has been poking around in my past and even if I can't blame him, it's infuriating. And it means I can't trust him.

As soon as he is fully committed to the 97 I will begin my

interrogation. The anticipation of having the upper hand, having the dirt on him, is inappropriately rejuvenating. I close my eyes, preparing, but then he says, "Coffee?" and drives right past the freeway entrance.

I open my eyes and look at him. Against my will, I really look at him. Cool as a cucumber. He's almost too nice to be hot—he is handsome, but like Adam Levine before the beard. I love him. I know it immediately. I can feel it in my relief.

Yet. I'm still suspicious. Did his mistake just dawn on him? Or was a coffee stop his intention all along? He pulls into Tim Hortons, past the drive-thru and parks.

"Think we should pee?" he asks with a grimace. "It's a lonnnnng drive to Forksdale."

My face falls.

Dammit, Will. Not you too.

CHAPTER TWENTY | *Will*

I realized my mistake as soon as I said the word. I'm just no good at deception. She knew too, possibly since the initial U-turn.

Grandad's hospital was named after the original name for Merritt, The Forksdale Hospital for Children, dating all the way back to 1965. Even though he privately funded the hospital, hospitals in Canada are public. Unlike my father, Grandad wasn't concerned with acclaim. Most of his publications gave credit to the hospital as a whole, citing other doctors' names more than his own.

The exception was one of his most effective treatments, known at the hospital as the Sutherby Method, about which a decades-long study is set to be published later this year.

Jill's eyes are burning holes in me as I skip around the car to open her door for her. What a fucking idiot. If I'd owned it immediately and said I'd done some research … "I figured it must be the place," …I might have bluffed my way through. But no, I freeze and say nothing.

I was starting to worry on the plane, the way she kept looking over her shoulders, smiling her pretend smile. But once we got in the rental car, she seemed more relaxed than I expected. Until my blunder. Now I reach for the handle of her door with a million excuses sandblasting my mind to the point that I have nothing to offer. Play dumb, I think.

I guess it's my natural default.

"After you," I say, gesturing for her to rise. But she doesn't. She slowly turns to face me. Her eyes are steel, cold and tough. For a second, I'm relieved she's still got it in her.

"Take me to the airport," she says tonelessly, reaching to re-close the door.

I stop her. "What is it?"

"Really, Will? Do you think I'm clueless …"?

She's furious. She steps out of the car now and seems much taller than usual.

"Forksdale?" She crosses her arms.

"What—the hospital? It was your idea …"

"How do you know which hospital? And don't say you looked it up. It's not even called that anymore!"

It's hard to lie when someone is glaring at you so intently.

"What is it called now?" I ask coyly, but it's not a good time for funny.

She slams her door behind her. "Give me the keys!"

I try to slow my thoughts. How would I know? I'm taking too long. She's done. She grabs the keys from my hand and heads for the driver's side. She is going to leave me here. I wouldn't put it past her. She's a hundred percent fight or flight.

Then it comes to me.

"The photo, babe."

She stops. "What photo?"

"You showed me a picture of you with your sister's doctor in front of the hospital, remember?"

I never wanted to bring up that photo again. I briefly saw it once, so I could have denied looking closely enough to see my grandfather. Mentioning it now incriminates me. But it's all I've got.

She's thinking about it; her body softens somewhat. Finally her shoulders drop, and she glances around, checking for witnesses the way you do after the adrenaline settles.

"Shit, Will. I'm sorry." She comes toward me and wraps her arms around my neck. "I don't know what I was thinking."

But I do. And she's right to think it.

She uses the restroom and I grab us a couple coffees, a vanilla dip for her and a Boston cream for me. Then we hit the road.

Why I thought this might be a good idea is beyond me right now. Sure, we both want answers—but aren't those answers going to reveal me as the traitor I am?

The drive is a little over an hour. Jill uncharacteristically fills the time telling me about Cedar and her Aunt Jen. I know she has suffered a lot, but listening to her stories, I realize she's had more of a family life than I ever did: dandelion crowns, hide-n-go-seek in the laundry chute, rainy day tents made out of blankets in the living room.

I don't say it, though. I let this be about her. I sit back and enjoy the stories, but mostly the happiness on her face as she recites them. She doesn't offer much about her mother, but her father comes up from time to time. He liked to sing old Scottish songs, *I loved a lassie, a bonnie, bonnie lassie*, especially while he cooked dinner. Roasts, hens and pork chops smothered in Campbell's mushroom soup.

It's the most Jillian has ever talked about her family. Even before their once-ever visit to Vancouver, when I finally met them after Jill and I had been living together for more than a year, she said only that they weren't close. That was an understatement. I'm not sure I've ever seen three people more awkward together, except for my parents and me.

My palms are sweaty as I take the exit to Merritt.

Most of the roads are named after the early settler families. Charters, Chapman, Cleasby, Garcia, Voght, Granite—I found this out more than ten years ago when a university buddy and I came out for the Merritt Mountain Music Festival, back when it was still a scene. They passed out flyers full of municipal history to nearly two hundred thousand totally disinterested concert-goers. For the most part, it was early settler bullshit, the surveyors and small business owners—but the blurbs about it being the gateway to the interior of BC got my attention because Grandfather's slogan was, "The Forksdale Hospital, a gateway to a healthier mind."

It's cooler here than in Kelowna. We roll our windows up, but the chill lingers. Merritt is situated at the exact point that the Nicola and Coldwater rivers merge into one indistinguishable body of water. There is an unsettling parallel: the idea of losing yourself here by melding into one concept of mental appropriateness. Perhaps it was the perfect location for Grandfather's hospital.

We're close now. Jill has stopped talking and I can see by the tension in her hands that she's getting nervous. She keeps her eyes on the yards we're passing, perfect in their shabbiness, houses built far back from the streets behind weathered wood fences. As we stop at a light only blocks from the hospital, I pretend to consult the GPS. Of course, I know exactly where we are—turn right at the white house with the large front porch and triangle of silos in the back, then follow the long, pine-tree-lined road until you get to the hospital. I could throw up with the fear surging through my body as I study the directions on my phone. I'm about to share some local history with Jill when I see it beaming off the map like a lighthouse among a sea of other names: Sutherby Road.

I look up from my phone and it's right in front of us: an ordinary green street sign looms like a Times Square billboard.

Jesus. I'm not sure if a man can tremble, but I feel every part of me roiling against itself. I pray the light stays green, that we can cruise through the intersection, but it's unlikely.

This will end us. I finished my coffee ten minutes into the drive, but I can tell by the milky liquid seeping through the lid that Jill's is still close to full. I watch my hand slice through the car like it isn't attached to me. Instead of the minor spill I intended, the cup explodes. The coffee is cold now, but she jumps as if it burns her. She's yelling at me but I can't make out the words. We're twenty feet from my surname and she is desperately looking for napkins.

"The glovebox," I tell her with an urgency that makes me sound angry. "I'm so sorry—there was a mosquito about to land on you and I forgot about your coffee."

The more I try not to look at the sign, the more it pulls me to it. Only ten feet away from our turn. I change the car display from map to radio while she dabs at her stained jeans.

The light is red. There's a young girl sitting on the porch of the landmark house. She's looking at me with hostility, like I'm an outsider, an intruder. The Mercedes passenger van in front of us turns and I see that it's marked with the name of the rehab center.

I force myself to make eye contact with Jill.

She's calm but annoyed.

"What a creepy kid …" I nod toward the porch, manipulating her eyes away from the sign.

"Not as creepy as the ones up the road," she says lightly, waving hello to the child.

Disaster momentarily averted.

The final stretch is like climbing the hill of a rollercoaster, both of us scared silent, anticipating something amazing or altogether awful. The heavy wrought iron gate manned by lab-coat-clad orderlies has been replaced by a wood-framed automatic gate that instantly makes the place feel more resort than institution.

The deep woods on either side of us that I used to imagine patients fleeing into are now sparse, subdivisions peeking through the branches.

"I barely remember any of this," she says, tucking her hair behind her ears and leaning forward.

"It wasn't like this before?" I ask, trying to sound sincere.

"So different." She rolls down her window. "But the air smells the same."

I pull up to the intercom. It takes some convincing, former clients taking a reminiscent drive around the property, but eventually someone at reception opens the gate.

The grounds are the same: impeccably maintained, from the pristine lawn mower lines to the precisely trimmed hedge tops. A few residents wander, some in hospital pants and gowns, others as if they're on their way to yoga. The fountain is still circulating water up and then back down.

Jill's eyes are scanning quickly, and I can see the wheels turning in her mind along with them. For a moment I wish desperately that I could just be honest with her—that we could share this experience of coming back to a place where we'd both spent time as children. Rage rises up in my chest, and for a moment I fantasize about strangling my father, just until he feels as powerless as I do in this minute. Then I realize I'm angrier at myself. I've always had the option of just getting my own fucking life, haven't I?

There is a black Escalade in the roundabout ahead of us. I hang back and observe what looks like a mom and dad dropping off their twenty-something son. I half expect my grandfather to come out and greet them with his firm handshake and a stethoscope around his neck. Instead, it's just a valet attendant and a distracted woman on her phone. The bench to the left of the front doors is still there. As inscribed, it was donated "With gratitude from the Rose family."

I remember sitting there for hours, preferring it to the stuffiness of the hospital corridors. Twenty years ago, patients often arrived in wheelchairs or ambulances—twenty years ago there were injected sedatives and restraining devices and it all made me want to leave as fast as I could.

Luckily, there are no statues of Dr. Sutherby in sight and all the signs point to recovery and rehabilitation. I'm about to continue around the circle, but Jill says she wants to go in. Before I can park and we can rehearse our story, she opens her door and gets out, as if she's under some kind of spell.

Fuck.

"Can I help you?" The valet walks over. I have Jill in the corner of my eye and can see the lady on the phone approaching her. I beat him to my door and hop out.

"A tour," I say. "The keys are in the ignition."

Jill and the intake person are moving toward the front doors. The woman's body language is relaxed and welcoming, so whatever Jill is telling her must be working.

"I'm so sorry … she was your sister?" she asks, placing her hand on Jill's shoulder.

"Yes, she was a patient of Dr. X for a long time."

"Dr. X?"

"He was the head of the hospital back then."

"Oh, you mean …" she starts, but I make it to them just in time to cut her off.

"Is it terrible if we have a quick peek around?" I blurt.

She turns to me, startled, looking from me to Jillian and then back to me. My presence hardens her, as if she can sense my dishonesty in contrast to Jill's surprising vulnerability.

"Absolutely. You'll have to get visitors badges." She walks and talks, leading us through a Four Seasons-esque foyer.

"There may actually be some old articles and photos still up in the original wing …" She trails on but my pulse is roaring in my ears. I have the urge to turn back, to fake stomach cramps, to be the coward I am and allow Jill to discover my family's deception on her own.

CHAPTER TWENTY-ONE | *Jillian*

Everything is different.

The hallways are wider, and the black-framed windows are new. The sun pours in, bouncing off the bright white paint as if the light were radiating outward and not the other way around.

This building can't keep secrets like the old hospital could. Its corridors swallowed you up, seeming to narrow even more as you walked deeper into the building.

Besides having to sign in, we are free to wander; freedom is not something my memories associate with this place. You would never guess these were the same walls that kept the odd children hidden only a decade ago.

I'm different, too. I sensed it as soon as Will pulled the car through the entrance. For as long as I can remember I've wavered between dreading this institution and wanting the sick comfort of Dr. X.

This is the only place where Cedar's light faded. Everywhere else she was confident and colorful, but here she seemed to slip away, almost blending into the beige cinder block walls like a ghost being called home. The more I visited her here, the less I truly saw her—the more she was here, the less she wanted to come home.

How I hated Dr. X for taking her away from me, and my parents for sending her here in the first place.

Collectively, my family spent a lot of time on this property. Aunt Jen came first. Before filling the vacancy left by my mother's depression and medication, my aunt was one of Dr. X's nurses. She didn't work at the hospital long, but long enough for her to present Cedar's case to Dr. X. He was immediately intrigued and after they met, he became obsessed with fixing her, with just being around her, eventually, it seems, convincing my weak parents to give her to him.

There is something euphoric happening to me now. Triumphant, perhaps? During the time I spent here, I was a shadow of who I am now. I was unable to foresee a future for myself, even a bleak one. Yet here I am, strong and, shockingly, not alone.

My feet are guiding us back to the oldest part of the building. They know it well. They remember running with Cedar through the halls, holding hands, giggling between sedations. We had already been coming here for nearly two years when Dr. X commissioned the plans for the atrium, a small outdoor oasis tucked into the back of the middle wing of the hospital. Not many of the patients were allowed to use it, but on good days, my sister and I spent hours out there, talking without the fear of clinical judgment, lying on our backs in grass prickly from dehydration, staring up at clouds from our roofless cell.

We're close now. Will is following me, but I am barely aware of his presence, my anticipation driving me.

Cosmetically this is a new building, but the bones are the same. So much so that if I close my eyes and trace a finger along the wall, I could make it to the atrium.

I'm used to people staring at me in the way I imagine all attractive women are, so I disregard the questioning faces we pass, wondering if I'm a patient or nurse, a drunk or druggy, the newest potential conquest for the sex addicts. In the end, these new patients aren't that different from the old. Addiction is also mental illness. But today's residents are encouraged to share their fears and urges without judgment, I've heard, while the earlier patients were punished with disabling treatments if they weren't able to quiet their vices, their differences.

The closer we get, the emptier the halls become and the shabbier the renovations look.

"Did it just get hotter?" Will asks, still lagging.

"I don't think this part of the hospital is in use." I point up toward the recessed lighting, dim and flickering beneath a stained tile ceiling.

"It certainly has a different feel back here," he says, slipping his fingers through mine.

"Scared?" I tease, squeezing his hand.

He gives me a half-assed chuckle. "No. But I wouldn't want to be the patient in 506."

He's referring to the room to the right of us. The sun must be blocked by a tree outside; in the wind, it casts eerie shadows towards us and then pulls them back like something caught on a giant hook.

"Were we supposed to wait for someone?"

"It's fine," I say, pulling against his hesitation. "We're here."

Straight ahead of us I can see the sharp glass corner of the atrium. You would think it would be a great source of comfort to the current residents, oxygen and a surge of fresh blood to their hearts, but even from here I can see the buildup of dust on the once crystalline windows.

I'm struck with sadness at this waste of Dr. X's gift, mixed with hope that perhaps it means that something of my sister has been preserved here.

I'm tempted to ask Will to return to the foyer to wait for me, but I've missed the chance. His hand is firmly attached to mine. Even more, he is a part of my life now, maybe the only part that really means anything to me. Asking him to leave me now might very well break my heart even more than his. So, we move forward together into this place I imagine Cedar usually felt very much alone.

The woman who greeted us like a bubbly restaurant hostess was right—some of the past does linger here in the old wing. But the area said to be left as a tribute is overgrown and uncared for. The wall adjacent to the atrium is hung with old photos, framed newspaper clippings, award and achievement plaques; blah and blah and blah. I will get to it, but right now I'm only interested in getting outside, despite the untamed vines left to overrun our once serene garden. As I stand in front of the door, I can feel Cedar rising up inside me, moving swiftly from the deepest part of my mind. She's fighting through the giant weeds and pulling past tall grass to come into focus. And then she appears, standing on the other side of the marred glass like a polished reflection of me. She's sad to be in there alone, away from me, and I am drawn to switch places with her, to be freed from the sounds of commercial air conditioners and Will's nervous breathing behind me. My heart and breath quicken like they do whenever I'm scared, panicked or excited. I am all of those things. I'm scared because she seems so real, watching me calmly; I'm panicked because I know, especially now, that she isn't really in there; and I'm excited because, for once, I don't care what is or isn't real.

I needed her here and here she is, even if she isn't. So, I hold my hand up to hers. We smile at each other and it's like saying hello and goodbye at once. Then I allow her to fade back into the recesses of my mind.

The door is stuck. I hadn't considered the possibility that it might be locked. Like a disappointed child or a dog left outside a store, my reflection deflates, hunched and pouty. I'm about to move onto the homage wall when Will flies in front of me, hip first, slamming into the jammed door like a WWE wrestler. Unexpected. But it works—marginally. He is able to push the door open seven or eight inches through the years of accumulated debris.

"Babe!" I say, looking at him awestruck, his shoulder now imprinted in the dust on the door. "Well done, sir."

"Can you fit through here?" he asks nonchalantly, studying the door and pretending not to be impressed with himself.

"Yeah—yes, definitely." I turn sideways and squeeze through the opening.

Before I take another step, before I inhale the air, sweet with mildew and dried leaves, I reach back for Will's hand. I want to do this with him. Not only because he pushed for this adventure or because he broke down this particular barrier for me, but because I now realize I want him to know me. Even if it scares him off.

He's back to normal Will after busting down the door, looking back over his shoulders before shimmying inside.

"Shit, babe. It's a jungle in here." His steps are careful, like he's never been outdoors before.

I feel irrationally embarrassed, like he's just walked into my messy house or tasted my shitty cooking.

"Well, it wasn't always like this."

I lead him toward a clearing and feel the coolness for the first time—it sharpens the nostalgia.

"There used to be a bench right here, and a garden that ran along the perimeter."

I breathe it all in. The bad memories, the awful ones. But mostly Cedar: her companionship, our daydreams and our banter.

"Right here," I say, sinking to my knees beneath the only tree left, a beautiful dogwood. I clear the ground to uncover a large rock. I blow the dirt off and use the sleeve of my Club Monaco sweater to reveal now faint lettering.

Take my roots with your roots,
you, me
and the Cedar tree.

"She stole a Sharpie from the nurse station—this is sort of like a tree that grew at home."

Will sits beside me and drags his finger across my sister's words. I'm happy to be sharing this with him.

Part of me believes she was just with us in the city, watching, tormenting me for forgetting her—perhaps for finding happiness, for loving Will.

Or maybe it wasn't her at all.

Whatever is going on, in this place where we giggled about boys and fantasized about a different grown-up life than our parents had, I feel closer to her than I have in a very long time.

"She would've liked you, Will. In fact, if she were still here you two would probably be together."

I rest my head on his shoulder and he winces playfully.

"Hard door …"

I feel his lips on my forehead.

"No chance, babe."

It's quiet for a while. I let him hold me and settle easily into his arms, utterly relaxed by the steady rhythm of his breathing. Before Will, being this still scared me. There was always fear that I might melt into the earth, disappear like my sister, float away like a leaf caught in the wind.

Cedar was special, though. She was different and gifted. Maybe it made sense she would be taken, by God or otherwise.

"Jill," he says, breaking the silence. "Why was Cedar hospitalized?" His breathing quickens and the euphoria ends abruptly.

"I told you, she didn't speak. Mute, they called it, even though she could hear."

"Yeah, I remember …" he sighs, pushing me gently from him to look in my eyes. "But a lot of kids don't talk, right?"

"Really?" I snap, defensive. "You know a lot of kids who don't speak, Will?"

"Well, not personally, but I don't think it's that uncommon, is it?"

"My parents only wanted her if she was perfect, I guess." I stand and begin to pace a tad theatrically.

"I've always known they were lying to me about the accident—I just don't know why, or what they're hiding. I think that is what this is about—Cedar needs me to find out."

Suddenly I feel the anger I felt all those years surface as rage.

"It was my mother—there was something wrong with her."

"Your mother?"

"She wasn't much of a mother …" On cue, a woman inside walks by the window pushing a stroller. She seems out of place in the deserted hallways, probably trying to put the child to sleep. I imagine she is visiting the baby's father, an alcoholic who lost his job, turned her life upside down.

I lower my voice and continue. "Cedar was really smart; she knew things other kids didn't. Her doctor said she was the most brilliant child he'd ever met. The most, Will!"

I don't mention the telepathy. Dr. X said it was best to keep that between us: Cedar, me and him. It's too big an idea for people, regular people, to process. There were other special children at the hospital, but none like Cedar.

Dr. X said he knew it the first time he came to the house.

The hardest part to swallow is how much they tried to brainwash me after, how tirelessly they tried to convince me my sister was not who I thought she was, who I knew she was.

Sick. Distant, unhappy, disassociated. All bullshit.

The hairs on Will's arm are standing up. He's covered in goosebumps, but he doesn't complain. I tell him it's time, and it sounds like we're about to say goodbye to someone very sick, like Cedar's dying all over again. But this time I feel at peace. Because I am certain of one thing: the Cedar I remember doesn't exist anymore.

Nothing has been preserved out here except a rock she wrote on. The wild has taken over our spot, as if nature has been given its chance to reclaim ownership.

Will tries to pry the door open wider for our exit. It doesn't budge, but I pretend not to notice and gratefully leave first. Surprisingly, I'm not sad. In fact, I feel uplifted.

I approach the tribute wall casually, scanning the photos. I see a picture of Cedar and Dr. X first. Except it isn't Cedar—it's me. Why would they choose that picture?

I'm grappling with how I can explain it to Will.

But then something else strikes me with such force I feel blindsided, as well as just plain stupid.

DEDICATED

TO

DR. XAVIER SUTHERBY

CHAPTER TWENTY-TWO | *Will*

I managed to shut the atrium door behind us.

I don't know why I was so nonchalant. I knew she was heading to the wall. I haven't the slightest idea why I didn't prepare, evade—pull the fire alarm, for Christ's sakes.

It happened in slow motion: her body pivoting toward me, her face already angled toward me over her shoulder. Her eyes, first pleading then storming, locked on mine.

When I was a boy, say thirteen, I made friends with the neighbor's grandson, Theodore (Teddy) Robertson. He was more spoiled than I was, perhaps more neglected. The two of us dabbled in mischief and petty theft, the way entitled kids show the world their toughness, small pranks with eggs and spray paint. Other than our alcohol-fueled fathers, we didn't really know what trouble was, the fear of getting caught red-handed.

One night, close to the end of that summer, Teddy dared me to break into the house at the end of a dirt road a couple blocks over. The house was famous in our neighborhood—the owners, an elderly couple who had since moved into a nursing home, were the only people who held out and refused to sell to a developer. To my grandfather's generation, it was basically criminal to replace historical architecture with cookie cutter houses. To my father and his profit-driven buddies, selling out should be a no-brainer if the price is right.

I'd been called a loser and a chicken more than once, so I couldn't risk Teddy's taunts heading into high school. To be honest, I don't recall giving it much thought at all. Sure, it was dark, and I was likely nervous about the night noises and shadows, but I definitely didn't stop to think about any potential consequences.

Teddy stayed at the end of the driveway. I made my way to the house, accumulating mud from the dirt road on the bottom of my tennis shoes. Perhaps at one point the property had been properly maintained, but on that night, it was like walking through a swamp. My feet got heavier with each step, sticking to the ground like they were signaling me to stay put. By the time I reached the front door I was wearing mud platforms.

I remember this clearly because of the sheer ignorance of my actions a bit later.

Maybe it was escaping the dark that propelled me forward, or maybe it was just immaturity, but when I reached the house, I turned the front door handle as casually as if I were arriving home. Surprisingly, it opened, and I walked in.

It makes my stomach turn now to think of their wood staircase, how I scraped one Nike sole and then the other against the bottom step, the mud curling off in big wet slices that crumbled and smeared on the old wood floor. I didn't think about how it would make them feel to discover this assault, not just to have their home invaded but so disgustingly soiled as well.

The dare was that I had to spend ten minutes inside. I kept the lights off, flippantly flashing my Motorola phone across a gallery wall of family pictures, the kind you would never find in our house. Despite the photos, how flesh and blood the people in them appeared, I still didn't grasp the invasiveness of being there—inside their private world, where their children woke up Christmas morning and laid watching cartoons when they had fevers.

My concern was my shoes. I fucking hated dirty shoes. Like a dog covering its feces, I laid my final assault by wiping them over and over on their carpet. And then I looked up.

I don't know how long she'd been standing there, cowering in the corner of her living room, dressed in a pink fluffy robe and matching slippers. When I saw the fear and disgust in her eyes, I also saw the gravity of my selfishness and the value of what I'd overlooked and regarded as beneath me.

It may have also been the first time it dawned on me that I was becoming my father.

She was old and defenseless. Her voice quavered. She didn't threaten to call the police or my father.

She just wanted to know why I was there—if I was okay.

I couldn't think of anything to say. My head was the buzz of the TV when the network goes off for the night. I couldn't blame Teddy—he hadn't told me to rub dirt all over this woman's home, a home with family on the walls and coasters on the tables.

As much shame as I felt, I didn't apologize or offer her an excuse that might ease her mind. Instead, I ran out without cleaning my mess and never looked back.

Since then, I've avoided that road altogether. Refused to even look in the direction. From time to time, I heard something about the couple, their children, the for-sale sign that eventually went up. But until now, I could never bring myself to think about that night, could never joke about it. I never even told Teddy what I found inside.

We stopped being friends after that. The look in that woman's heavy-lidded eyes was the most trouble I have ever been in. It was a look that told me my personhood was in trouble, my character. I swore I would never do anything so low again, that I would do whatever it took to never see that look again.

Yet here it is. In Jill's eyes. And once again, I deserve every bit of disgust and disappointment.

"Jill," I hear myself plead, meager and pathetic.

She immediately knows she has made the right assumption. I go to her, but she backs up. Her eyes are still locked on mine, but I can see she is going through her mind like a computer program scanning for viruses. Her face changes every time she makes a connection. Sad, angry, confused. I repeat her name over and over until she tells me to stop. She holds her hand in front of her and it shakes like the old lady's voice. I knew this was coming, that it was only a matter of time.

But somehow, I thought that if I could buy myself a few days, a week maybe, there would be an opportunity to explain, to gently tell her only as much as she needed to know.

"What the fuck, Will?" She's trying really hard not to cry.

I love this fragile girl in her strong woman's body. I want so badly to tell her the truth. But it's not possible. This type of confession is for a deathbed, a suicide note. I'm back in that old house again, stunned at being caught and silenced by shame.

She keeps talking, demanding to know who the hell I am. Finally, I lie.

"Listen, babe …"

"Don't you dare call me that!" She turns to leave.

"I just made the connection myself!"

"What connection? Who the hell are you? What do you want from me?"

Her back is nearly against the wall now. My grandfather's legacy is mapped all around her. The gravity of our bond becomes so real I don't think I could move if I wanted to. From the way she's looking at me, it's clear she thinks I've played a role in her sister's disappearance, that I am part of the reason she has suffered so long.

It's just not true.

In so many ways, I am as clueless about all this as she is.

"The other day, when I saw that photo …" I start spitting out bits of truth. "I didn't know your sister's doctor was my grandfather."

"Your grandfather?"

She covers her face with her hands.

"How could I have known, babe?" I take a tentative step toward her.

Her breathing is exaggerated, her chest visibly rising with each inhalation. I don't know if she's building to rage or tears, but I pray to God for one or the other. Anything but the third option, frozen Jill. As long as I can keep her raw and engaged, I can keep fighting.

Shit.

She drops her hands from her face and the eerie calmness,

the pretend indifference, has returned.

"You knew three days ago? You knew when you booked this messed up trip down memory lane." She manages to keep her voice steady, save a bitter laugh.

"So that's how you knew how to get here? So—you're a liar. You know that, right?"

"I am. I'm a liar. But I swear I don't know anything about where your sister is." I put my hand on her shoulder, but she throws it off.

"She's dead. D. E. A. D," she spells it out like a poker-faced cheerleader. "You said it yourself. Has that changed? Do you know something?"

She slides down the wall and reburies her face in her hands. "Not you, too. Not you, Will."

I sit beside her, noticing a photo of my grandfather on the way down. If anything, in a different world, my being related to him would be a good thing. Of all the men I've known, he was the best. She has to know that.

"I don't actually know anything, but I found a picture …"

She lowers her hands from her face again, this time with much more emotion in her expression. "You what? What picture?"

"Listen, after I saw the picture of you and my grandad, I went to my parents' …"

This wasn't premeditated, obviously, so I have to choose my words carefully. "I didn't know what I would find or why I even went—I just wanted to know more, I guess, before I said anything to you."

"But you didn't tell me?"

She has every reason to hate me. What she does know—that

I sat beside her on a plane, in the car, and here at the hospital, and said nothing about my grandfather—is reason enough, never mind the rest of it.

"Yes, I didn't tell you and I wish I had a reason." As I try to explain, the sun passes through the atrium window and its light dances above her face like a halo. My gut knows we won't recover from this. It's inevitable. All of the shameful facts will crawl out of hiding like a corpse, one sinister limb at a time.

I just hope Jill will let me help her sort it all out—I owe her that, my family and me.

"My father still has some files in his office. It used to be my grandfather's. I found Cedar's. It's in my car at home."

"What? How could you not ..." She stands, furious.

I grab her arm. "I'm awful. It was stupid—but listen, I found a picture of your sister in there."

"Well, it is her file ..."

"No. I mean I found a current photo," I lower my voice, "like—she's an adult in it."

"What are you telling me, Will? What the fuck are you saying?" Her eyes are glassy, and I can almost feel her adrenaline burning my face. My heart lurches for her.

"I don't know what I'm saying, which is probably why I didn't say anything ..."

"Not good enough. We have to go back. Now!"

She turns away from me, crying, her arms wrapped tightly around her body like she's desperate to keep her insides from falling out. I picture her here all those years ago, a child manipulated with lies, white ones and black ones. Heartbroken and alone. The medicine, all those pills scattered on our kitchen counter—they were Jill's. It's obvious to me now why she stopped taking them. They convinced her that her sister Cedar was dead. And now she's back?

What the actual fuck? Why didn't I bring the file? Why did I bring her here and leave the file at home?

Now that she knows, I can't imagine how I was okay with leaving her in the dark. The cruelty is shocking and my disloyalty is disgusting even to me. Worse still, I hadn't even bothered to read the rest of the file. I left it underneath my driver's seat like I hoped it would all just go away—truthfully, that Cedar would just go away.

I attempt to catch up with Jill, frantic, but someone's watching us. I notice her through the far side of the atrium, standing behind a darkened window. I pause to process what I'm seeing, conscious that Jill is getting further ahead of me. My mind is playing tricks. All this talk of Cedar today, seeing the photo of her, almost indistinguishable from Jillian. I could swear that I'm now looking at her. I shoulder check to make sure I'm not just seeing Jill's reflection in the dingy glass, but Jill is out of sight. I look back and the image remains: mahogany hair framing a perfectly symmetrical face, an almost cheeky smile. She stares right at me, perhaps through me.

"Cedar?" I call out, before I've given it any proper thought. My feet start moving in her direction. I don't take my eyes off her because I feel like she might vanish, like she might not be there at all. She does the same, her eyes locked on mine. It borders on erotic, but I push sex from my mind and focus on moving my feet. I lose her for just a second as I turn the final corner. I half expect her to be gone, but here she is, mere feet in front of me, her gaze swallowing me up with its confidence.

"Cedar?"

"I thought I was the only one who knew about this place," she says, turning toward the sun as if on cue. She is beautiful, breathtaking actually, and could certainly be mistaken for the Cedar I saw in the photo. But this woman is Cedar like Michelle Williams was Marilyn in the movie. And I've allowed myself to lose sight of Jill while chasing a ghost—like she has her entire life.

I'm unreasonably disappointed. For a moment I had thought discovering Cedar would make me a hero, or at least a forgivable villain.

I manage a smile and a proper greeting for this would-be angel and then turn back, fast. She shouts something at me as I leave but I can't make it out. She starts laughing and it bounces off the walls like it's chasing me. Once a mental hospital, always creepy as fuck.

I can't help but feel uneasy alone in these corridors. It's as if the new owners have left this part of the building to die with its bad memories.

There is a very distinct border and I know immediately when I've crossed over. I have to slow my pace to blend into my new surroundings. I'm more or less as familiar with this place as Jill is, so I find my way to the lobby easily.

Ahead of me, a teenage boy sits outside his room rolling a pen through his fingers like a makeshift spinner. I can't help but remember Grandfather's rules: no pens, paper clips, scissors, utility knives. Times have changed. They're clearly not worried this kid is going to stab himself in the jugular. But I don't care if the walls are cheerfully painted and the orderlies smile a lot more—this place is still a prison. I can't get out of here quickly enough.

I give the kid a reassuring nod, something I intend to say, "They can't keep you in here forever." He nods; I'm reasonably sure it intends a blunt FU.

I see Jill ahead of me. Thank God she is still in the building. I can see from here she's upset, talking to the woman behind the counter with more expression than usual, her hands gesturing wildly. She turns and points in my direction. Our eyes meet, and she throws me a look so cold and accusatory I feel as if she's slapped my face.

CHAPTER TWENTY-THREE | *Jillian*

In the weeks before my sister's accident, they kept her from me. Tucked away at Forksdale, alone. No visitors. She was coming home soon, so they'd said she needed to be alone with her doctors, no distractions or interruptions. They told me how much progress she was making, and how that progress depended on our being apart.

"Cedar relies on you too much. You're enabling her sickness," my father said, hanging up the phone with the hospital. He didn't look me in the eye.

I knew he was keeping something from me. It was just the way he was. He couldn't tell a joke without laughing before the punchline, he couldn't keep a gift hidden and he could not lie.

Up until that point, Cedar and I had only been apart five days at most. Each time, they kept me occupied, avoided bringing her up at all costs and praised me for the littlest accomplishments. I didn't know it at the time, but I know now they were preparing me for her loss.

She had only been home one day before she died.

My mother kept calling her out of the room. It was strange

because, besides our meetings with Dr. X, I can't recall Mom interacting with Cedar much at all. Dad said they were bonding, spending much-needed time together. I couldn't complain, couldn't take that from her. I'd always felt guilty about how awful Mother was to Cedar, confused by how she could neglect her own child.

Don't get me wrong. My mother was cold to me, too. But she treated Cedar like she didn't exist.

I was so used to having Cedar to myself, I was jealous, irritated even, that she would want to spend time with them. To me, she was acting like a neglected dog that kept trying to please its owner anyway. I didn't say as much because this was progress, this was healing. She wasn't talking to them, but at least she had a relationship with them.

She went out with my parents the morning she died. They took her shopping for new clothes. They said that if she stayed well, they might let her come to my school in the fall. Aunt Jen stayed with me and, as a treat, we had cucumber sandwiches and hot tea with milk on the porch.

She told me that my parents had hinted that she should move out, get her old job back. I could tell that, like my father, she was only pretending to be happy about it. She was so clearly sad.

Later, they all whispered together in the kitchen, huddled around the phone. I didn't remember until years later that I saw that Aunt Jen was crying.

Mom had scolded her, barking, "This isn't about you!"

How could asking her to leave not be about her? Unless that's not what they were talking about at all.

Mother was chipper, obnoxiously so. She made Cedar do a

spin in her new yellow dress, then clapped theatrically. My sister hated yellow—someone as bright as her didn't need to dress in basic crayon box colors. Yellow is for people like my mother. Cedar must have agreed to wear it to make Mother happy, and it worked. My mother beamed all afternoon, more smiles than in the previous year combined.

I was nearly thirteen years old, so I should remember the day clearly. But I don't. It's hazy—like a night terror in broad daylight.

We were sitting on the cement curb that ran along our driveway, Cedar still in the yellow dress. She had a stick and was drawing hearts and letters in the sandy gravel, flashing me smiles as I prattled on and on about how much fun we were going to have now that she was home.

Mom came outside. I heard the screen door slam; Aunt Jen and Dad were calling after her. I stood up to see what was happening. Mom was running toward us, her long white skirt blowing between her legs like palazzo pants. She looked ridiculous. She started screaming and pointing, so strangely frantic.

That part of my memory is in slow motion.

Then behind me was a noise so loud I felt it before I heard it. I stood frozen as the street filled up with people. Neighbors who lived nearly a mile away were there, two teenagers I didn't recognize, and a paramedic who happened to be passing by.

My sister was no longer sitting beside me. The twig she'd held like a paint brush lay at my feet. I slowly came to understand that she was under the blanket on the road, unmoving. Someone pulled me away, and, for whatever reason, I let them.

Then there is nothing. I'm told I slept for a long time, days and days. My next memory is of being at the hospital. Cedar was gone. *Ladybird, Ladybird fly away home. Your house is on fire and your children are gone. All except one and her name is Ann. And she hid under the baking pan.*

I'm so angry at Will. The more I think about his playing-stupid charade, his clever, "Does the hospital look different now?" the harder it is to imagine ever believing anything he says again.

Sadder yet, anything he has ever said before. I think of our nights curled together at home and realize even that doesn't exist now. I have no home.

Not only did he lie repeatedly, he lied well.

I can't believe I left the city. That's the problem when you can't trust your mind—you start trusting other people too much.

It has only been in the past two years that I started to see things differently. Maybe my happiness helped me see clearer, to finally accept that Cedar was gone.

And then I saw her.

I did. But the thing is, I sleepwalk. So even though I believe it was her, I have doubts, too. It was those doubts that allowed me to get on a plane, to leave the city that she may be in right now.

I came back to this place to try and let her go, with this man I loved—and thought I knew.

Then we get here and he tells me my sister is alive. And his family has something to do with her being taken from my family.

I'm furious with Will, but I'm angrier with myself. This is exactly why I have spent my life alone. I can't trust anyone. My parents lied to me. They gave away my sister and convinced me she died. When I didn't believe them, they had me drugged and brainwashed.

Now Will is lying to me.

What does he know? I'm tempted to leave here alone. In fact, as soon as he confirmed that Dr. X was his grandfather and he'd been hiding that from me, I decided I would never speak to him again.

Now I understand that isn't the smartest play. I need to see that file, all the files. If they did this to my sister, how many other children might they have taken?

When I reach the lobby, the woman at reception looks startled, as if she can't place me. She has a perplexed look on her face, and I wonder if she can tell I've been crying.

"Are there any cabs around here, or do you have a shuttle?" I ask, slowing my breath, trying to sound composed.

She doesn't answer but looks toward the valet stand and then to the hall behind me.

"Is something wrong?" I ask finally, catching her eyes.

"No. Ummm," she says, and puts her clipboard down with an unexpected thud. "But—didn't you just leave?

I don't have time for this. "Obviously not. We just got here, remember?"

"But then you left? Right? You signed out?"

"No," I say flatly, trying to be patient. This woman seems distracted and confused, like she's lost a patient or something.

"Shall I just speak to the valet attendant?" I start to back away, but she stops me, coming over to my side of the desk.

"Wait! I'm sorry." Her manner has changed. "It wasn't you,

you're right, of course." She shakes her head and smiles tightly but then stands in front of me.

"Thanks?"

"I just need you to sign out and then the valet will see you have a ride to wherever you're headed."

She meekly passes me the clipboard and I somehow refrain from rolling my eyes. She doesn't move but keeps her eyes on me as I scan the page.

"Do you have a pen?" I ask. I'm growing suspicious, thinking how normal she was less than an hour ago. Does this have something to do with Will?

"Oh, yeah," she laughs nervously. "Here." She passes me a ballpoint.

I turn my back to her and place the board on the sleek black counter. There is an oddness in the air that I've felt before; in a fishy place like this, I'm not about to nonchalantly sign anything. I won't be involuntarily committing myself, thank you.

I don't see it at first; I just scroll down to the bottom expecting to see my name. It's funny, I must go up and down the list three times before I notice, and then it is glaring: Cedar Gannon. I drop the pen. In shock, I swing around.

"Is this some sort of joke?"

She jumps back and practically squeaks, but I continue. "Look, I don't know what kind of game you're playing at, but this isn't cute."

"Ms.?"

"Who did you think I was? Why were you asking me if I left?"

I try to steady my voice, but I can hear the aggression in every word.

"Ms., please …" She's at a loss. "It's just that someone who looks an awful lot like you just left, I mean, not even a minute before you …"

"Why didn't you just say that then?"

Suddenly I feel like everyone's eyes are on me, like I'm being followed. I look behind me and there is Will, coming down the hall. My reaction is double-sided—I hate him like I've never hated anyone, not even my mother. But like my mother, I love him still. So much.

"I g-g-guess I only remembered one of you signing in?" She stammers but it doesn't soften me. This woman is beyond frustrating, from her tiny stature to her large, too-white teeth.

"Is this the woman?" I ask, tired of all of this.

"Where?"

"Here!" I shout, losing all patience, pointing at my sister's name in the place where mine was.

Now she looks even more confused. "Isn't that your name? You signed it."

Will is with me now, both comforting and infuriating me. He asks what's going on but I just glare. Minnie Mouse starts explaining the situation to him in a ruffled voice and it's all I can do not to slug her.

"You wrote it, Ms."

"I absolutely did not."

I have survived on moments like this most of my life—when someone says, "Hey, is that your sister?" or "You look just like my friend."

Hope.

Yet this time, when it could actually mean something, I'm

angrier than I am intrigued. I'm too worn down, emotionally and physically, to even try running after her as I did at my office. I don't have the energy to play chase. For the first time in my life, I'm furious with my little sister.

As children, we played Hide-n-Seek for hours. Being older, I was always "it," stuck counting beneath the cedar tree, breathing in its sweet, earthy fragrance as she giggled her way into hiding. But we're not children anymore and this game, whatever it is, isn't fun.

Begrudgingly, I take Will's arm. He's as shocked as I am at my touch, but he easily obliges and follows me away from the lobby, away from the woman who suddenly can't stop talking.

"Get the car," I whisper to him, not trusting my voice to say more. He nods and then disappears behind the burly attendant. I release my arms from around my chest and force myself to look straight ahead instead of surveying the property. In my mind, I'm standing in the crossfire, standing here with a target on my back. My sniper is watching for my panic, because that has to be the point of all this, right? Someone wants me to lose it?

I'm used to people expecting the worst from me. I'm equally used to rising to the occasion: cutting my hair off and strewing it over the floor like rose petals, ripping the heads off all the flowers the night before the funeral, refusing to eat until my whole body ached and burned, until my arms grew furry. Not this time. The car can't come fast enough. I won't allow myself to crumble, not here in this place where I may have cried more tears than I took breaths.

Instead, I count. Just as I used to, slowly and patiently. This time the endgame isn't to find her. It's to find answers. Once and for all, I'm going to find out what happened to Cedar.

The car pulls up and I even wait for my door to be opened, managing to look composed for whoever is watching.

If Cedar is following me, she'll have to keep up.

CHAPTER TWENTY-FOUR | *Will*

The fact that Jill got into the car with me is already more than I deserve. But since then, she has barely spoken, beyond giving me the address to her family home—and even that came with a remark about me probably already knowing it. Which I don't.

When I met Jill, I assumed—because of her appearance and the way she carried herself, with the poise of an older woman—that she was from a big city, perhaps a US transplant. Even when she said she was from a small town, I didn't picture this. Ravenscliff is a village, not so much up the hill from the lake as in the hills.

We turned off the 97 and headed away from the lake and straight up. The roads dipped and curved like they were trying to hypnotize us; I had the feeling that once you got in, you weren't getting out easily. I imagine that towns like these, deep off the grid, are either completely wholesome or completely fucked.

In any case, I keep my mouth shut tight and my door locked. We pass Townline Road and it's as if we have driven fifty years into the past. I pull over by the wooden sign that says "Welcome to Ravenscliff." It sways back and forth with the rusty screech of a lone playground swing in the wind. Otherwise, it's quiet.

She speaks first, something about not caring what I think. I don't bite because I know she's looking for a fight, and even though she deserves one, I also know it's likely a defense mechanism.

I'm in a tight spot here.

For one I'm a liar and therefore don't get an opinion, and for two, this place sucks. I suppose if country bumpkins and backwoods are all you know, it wouldn't be that bad. It might even be a blessing to not have the corruptions of city life, if the isolation didn't drive you mad.

The downtown is over before it starts: a small grocery store with three or four modest cars in the lot, a drug store (aptly named Drug Store), and an old-school post office. If there are thirteen thousand people here, most of them are rural and they all shop in Kelowna.

Jill tells me to turn left just before the elementary school. It is a strangely modern-looking building, complete with an over-the-top American-style football field, a track and a large digital sign wishing Principal Lewis a speedy recovery. "What's the deal with the school?" I ask, noticing Jill's eyes fixed on the soft turf playground. I can tell she's fidgety. She keeps still, too still, like she's afraid to move, afraid to let her guard down. We may be in the same car, but her body language makes it clear she wishes was anywhere else.

"Private donation."

Her voice is flat to the point I can't tell if she feels this is a good thing or not, so I follow suit and offer no comment beyond a neutral, "Oh, yeah?"

I turn as directed. Although the sun is reflecting brightly off a dried-up cornfield, everything here is reminiscent of a sepia photograph. The houses all seem to have detached garages and enormous yards.

She tells me it's the next house, about a mile away.

I know her sister's accident happened outside of their home, so I slow the car to a crawl. Whatever the story, I'm certain this road holds a lot of bad memories and dark secrets for Jill. More than anything, I want to hold her hand.

I'd hoped this trip would bring us together, allow her to open up to me. I wanted so badly for her to lean on me and let me support her. Instead, I've created this frozen woman beside me. Returning to a place that is riddled with pain and love for her, she seems entirely emotionless.

Her expression has not changed the entire drive. As we get closer to the long driveway, I half want to ask if we should turn around, if this is all too much. But then I hear her whisper, "Home sweet home," under her breath. I take it as a nod.

Strangely, given real estate prices in the Okanagan, Jillian's parents still own this property. Jill told me that a neighbor lady checks in on it, dusts and runs the vacuum around while her husband mows the lawn, in exchange for a hundred-dollar cheque that arrives in the mail by the first of each month.

Otherwise, the house sits empty; no summer picnics, pumpkin carving, stockings hung by its fire. It's sad to think about this lonely house in the middle of nowhere collecting dust instead of memories.

But Jill's heavy sigh seems less wistful and more let's get this over with. It's a front, a heavily fortified front. I know—I helped her build it.

The sound of the tires on the gravel as we pull in couldn't be more small-town. I'm guessing it's the sound of teenage trouble approaching in the middle of the night, or the excitement of Grandma arriving with donuts on Sunday morning, just as much as it's the everyday sound of Dad arriving home from work. Today, it's the sound of our arrival.

I park halfway down the drive and turn the engine off. Jill turns to look at me, possibly for the first time since we left the hospital. It's a tough face to read. Angry for sure, but more scared than anything.

She gets out of the car and, somehow, she too is transported back in time. Her movements are so graceful, and her hair moves gently about her face in the cool mountain breeze—she is the cover girl on a paperback romance, dancing in a field of dandelions.

I've never seen her look lovelier. I can't help thinking about being inside of her, holding her tightly, maybe in the thick moss of the forest behind the house. It's hard to believe now that I thought she was better suited to the city.

Stepping out of the car seems to free her, like releasing a tiger or an orca into its natural habitat. She waits for the sound of my car door shutting and then starts off toward the back of the house.

The ground crunches under our feet and the wind rises, pushing us backward toward the car. Unlike home, where all weather is muted by towers and underground garages, the seasons are alive here. And winter is coming. Soon this lane will be covered in snow, but now the verdant summer is dying.

Just inside what looks like the border of their property is a soaring cedar tree, its branches reaching majestically in all directions.

Before we got to the hospital, Jillian told me that this tree, Cedar's namesake, is also the resting spot for six tiny gravestones. As if on cue, a gust of wind dances through an eerie moon-and-stars windchime hanging at the back of the house, releasing a cascade of nursery rhyme notes.

"Don't worry, they're not buried here," she says, dropping to her knees. She uses her hands to brush off the dirt and leaves, and the remains of a plastic bouquet.

"Meet Mama's babies." She brushes her hair from her face and crosses her legs in the grass. There is something almost frightening in the way she says it, and for whatever reason, my mind goes back to the hospital, where Jill signed in as Cedar.

"There are so many," I reply, hoping she can hear the sympathy in my voice. I feel incredibly sorry for Jill and her poor parents, especially her mother. You have to wonder why she would subject herself to so much pain.

"Two came before me …" she stops mid-sentence to dust the remaining stones, "and four came after."

She gives me a peaceful smile as I lean forward to read them, but this is extraordinarily harrowing. All of them are marked with a name. Jill's mom must have been either pregnant or grieving for Jill's entire childhood.

Jill collects a handful of dandelions.

"This is why they won't sell the house." Her voice is hushed, like she doesn't want the babies to hear her. She drops all the little weeds save one. Softly she sings what sounds like a dark nursery rhyme of some sort, "Mamma had a baby and her head popped off ….” She looks me dead in the eye and then force-fully decapitates the dandelion with her thumb. “My mother says it’s their home now.”

Jesus. I silence a shudder.

“But they’re not actually in there?” I manage.

“No. At least I don’t think so. My dad didn’t put these stones here until my mom was safely pregnant with Cedar. And then …” She shrugs her shoulders and stands.

“I’m so sorry, Jill.” I take another moment under the tree and uncharacteristically touch each plaque with two fingers. I stand beside her and add, “For everything.”

“Just don’t. I can’t right now.” I can see she’s about to cry but she doesn’t push me away. Instead, she wraps her arms around me. “Not here.”

It’s so small town, right down to the key hidden under a clay pot that holds three oversized faux sunflowers. Jill has mentioned her mother’s fake flowers more than once—it’s the only thing the deer won’t eat. As a city kid, I was lucky to spot a deer in the woods up in Whistler, but here they’ll apparently come right to your front door and eat your geraniums.

Jill takes a long breath and then turns the handle. She starts talking before we’ve made it over the threshold.

“This door was triple locked when I was little,” she starts. “My parents were pretty overprotective. Cedar and I figured out early that if we dragged a kitchen chair over, we could reach the top lock and sneak out.”

She drifts into the kitchen, chatting while she moves like a tour guide. “She was standing right here when she lost baby number three. More than anything, I remember the color of her face—it was like all the blood drained from it. She was ghost-white, and then I saw blood dripping down her legs. She didn't say a word, just held her stomach and cried."

"That must have been really scary for you, too." I walk toward her, but she moves away.

"It was. That first time especially. Mostly because I'd never seen her cry like that before, hunched and sobbing like a child. And then all her laughter and silliness just stopped."

She shows me the family room. It's small and cluttered with knick-knacks and plaid, but beyond the shabbiness, you can tell it was once a cheerful room.

I've seen photos of her parents, but none of the family together. On the wall behind the old TV set is a fairly large, Sears Studio-looking family picture. I'm not any good at guessing kids' ages, but Jill looks about ten, which would make Cedar five-ish. Yet only Jill and her parents are in the photo.

She follows my gaze. From her expression, her eyes squinted and solemn, I know she's thinking the same thing. I don't say any-thing—by the tilt of her head, I can tell she is puzzled too, trying to work through it.

CHAPTER TWENTY-FIVE | *Jillian*

Que sera, sera …

My father used to sing the old Doris Day song to us so often that Cedar joked that it was the only song he knew the words to. I think it was his way of being present, of trying to salvage a broken childhood by not agonizing all the time like my mother. It was his way of saying that he trusted that, whatever issues Cedar had, that Mother had, that I had, we would work through them together.

I often dream of this old house, of running my fingernails over the rough red brick and feeling the spongy yellow linoleum floors under my feet in the morning. The smell of rotting corn in the fields after the harvest, my mother blank-faced in the bathtub. Once in a while I dream the house is full of children with dark hair, bright smiles and dirty feet. In those dreams, my mother glows with exhaustion and pride; my father chases us around the yard with his pant legs rolled up and a scruffy beard that tickles.

It's as if I've invaded my mother's dreams, like I'm in her mind, living the life I couldn't give her.

Today, everything is different than I remember, and yet it's all the same. My parents left almost everything behind, part of their effort to start a completely new life, surrendering this house to the past like the set of a TV show. They're not coming back. They'll leave the house to me in their will and I'll have to confront these memories all over again.

I don't want to be mad at Will. The truth is, I need him here. I have to believe he loves me or face the fact that my life is as empty now as it was when I lived within these walls.

He told me Cedar is alive; he saw a picture of her. Of course, his grandfather is her doctor and my number one suspect in her disappearance. But maybe Will is telling the truth when he says he knows nothing about it.

Strangely, I feel closer to him knowing we have this connection, even if it's weird and toxic.

I don't trust myself to say it out loud, to even think it, but my memories are different here. Particularly the way I'm remembering Cedar—they're foggy, I guess. She's foggy, and the closer I get to her the fainter she becomes.

Then there's this photo.

I try to scan past it, but I can see the spot where she used to stand as if a red circle had been drawn around her invisible toothless grin. She's been erased, and what's left is a sad family trying to smile at the camera. There is a chance that Aunt Jen is behind this, sneaking around with Photoshop, one step ahead of me. Although with her twins, her job and Geoffrey, her 1950s-style husband, I don't know how logical that theory is.

When would she have time?

So here we are, staring at another elephant in a house full of elephants, yet another explanation I have to somehow come up with. Will doesn't move, waiting for me to say something, but what am I supposed to say? That we were a cold family and excluded my mute sister from our Christmas cards? Or that my crazy family had Cedar removed from all our photos because they believed it would help me get on with my life?

"I don't know what to say. She was in this picture before. I mean …"

I close my eyes tight to access a clear memory. I see the two of us sitting side by side, flipping through the toy section of the Sears Christmas catalogue. I focus in on later memories, myself as a pre-teen, zoned in on the TV. She's there, my hand on her shoulder the way I remember. But just as I open my eyes, the scene flashes and she's gone. It's just me.

I rub my forehead and then pinch the bridge of my nose, trying to focus my brain. The image in my head is flickering as if the lights are being turned on and off. She's there. She's gone. She's there.

Sensing my stress, Will quiets my head by pulling me into him.

"Babe, it's okay. This …" he gestures to the room, the house, "would be hard for anyone."

It's too late. I am completely freaked out. I can understand misinterpreting the way things are when you are a small child. Children experience things differently, so it makes sense they would have different memories of the same events. But I was nearly eighteen when I left here.

I make my way to the staircase at the back of the house. I'm overwhelmed, and trip on the first step. Will is there to catch me. He asks me if I need to sit, if I need water.

I nod. I need a minute to collect my thoughts. I breathe methodically and attempt to slow my mind.

What's changed?

I think back to the last few days, seeing Cedar in the window, and then in the office. I heard her first, didn't I? I mean, I'd never heard her adult voice before, but I am certain it was her. The other night in the apartment, it was the same voice, even clearer. She'd called me Jillybean.

Please God—I want to jump out of my head, I want Cedar to take over the way she did when I was in school, to make sense of this for me. I think of the kitchen in our condo, my medicine spread out for Will to find.

Why would Cedar do that? What was she trying to tell me?

Then it hits me. The medicine, that's what's changed. The last time I was here, I was taking the prescription meds Dr. X ordered and my parents enforced. Did the drugs erase my memories of Cedar the same way Photoshop erased her in photos?

I try to remember that my parents and Dr. X were trying to help me, but I'm enraged, too. How fucking sick do you have to be to think it's okay to take a kid's memories away?

Will hands me the water. I heard him let it run for a while before filling the glass and yet tiny particles still dance in it. At this point, I'm not worried about unpurified water and I swallow in gulps. The specks get closer and closer to my mouth, but I'm too thirsty to stop. Just as I take the last swallow, it dawns on me that it would be very easy for Will to drug me too.

I hate myself for considering it, but does it not make more sense that I'm hallucinating now?

In my mind I see Will handing me the allergy medicine, the take-out sushi the night Cedar paid me a visit, the coffee. This dirty water.

He takes the glass, smiling like he's proud of the way he's taking care of me, and sets it down on the table that my father always left his reading glasses on. Dad used to drug my mother, too. More than once, he crushed her pills between two teaspoons before sprinkling it in her orange juice.

"It will make her feel better," he'd say, with the tiniest wink.

I feel foolish for not putting it together before. Everything I thought I knew is too choppy, too fluid.

We make our way upstairs. For the life of me I can't remember what Cedar's side of the room looks like. We shared a bedroom in a four-bedroom house, I know that much to be true. I get that some girls love their own space, their privacy, but I only wanted to be near her.

Our room is at the end of the hall. It's smaller than the one Aunt Jen stayed in, but it gets the best light. The bay window overlooks the cedar tree and provided a dramatic perch for our daydreaming and stargazing.

The floorboards are dry with neglect and cry out with each step we take. It sounds like the whole house is crying.

The door is open a few inches. Bright light seeps through the crack in an otherwise dark hallway, a hallway that seems to get longer with each timid step. I push through the door to our room, the hinges grating against the quiet of the house.

Will hangs back, watching me, looking for signs that I've lost it or maybe that the drugs he slipped me are taking effect. Or perhaps waiting for me to have some sort of epiphany?

I've had people watch me before. I know how to fake it but it's shocking how quickly the paranoia takes hold again.

At first, I stand still and take it all in. There is a kind of serenity in this room, and the sun warms me as it always did. The walls my mother painted a soft yellow seem juvenile now, but welcome and soothing just the same. Our beds in matching quilts still sit on either side of the window, each with a proudly displayed, much loved stuffy.

I carefully step into the room like I'm fearful I might fall through the floor, like maybe the floor isn't even there. This is the location of my most beloved memories—I don't know if I can handle something happening to them. I can feel the crazy creeping into me; I know that things are not right in my head. Each discovery only complicates things more.

If only Will had shared the file with me. Even more than finding out where Cedar is now, I need to know where she was. What happened in this house? What did they do to us? Why?

I sit on the edge of my bed, clutching my old teddy in my arms. From here, everything is as I remember it: the same books on the shelves sandwiched between two bunny bookends, my alarm clock still on my night table, the baby blanket Mom knitted for Cedar still folded at the foot of her bed.

Will stops lurking in the doorway and plops down into the rocking chair where Cedar and I read together so many nights. He starts to rock, and the seesaw sound of the movement sends me back in time. I see myself alone in here, talking to myself while I color in two Care Bear coloring books. I see Mom in the background, watching over me with an irritated expression.

"This is a great room." Will lifts himself from the chair and it wakes me like the snap of a hypnotist's finger.

"Sure is," I say, standing and making my way to the closet.

I nearly open it but stop. As delicately as I can, I ask Will for some privacy. I know what's behind these doors and I don't know if I'll survive opening the door to a fresh coat of paint. Surely even my mother wouldn't stoop that low. Of course, she'd say Dr. X made her do it, just as she had when I caught her throwing away all of Cedar's drawings from the fridge as if they were trash.

But I've come too far to turn back. I know hurt. I know the feeling of having everything ripped away without any reason. I am strong—I've had to be, and I have to be now.

After Will leaves, I pull the accordion door open to its limit. I start from the top, the shelf that Cedar never got the chance to reach on her own, still lined with boxes of our toys and collectibles. The rod holds a few of my old things but mostly it's just empty hangers, swinging in an unexplained draft.

My robe and a few dresses block the furthest wall of the closet. We used to pull back our clothes like stage curtains to reveal our masterpieces, ta da!

I got a paint set from Aunt Jen for my birthday one year. She said it was for real painters and to make her something wonderful, but Mom and Dad asked me to paint my feelings … Blah. It was Cedar's idea to paint the closet instead. I was the eldest and I knew better, as they later scolded; all the same, the idea made her giddy with excitement and that kind of joy is never something you should turn your back on. She squealed at the way the paint felt on her hands as she pressed them into the paper plate, cool and goopy. Just like I showed her, she positioned her hands like butterfly wings and held them against the wall, first in purple, then bright green. I used my finger to make a caterpillar, my thumbs to make leaves. The result was the happiest closet garden ever. It was so beautiful, in fact, that we hardly got in trouble at all.

Thankfully, here it is. The room instantly cheers up, like a kindergarten. Cedar's words echo in my mind: I wish we could paint the whole house like this.

Cedar made life fun. I taught her things I learnt at school, braided her hair like Aunt Jen braided mine, mothered her in the way I wished I was mothered.

Sure, our artwork isn't as magical now as it seemed when we were kids; the caterpillar doesn't look as real as it was in our imaginations. But it's still here. It's survived whatever it is in my mind that is changing facts into dreams.

Against my will, I look critically at the handprints. There is an obvious difference in the skill level. Cedar's butterflies are less sharp and more smudged, my petals are more defined. But—is it possible our hands were that close in size? The shapes of our fingers, the creases where the paint didn't catch, even the tiny swirls in our prints are so similar. It's as though the same child did it all.

I catch myself holding my breath and dizzily back up to sit down on the bed. I try visualizing myself painting alone and the images are so easily evoked, I force myself to stop.

This is what they always wanted.

They're wrong, they always were. Cedar is alive, Will said so himself. The reminder makes me long to be next to him. I close the door to the closet tight behind me to keep our happiest memories safe inside.

CHAPTER TWENTY-SIX | *Will*

She asked me to leave the room. I wanted to stay, to keep an eye on her, but then I'm lucky she even let me in the house. I'll probably never know what's in the closet, though I suspect it must be something to do with Cedar.

Maybe it's the stillness, the way this house has literally been abandoned, but there is something creepy in here.

This isn't exactly the way I imagined Jill bringing me home for the first time.

First, a walk through the baby garden, then the family portrait hung proudly without her kid sister, and then, just as if we were in high school, I'm forbidden to be in her room. All of this is made even creepier by Jill's behavior. Mind you, I don't know how you could grow up here without having some oddness attach itself to you.

I'm unreasonably awkward given that I'm alone out here in the hallway. There is something that makes me uneasy about all the closed doors—it's so much easier to snoop when the doors are open. Regardless, I can't just stand here.

I open the first of two doors on the right and the hinges creak as if it hasn't been opened in decades. At first glance, I take this to be the guest room—Aunt Jen's room. It's nice enough. There's a large window in the corner that has been left open a crack to allow some air into the otherwise stale room. The late November temperature cuts any warmth that might have accumulated over the summer months, so much so that a visible cloud of my breath floats away from me. The sheer white curtains lift away from the window; this slight movement is the first sign of life I have seen in this house. Aside from a floral throw draped over the bed and a lavender candle on the night table, the room is completely devoid of personality. I suppose it's a perfectly functional guest room, but I don't know how welcome anyone would feel in here on a cold winter night.

I'm just about to shut the door behind me when I remember a story Helene told me one night when she was two bottles deep. I couldn't have been older than ten at the time, so it frightened me more than it should have. As we lived in an old mansion, complete with a private staircase for staff and a suspiciously locked room in the attic, I was accustomed to being scared.

My mother, however, adamantly claimed the ghosts we shared the halls with were hospitable. Aside from late night faucets being turned on and off and the terrifying sound of kitchen chairs being dragged across the floor, I did feel safe enough.

The story goes that Mom was alone in the house one afternoon, coming up the stairs from the basement with laundry. (From the wine cellar with a pinot.) When she reached the top, she was about to shut the door behind her when she heard a small voice beg, "Please—don't close the door."

While she told me, Mom's voice quavered, and she picked

at her nail polish. "It was as clear as if she were standing right beside me," she said.

The voice was desperate, pleading in a childlike, unthreatening way. It was so convincing that from then on, the idea of a young child trapped in the cellar would make Mother rise from her bed late at night to go open the door.

As I do since hearing that story, I leave this door unlatched just in case. And I remind myself to be a little more generous about Jillian's fixation on Cedar.

Three doors remain unopened. I'm expecting at least one to be a bathroom and one a master bedroom. The third is a mystery. If I was a betting man, given the way this house seems suspended in time, I would wager a hefty amount that it is a sewing room.

Now, which door leads to which room? Sure, it's a juvenile way to kill time, but what the heck. I like the way "immature" feels—so much more comfortable than L. I. A. R.

I open the door directly across the hall next. I open it slowly to soften the inevitable crrrrrreak, but it only makes it worse and the hinges scream out at the nerve of me. The door's agitation isn't justified by the room it guards, pale pink tile with matching tub and pedestal sink.

I step inside, think about peeing and then think better of it. I hold onto the sink, bracing myself as I look into the oval mirror Jill, Cedar and the rest of their family must have looked in thousands of times.

I doubt Jill ever appreciated how beautiful she was. Is. I wonder if her mother could see the sadness reflected back as she brushed her teeth, if it was as clear and painful for her as it was for her family. I have no business judging this woman who suffered so much, who endured the physical pain of labor and loss, over and over. I know that. But I'm angry for Jill. In fact, the antique-looking painting of a mother embracing an infant on the wall behind me irritates me instead of sparking my empathy. It seems a bit overkill.

Before I open door three, I press my ear to Jill's room, listening for a signal that she needs me.

She doesn't.

Eeni, meenie, miny, mo … I choose the door one down from the bathroom. It's not the master. It's not a sewing room or linen closet, which was my second guess. There are two beds in Jillian's room, so I assumed it was their shared space, but a stencil on the wall in here reads CEDAR, painted in pale-purple lettering. It's a nursery. It has all the props, a crib placed in the center of the room. There's a rocking chair like the one in Jill's room, but this one has an etched drawing of Winnie the Pooh that matches the pad on the change table and the quilted characters suspended from the ceiling.

You might think that the Winnie the Pooh theme would take away from the totally fucked-up-edness of it all, but it doesn't. Why keep a nursery intact this long? Is it a coincidence they left Cedar's name on the wall? It unnerves me.

"They kept this door locked."

Her voice startles me. Less from fear than guilt—guilt that I am in here, that she somehow knows the awful thoughts I'm thinking about her mother, this room, this whole screwed up situation.

She lingers in the doorway and gazes around with a curious

expression, one I'm not sure I have ever seen before. It's almost as if she's seeing the room for the first time.

"Did you know they still had it set up this way?"

"I can't remember. I can't really remember being in here much after Cedar was a baby." She steps forward, inching into the room, then stops abruptly like she's been zapped by an invisible electric fence.

"I wasn't allowed in here after …"

"After what?"

She doesn't hear me. Or, she's not listening, her eyes blankly fixed on the crib.

"She's the only one of my mom's babies I remember. Her legs were so chubby she got little rashes in the creases."

She brings her finger to her mouth. Her eyes are bright but seem empty, too. She's proud, like an old lady romanticizing rashes and sleepless nights when her children were small and loving.

"We used to play this game—every morning I would sneak in here and try to catch her asleep." Still in the doorway, she slides her body down the frame to sit on the carpet.

"I guess it was more my game, but I swear she knew," she laughs. "Even when I thought I'd caught her, she'd give me this adorable little pirate-eye."

Maybe because she is sitting on the floor, or the way she's folded her knees into her chest, she looks so young and small. I want to pick her up and keep her safe. She keeps talking but I've stopped listening; instead, I'm just seeing her soft smile and the way her feet point inward. She is so vulnerable, but it also feels as if there is something … off.

I realize that, whether Cedar is alive or dead, Jillian needs help. This is more than mourning. All this death has marked her to the point that she is either an iron tower or a cowering child.

I have had glimpses of Jillian on even ground and she's amazing. Jill in the middle is perfect.

My thoughts are interrupted by the sound of an engine outside the window. It could've been there the whole time, like a fan running in the background of a room, but we both acknowledge it now. Our eyes finally connect and it's as if we synchronize our steps across the nursery.

Someone in a car is watching the house, or us. It's not particularly surprising, as we did just break in. In a quiet toy town like this, it doesn't shock me that our arrival has been noticed.

Jill's breath is steaming up the glass. She doesn't seem to notice and continues to stare intently at the woman behind the driver's seat. At first, I figure she is trying to place an old neighbor or a high school friend.

Then she mutters, "It's her."

She frantically tries to lift the old wood-paned window, trying to pry it open even though it looks as if it has been painted shut.

"It's her," she repeats, more desperate. "Will, help me!"

Her panic snaps me out of my confusion. I don't bother apologizing, just muscle the window open enough for her to call down to the woman I am assuming she believes to be Cedar.

The screen is caked with an accumulation of dust and cobwebs, but it doesn't stop me from recognizing the car immediately. I can't see who is driving, beyond a ponytail similar to Jill's.

"Wait, don't go!" Jill shouts as she tries to push the screen out, "Please, WAIT!"

Abruptly she turns away from the window and shoves past me. Her face is desperate as she begs me not to let her drive away.

All I can manage is a pitiful, "Babe?"

She's halfway down stairs that are too steep to run on, screaming, "CEDAR!" over and over until her voice carries outdoors with her.

She flies from the front door, jumps over a dry rose bush and sprints toward the black Cadillac sedan a hundred feet away. If I had any goodness in my heart, I would pray for this cat and mouse game to finally end, but I don't.

Instead, I silently urge the car on. I offer a pathetic "Stop!" but my voice is weak with insincerity.

The car speeds up and drives on, and Jill drops to her knees. She shoots me a look that shows exactly how disappointed she is with me.

I'm only half invested in her well-being; I know that now. The other half of me is one-quarter selfishness and one-quarter perverse loyalty to my father.

What I don't know is who is driving that car. If it is Cedar, then her relationship to my family is a lot more complicated than I thought. It's a company car, usually driven by whoever my father's current "fixer" is. Over the years the position has been filled by many different employees, all of whom have been large, surly men. Now it appears to be a woman, the woman I saw at the hospital. Cedar?

I don't take my eyes off the car until it disappears around the corner and then I have no choice but to look back at Jill.

She's still on her knees, sobbing hard, her whole body moving in waves. She's broken. Being here in this fucked-up dollhouse with all these memories is enough—and then this woman taunts her again. It's all too much.

Yet it's not enough to make me go to her side—to be fully on her side.

I've wanted nothing more than for Jill to open up, to soften, yet this degree of vulnerability in her is unnerving. It's like my father always said: when things get hard, I quit. Spoiled child syndrome, he calls it.

"I'll be right there, babe!" I shout from the window. My own voice startles me into motion and my feet fly the way they should have five minutes ago.

The stairs sing out, mocking me with each step. I can feel my phone vibrating in my pocket and realize that it has been vibrating since before Jill left the room. I grab it from my jeans: it's my father. He's been in my head all day—my whole life, poking and picking, blowing up my phone. I can picture the frustration on his face at my nerve. How dare I not answer him! For whatever reason, his "count to three" threats still resonate, and even as an adult I never make him wait. But this is different. He's not really waiting—he has eyes on us, on me and on Jill.

When he told me to take her out of town, I figured he wouldn't want me to bring her here, but I did it anyway. Before I hit the front door, his genius stops me in my tracks—this is what he wanted all along.

But why? Why do this to Jill?

Seven new voicemails.

I wrap my arms around her now, kneeling on the grass. The knees of my jeans absorb water from the ground. She has stopped crying and sits tall and still. If I loosen my grip or let go, I doubt she would sag or even soften. She stares longingly in the direction she believes her sister drove off in.

I'm focused on the phone in my hand. When is the appropriate time to release her and check my phone? Sixty Mississippi?

"I know what we have to do," she says out of nowhere.

Her voice is as flat as her expression.

"I need to see her death certificate. They wouldn't have been able to fake that, right?"

She doesn't wait for a response. I think she's done waiting for me to do or say the right thing.

She stands and takes leaden steps toward the house.

"Jill!" I call after her. Against my better judgment, I blurt, "It might not be what you think it is." I have no idea what it is. I pull myself from the grass and wipe the dirt off my jeans in pompous sweeps.

She stops dead.

"What are you talking about? What do you know?" Her eyes beg for answers, which makes me instantly regret opening my mouth at all.

"I don't know, babe …" My shoulders sink.

"Great, Will!" She slaps her hands on the sides of her legs. "I appreciate the input."

Fuck.

"Babe …" I lower my voice in an attempt to diffuse the tension between us.

I'm not saying this to calm her down. I thought the woman

in the hospital was Cedar at first, but when I got closer, there was no real resemblance to Jillian at all.

It is also possible I misread the photo in the file—maybe the woman was Jill's roommate Heather. Or someone who works for my father, the woman who is now driving his car and was hired, like me, to keep an eye on Jillian.

All of these possibilities—and I can't reveal a single one without giving myself away.

Jillian doesn't look well. Her skin is white against the red brick of the house and her pupils are huge. She keeps rubbing her neck and flexing her shoulder blades back, like the tension is starting to strangle her.

When we first moved in together, she was always perfect, even in the morning, her hair smooth and mascara in place. Slowly that turned into full on bedhead and morning breath, and it didn't bother me at all. But I can't remember a time she's looked worse than in this moment. Her arm is itchy, and she scratches it wildly as she stares at me. It could be the grass, or nerves. Either way, she needs help. She needs a doctor.

CHAPTER TWENTY-SEVEN | *Aaron*

It's almost laughable how easy Will is to play.

A simple getaway should have been an easy enough request to fulfill without too many questions. He is my employee and my son, for Christ's sake.

Predictable, William. Ha. I knew he would take her to that hospital and to play house in her little ghost town.

His need to be her hero, to solve this mystery, is apparently more important to him than our family. This is exactly why I can't tell him things, why it would be stupid to give him any details about his girlfriend.

He's my father all over again: the Sutherby disloyalty gene skips a generation, leaving me in the middle to deal with their fair-weather commitment to the family.

He's so obsessed with her he can't use his friggin' brain, which is ironic, because it was my father's obsession with that little bitch that got us in this mess. She could ruin us. God knows we're halfway there now. I hear the guys snickering at the club, slowly distancing themselves, looking down on me for doing exactly what I did to build this company in the first place. They forget who made them who they are, who threw them clients like breadcrumbs back when they could barely tie a simple half-Windsor.

Fucking kids these days don't know what sacrifice is, what must be done to protect a family's legacy.

My wife isn't innocent, either. She was so strong when we married—then she met a drink one night and they started a torrid affair that pushed everyone else aside. One drink to the next. Truth is, it's easier to deal with a bullheaded woman when she's drunk. I can't pinpoint when she changed, but one day I was leaving for work and the woman sitting at the kitchen table was frail and needy, demanding my constant attention.

Fast forward twenty years, and my son falls for a lunatic who I pay him to watch, not fuck. She is basically his mother; save the booze, add the meds. Predictable. Should I have known he would fall in love with her when I put him on the job? Perhaps. She is beautiful. Her eyes, the depth of the moody layers of brown on green; radiant in a way I've never seen. Those eyes alone have me questioning this whole thing sometimes. But unlike my father and son, I don't have the luxury of leading with my heart.

It's her or us.

Thing is, even if Will knew what was at stake, he would still choose her. That's why I now have to divert him as much as her.

He'll recover. He'll be set and I won't have to worry about him failing in business (in fucking everything) after I'm gone.

Will is lucky. Not every father would go so far to undo something as thoughtless and selfish as the shitshow my father put in place before he died. When this is resolved, my legacy will be preserved, and Helene won't be any the wiser.

Despite everything, all my shortcomings as a husband, I can't stand to have her think of me as a failure. After all, more than half was her money, her family's money.

Leave it to my father to entrust money I had counted on to some science experiment.

Cedar's file is a redundant read, almost exactly like Jill's, full of holes and blurred out records, aside from the difference in names, ages and personality traits.

I never put much merit in my father's work. His attachment to his patients seemed unnatural—not wholly appropriate even if it wasn't perverse.

The roommate indicated Cedar was back years ago, but her story is weak. And she wouldn't go on the record anyway, even turned down compensation. In her interview, she admits to only meeting Cedar once, which won't be enough.

I know less about Cedar, but as far as Jillian is concerned, my father has been playing puppet master even since his death. According to the file, her university acceptance, internship and apartment had all been arranged by my father. In part, I suspect this has something to do with his need to keep Cedar out of Jillian's life. Jillian stays busy and distracted and he tracks both girls at all times.

Truthfully, what Will and I have done is not much different. Sure, I'm sure my father would describe his interference differently, but from here it looks as if he had absolute power over their lives. Worse, he has subjected her family to a life of lies and heartbreak, all for some experimental therapy that has taken nearly twenty years to even publish.

I'm protecting my father's reputation now as much as the rest of our family. If Jillian decided to sue, I think she'd have a pretty damning case against the Sutherby Method.

It's like a bad movie.

But it turns out Jillian is a lot more malleable than I initially thought. The first time Will brought her home I took her for headstrong, not headcase. She held herself with the type of confidence that having nothing to lose instills. She shook my hand with adequate firmness, not too firm, to make up for her gender, nor with the listlessness I'd come to expect from beautiful women.

Her eyes beat me to the chase, locking on mine in a way that was almost a challenge. Later that night, I watched her and Will in the hallway through a crack in my office door. She had him up against the wall; she was kissing him hard, but her body was loose, completely comfortable with taking charge.

She is the type of woman whose presence makes everyone else fade into the background, so much that Will disappeared from the equation altogether and I felt aroused.

I pegged her as someone who was adaptable, strong enough to overcome any environment, to go through hardship and stay strong. It seemed she had it all together, mentally sound and unbreakable.

I was wrong. When Will started giving me reports, I learned Jillian still had doubts about her sister's death: the nightmares, the sleep muttering, conversations with the dead. Clearly, she was struggling. But she still needed a push.

Then we found her university roommate, who told my people about her encounter with Cedar.

It's not clear how much Jill's parents know about the money

my father left for her in his estate. But whatever they know, it all depends on Jill being mentally stable and healthy.

I'm sure Will has his hands full right now, but my third call going to voicemail is not acceptable. With no other choice, I leave another message:

"William, it's your father. Pick up the f-ing phone and call me right back. What were you doing at that hospital? Fuck, Will. Are you trying to destroy our family? Look, Jillian needs help. She doesn't need you making things worse.

"That's all I'm trying to do, son. There are things you don't know. She is not well. Call me back."

CHAPTER TWENTY-EIGHT | *Jillian*

Wake up, wake up, wake up.

How did I get here?

I'm looking down on myself sitting in the car beside Will, my knees tucked under my chin, my face buried in my palms. Will pulls his eyes from the road every few moments to check on me, telling me to breathe. He bites at his lip, reminding me of an expectant father trying to safely get his wife to the hospital.

The years of walls I've built around myself, the steps I've taken to overcome this feeling of being in pieces, it's all crumbling. In days.

I tell myself to straighten up, to stop fidgeting, but it's as though my brain refuses to communicate with my body, like I've been switched off.

Crying, yelling, slamming my fists on the dashboard—they would all be better options than sitting here vacant, shaking my feet over and over the way my mother always did.

I look crazy. Worse, I feel crazy.

"Jillian? I'm here. It's okay." Her words echo throughout my head, the car, and the space between where my body sits and my consciousness hovers.

I turn sharply to Will. He didn't hear it—he didn't flinch or blink.

My heartbeat races and the rest of my body joins my feet and starts shaking. I need to get out of here. I inhale deeply and close my eyes.

It's not her, Jill. It's just not. It was in your head. You did it.

"Jill, it's me! It's Cedar. It's Cedar. It's Cedar. It's Cedar. It's Cedar …"

"Stop the car!" My hands are in fists, trying their absolute best to push away this madness. I'm going mad again. Why would Cedar be in my head? She is nowhere near me; she drove off in the car. She is alive and I am fine. I am perfectly sane. I employ the self-talk I got so good at during all my cognitive therapy with Dr. X—Grandad X. Jesus.

The car is at the side of the road. Will jumps out and comes over to my side. I need to scream or have a really good cry. That always used to help discharge the anxiety, but I'm too far gone now to do either one of those things. I have to pull it together.

"I thought I was going to throw up," I blurt as he opens my door.

His face is blank. He is neither annoyed nor sympathetic. His eyes and the cool air smarten me up. For a moment we are as we were a week ago; I'm equal to him, if not stronger.

But the way he is looking at me makes me feel ashamed. It's so familiar, that concern and disappointment. I tell him again that I'm just physically unwell—perhaps I need to eat. He nods as I explain, yet the look still lingers.

"Well," he says, before heading back to his side of the car, "let's get you something."

I'm scared, but at least I feel like I have some control again. I swallow hard before he gets back in, hoping to dislodge the confusion that lingers.

He sits down hard, raises his hand to start the ignition and then stops. He looks down at his lap and sighs. Had this been a different scenario, had he been a different type of man, this might signal the "this isn't working" talk.

As difficult as this past week has been, I know Will loves me. Everything in my life is jumbled, worse than ever maybe, but I am certain of Will's commitment to me.

What he says is worse.

"You need to see a doctor, Jill. You're not well."

Anything else. He could've said anything else and it wouldn't have hurt this bad. My face burns red hot. It's as if I've been punched in the stomach and it sends its contents flooding into my mouth. I bear it and swallow. A few disloyal tears spring into the corners of my eyes.

I cheated on you.

You're fat.

Get your boobs done.

You're stupid.

Literally anything else.

"Don't take it the wrong way, Jillian."

I don't know what hurts more: what he's saying, or that he is looking ahead at the road while he says it. Which way does he intend me to take, "You're not well?" Is there any translation in which that doesn't mean, "You're mentally ill"?

Either way, I'm hung up on how quickly it's happened and how I wish he'd call me "babe" instead of Jillian.

He's saying something about his mother's drinking. The association with someone he loves softens the pain for a moment but then he says "unstable" and I realize that's where his mind has gone.

I cut him off mid-sentence, silence him by bringing his hand to my mouth and kissing the back of it.

"You're right. You are. Just help me find her death certificate and then I'll see anyone you want."

There, that was good. I can't be lost if I can turn it off. Except he doesn't seem as relieved as I expected.

"How do you do that?" He turns to face me, finally looking me in the eye.

"Do what?"

"Switch back and forth so easily?"

What does he mean, switch?

"Well, I'm not bipolar, if that's what you're suggesting."

I can feel myself hardening. I can hear it in my voice, but I'm careful not to make any sharp turns.

"I'm not saying anything like that—"

Before I can stop myself, I'm laughing. I hear the pitchy peals about to give way to full on sobs and I fear I am no longer in control. How is someone in this situation expected to behave? My frustration with Will is bordering on rage—rage that he is somehow connected to my sister's disappearance and has the audacity to question my sanity.

It's all I can do not to propel myself from our now moving vehicle. Fuck you, Will Sutherby. Fuck your whole family. I catch his side-eye glare as my laughing subsides into a drawn-out sigh.

"I'm not handling this well, I know. But I would dare you to handle it any better if our situations were reversed." I keep my gaze on the roadside as it passes by. "Bear with me, or don't." Another laugh escapes. "Stay and help, or please just drop me off and leave."

I'm done explaining any of this to him, done rationalizing what is clearly not rational. As much as I love him, I will always love my sister more. And right now, I have to love myself most. I don't have Dr. X to confide in anymore and Will is not his grandfather. Is simply pretending this isn't happening any better? Ignoring Cedar, giving up now, is not going to make the events of this week any more acceptable to him than all the screwed-up memories that haunt my life, that have attached themselves to me like a shadow.

We're close to town now. Will's only response to my declaration is to clench his jaw and stare ahead. I do my best to distract myself and focus on the homes we're passing, their yards exploding with toys, clotheslines, tire swings and dog houses. I feel sad once more that things were so different at my house.

I catch my eyes reflected in the car window and they're so like those of the young girl who rode the bus on this route to school every day twenty years ago.

"Which way do I turn at the light?"

He speaks.

"That depends, are you staying, or going?"

"We're in this together, Jill. I'm sorry." He rubs his eyes with his free hand. "I'm a jerk."

Ha.

"Then left—if it's still even open."

His apology is a relief and I feel my betraying lips curl upward on their own. It's amazing what a smile can do for your psyche. It was one of the only bits of wisdom my mother was able to give me: When you're feeling down, even so down you don't want to go up, smile and breathe, long and deep. It's odd, but every morning when I sit to pee, I hear her voice and I smile to myself. Somehow, even if it's temporary, the smile pushes the darkness back under until about thirty minutes later when I'm drying my hair or buttoning my blouse, and then I do it again.

In this moment, my smile is genuine and Will loves me again. It makes me forget his insensitivity.

"We're heading to the community center, about five minutes down that road."

"There's a community center here?"

He's trying to be funny. He's definitely not forgiven, but I'll gladly take a break from the tension.

"It's the arena, really—the town hall is in there, a small closet-like room run by one employee. Tim Hortons is across the street. I'll buy you a donut if you stop calling me crazy?"

I hear the excitement in my voice and take note of my energized posture and relaxed shoulders.

Will is right to question me, although I wouldn't say this is necessarily a switch, as he calls it. I'd describe it more as a well-practiced coping mechanism—and my attempt to prevent history from repeating itself. Not to push everyone away again, to be alone again.

"I didn't say you were crazy," he says, as he takes a left turn that feels like a rollercoaster to my shattered nerves.

"I'm just not sure I'm doing the right thing encouraging this. It's too much for anyone, Jill. And, honestly, I'm afraid that you want Cedar to be alive so badly you're turning a bunch of weird coincidences into something it's not."

It kills me to admit, but I say it anyway: "So am I, Will. So am I."

As expected, the entire town hall is still more like a doctor's waiting room. There are no bells and whistles aside from a gallery wall of newspaper clippings proudly displaying a collection of Ravenscliff Citizens of the Month announcements and photos of children participating in events that include a track meet and "The Happening in the Park." On the upside, there are also no numbers to be taken, no big city lineups. We're at the front of the line as soon as we enter the room, before I have come up with a plan. The woman who greets us doesn't register any recognition when she looks at me.

"How can I help ya?" she asks, leaning across the counter toward us, bracing her weight on her folded arms.

Right now, I would prefer the robotics of an urban stranger to her relaxed welcome. I feel my throat close and my breathing quicken as she stares at me too closely. She reads my unsteady vibes and slides back to give me a second to gather myself. Finally, I manage, "Do you keep a record of death certificates here?"

My voice sounds much more assured than I feel.

"Oh dear," she says, a quintessential towny. "I'm very sorry for your loss."

"It was a long time ago …"

"Well, death certificates are a matter of public record and

while we don't keep the actual certificate, if the person is, was, sorry, local, I should be able to tell you when they passed."

"And, will it say, umm, how they died?" I ask, trying not to sound eager.

She smiles and nods, "It should," and then positions her fingers above the keyboard.

"Could you check the name Cedar Elizabeth Gannon, please?"

She looks up from her computer.

"Did you say Gannon?"

"Yes, G-A-N…"

"So, you must be Jillian, is that right?"

"That's right. I'm sorry, have we met?" I ask, feeling my feet go numb.

She looks different now, concerned.

"Not since you were little. I knew your mother and father … seems a long time ago. Where did they move to?" She's making small talk, but I can tell she is uneasy. Small town rumors, I'm sure.

"Umm, the island—could you check your records please?"

Rude, but this isn't a social visit and I'd rather she keeps any opinion she has about my family to herself. She slides a stack of sticky notes across the counter and asks me to write out the name. I can tell from the look on his face that even Will finds this bizarre, as she was about to type the name into her computer before she heard who it was.

She catches our look and explains, "This old thing is slow. I'll use the computer in the back. I just want to get the spelling right."

I carefully write out Cedar's name and pass it to her. She peels the note off the pad slowly and mutters the name out loud to herself as she turns from us to suspiciously head to the "back."

"That was odd," Will says, swigging his coffee. "Fuck it's cold in here, no wonder the computer froze."

Funny guy. He elbows my side and chuckles to himself but I'm too nervous to react.

"Relax, Jill, it's a small town, that's all."

A few minutes later, the woman returns.

"She was your sister," she says, still walking toward us, a somber expression on her face. Her use of "was" lands and I hear it over and over in my head like bells ringing. Will hears it too, and protectively drapes his arm around me.

I nod a few times, fighting tears of disappointment and relief and reluctantly repeat, "She was."

She comes over to our side of the desk and hands me a scrap piece of paper where she has jotted down some notes.

"Nothing more official?" I ask before reading it.

"That's all the information I have access to. Would you like me to read it to you?"

"No, no. It's alright." I'm not quite ready to know, to finally know. At least not with her looking over my shoulder.

Whether or not I will believe what is written is the real question. I fold the paper with one hand and slip it into my jacket pocket. We thank her for her help, and I do my best to play it cool. Meanwhile my pocket is on fire and I regret not reading her notes straightaway.

Will hasn't said much but he keeps his hand planted firmly

on my shoulder. I don't know how I feel but I know I handled the situation as calmly as anyone could.

My sister is dead. Which means I am seriously disturbed—or someone is fucking with me.

And, my sister is dead.

"Ms. Gannon?" I hardly hear her over the drone of the Zamboni and a flood of impatient children waiting to be released from their holding pens like cattle. I turn to see her behind us.

"Jillian," she repeats. "I'm sorry to keep you …"

"It's okay," I say, despite my anxiousness.

"I just wanted you to know I am so sorry for your loss. I know it was a long time ago, but I lost a baby a few years ago, and … I mean, it's none of my business, but I heard about your mom and her losses …"

I can see she is trying to be kind, and perhaps she needs to talk more even more than she needs to offer her sympathy. Either way, I have no choice but to hear her out.

"Our baby was two months early. But to lose a toddler …"

She's lost me. She's gotten the story wrong, gossip gone haywire like the telephone game. She touches my hand and says how sorry she is about Cedar and how she wishes I had been able to grow up with my sister.

"But …" I begin, about to explain her mistake. But what's the point?

Instead, I play along and thank her. Then, as briskly as I can walk without running, I bolt to the door ahead of Will, fighting the urge not to pull the paper out of my pocket until I am safe inside the car.

CHAPTER TWENTY-NINE | *Will*

I knew from the way she looked at Jill that something wasn't right. I'm not saying she recognized her, but there is definitely a story going around this small town.

It's hard to tell which one of us is acting crazier. My father's words and my grandfather's files are on my mind, driving every word and action I take, my love for Jill somehow redeeming me only to fail once again.

She's ahead of me. Clearly, she needs to get out of here, to get to the car, read that paper and figure out what to do next. I should be walking with her, but instead I let her get ahead. I'm not sure if that's the right call or she's up there cursing me in her head, "Hurry the fuck up, Will."

I'm shocked she didn't insist on reading the computer herself. The encounter did seem a tad on the shady side, but I'm not sure how smoothly asking for proof of your sister's death should go. Awkward is to be expected; doubly so, given that the poor woman on the desk had also lost a baby. But I was blown away that Jill didn't push for some explanation. A toddler?

I see Jill buckle her seat belt, pause, and then check her

phone. She is absolutely stalling, just as I am, standing out here fighting an urge to use the bathroom or go make an imaginary call.

My father is right—I don't know what the fuck I'm doing. And I don't know what the fuck he is doing—why would he choose someone who looks like Jillian to follow us?

Slowing my pace even more is not an option; I am barely moving as it is. I open the car door as gingerly as possible, aware of how fragile the atmosphere must be inside. I slide in and blow into my frozen hands, buying another second or two.

I wish she would speak first, or slide the paper over to me to read like a university acceptance letter: "I can't look."

I would read it, and everything would make sense. We'd hug. She'd cry. I'd call my father, tell him where to go and then book two tickets to Maui like I should have done days ago.

But that isn't going to happen. None of this was a good idea.

"Did you read it?" I ask, fully aware of the answer. She shakes her head no and bites her lip.

"This was a bad idea," she whispers. "I should never have come back here."

I squeeze her shoulder, completely agreeing with her but unable to say as much.

"You wanted answers, babe. This," I gesture to her coat pocket, "is what you were looking for."

"But you heard what she said about Cedar." Her voice cracks and she stops talking.

"Screw it," she says, more gently than the words imply, and throws her seatbelt off. She reaches for the right pocket, knowing exactly where the note is, and pulls it out. She holds the paper between her thumbs and forefingers, up high like she's reading the evening paper. I watch her eyes brighten and then shut tightly as she crumples the paper into a shape that looks like a failed origami flower.

Her delirious, almost menacing laugh returns.

"This is bullshit. It's bullshit."

Her voice is as emotionless as it could be saying those words, which may be why I feel comfortable asking what the paper says.

"Hmmm," she pretends to ponder, sarcastically. "What does it say?"

She's starting to break.

"What it says is that my sister Cedar died of accidental suffocation or late onset SIDS in 1993 when she was eleven months old."

Her face is animated, puzzled, like she's stumped on a Jeopardy question or wondering why a teenager might be wearing booty shorts while shopping with her parents.

She reaches for the door handle, about to jump out and storm back into the building, but I stop her.

"Jill, wait." I hold her thigh in place. "She's not trying to trick you."

She shoots me a look of disgust and then buries her face into her hands. "I don't understand, Will."

"I know, babe, me either."

She slumps over onto my side of the car. I hold her for a minute, searching my brain for something enlightening to say.

The truth … the truth is all I can come up with. Not the whole truth, but the only thing I know to be true:

"This is not your fault. Someone has done this to you.

Someone has purposely told you things that aren't true and you are very confused."

She starts crying. I can feel her tears on my neck. For just a second, I forget my role in this and hold her.

For the first time since we took off on this expedition of lies, I am present. I feel her weight on me and I hold her. As if struck by an epiphany or a crisis of character, I decide I'm all in. Whatever our next steps are, I'll confront them with her.

She abruptly sits up and presses her back against her door, her face brightening as if she has remembered something joyful.

"She used to talk to me," she says plainly.

"Of course she did …"

"No, I mean, she spoke to me in my head. When we were little, she didn't speak to anyone but me. My mother—" she pushes her tousled hair behind her ears, "was so jealous. She was so angry when I told her."

"I don't understand." I'm trying to keep my manner even keel, but my knee bobs against the rental keys hanging from the ignition. I'm afraid to hear what I know she is about to say.

"In my head, in our heads. Cedar was telepathic."

She keeps her eyes locked on mine, not giving me any room to process. I cough away my shock, clear my throat and mirror her position, pressing my back against the driver's side door, giving myself a bit of space.

It occurs to me that this could be some kind of elaborate prank, a test of my loyalty.

"She was telepathic?" Despite my best efforts, there is judgement in my voice. I try to distract her from it quickly and add, "Your parents knew about this … ability?"

"Well, they didn't believe me. They were so angry for so long."

"Why would they be angry, Jill? That doesn't make sense. Because they thought you were lying?

"Well, yeah. I guess. My mom did for sure. My dad tried to get Cedar to talk to him with white boards and stuff …"

Once again, I'm regretting not reading all of Cedar's file. What the fuck is wrong with me?

Jill interrupted me, freaking out when she thought there was an intruder in the apartment. But I could have read it the next day. I should have read it instead of booking this ill-advised trip. Surely, Grandfather would have included some of this information in his notes.

All I know for sure is that I saw a file on Cedar, and a photo of the woman who looks like Jill with Cedar Gannon written on it.

"Did my grandfather know about her telepathy?" I'm trying my best to be sympathetic and not skeptical. She knows how insane this sounds.

My mind is swirling and I'm wondering if Jill is coming to the same conclusion: What if it wasn't Cedar who was Grandfather's patient? What if it was Jill?

But none of this explains why my father is so invested. Why is this woman who looks like Jill's doppelganger following us?

"Of course!"

It's the first thing she's said with conviction.

"He was obsessed with her abilities, but I wasn't supposed to tell anyone, because my mother got angry and people like you would think I'm crazy."

"I don't think you're crazy, babe," I say. I know my next question will sound awful, so I yawn and stretch to try to make it sound more casual. "Did you ever spend any time at the hospital yourself?"

She slumps subtly. "I don't know what you mean by that," she says, trying to sound steady, "but yes. I did. After the accident. For a couple weeks."

"I didn't mean …"

"Yeah, you did. But it wasn't like I had to stay there. I wasn't committed or anything. I just felt more comfortable with Dr. X, with your grandfather, than I did with my parents."

"Why do you think that was?" Even though I wish none of this was real, that Jill, the woman I love, had a different upbringing, I'm happy she is opening up. She looks down and I can't help but notice how her lashes lay on her cheeks. She still somehow looks flawless—almost unnaturally so, the way clouds in a painting can look unrealistic when in fact the sky it portrays was just that beautiful.

"Honestly," she shakes her head like she is still in disbelief, "it was because my parents wanted to forget all about her. After the service it was like …," she dusts her hands together, "that's that."

"My grandfather let you talk about her, about how much you missed her?"

"Always. On some days, it was almost as if he mourned her even more than I did."

She draws a heart with her finger on the now foggy window. I turn on the engine and let the car idle, hoping she doesn't take it as a cue to stop talking.

"You do that a lot," I point out.

"Do what?" She moves her hands to hover above the luke-warm air from the heater.

"The heart on the window—I've seen you do that before."

"Just stop!" She smudges out her drawing with her sleeve. "All girls do it! It's not something I picked up in the mental hospital if that's what you're getting at …" She gives me a smirk and rolls her eyes.

"It's cute! And just the opposite—I mean, shit can't be that bad if you're drawing hearts on the window."

"Those hearts are for you," she says, making the kind of eye contact that simultaneously makes me feel worthy and self-conscious. "You make me happy, Will. You're the only person who never let me down."

Jesus. If only she knew. Regardless, I lean over the console between us and kiss her cheek, the warmth of it making me real-ize how chilled I am. The sun is almost completely set now, and the temperature has dropped to near freezing.

I'm waiting for a cue from her—if we're staying here togeth-er, or if we're heading to the airport. At this point, I'm even con-sidering driving the four hours back to Vancouver, although the Coquihalla is never a good idea at night.

"I'd like to get back to the city," she says, reading my mind and reaching for her belt.

"I think it's too late now. It's too dangerous to drive and seri-ously, I think we both need some sleep. I can get my own room if …"

"First thing in the morning then," she says, without acknowl-edging my offer. I'm almost relieved at how calm she is. It's as if she's entirely dismissed being told there is no record of her sister living past her first birthday.

At least she doesn't jump on the possibility that the records had been tampered with, or that the office lady is in on the Cedar accident conspiracy. How much influence did my grandfather have in this small town?

Unless we opt to stay at the Super 8 in Lake Country, we have no choice but to drive back to Kelowna. As soon as we cross over the town line, it feels like waking up from a bad dream. My head feels clear again, my grip loosens on the wheel.

Forty-five minutes later we check into the Delta Grand. Even by my standards, the place is charming. Once in our room, it is too dark and the mood too somber to take in the views, but I can see the outline of mountains standing tall behind the rows of boats, beneath stars that look almost make-believe.

Jill hasn't said much. I think leaving her hometown had the opposite effect on her. She closed her eyes for the entire drive but I knew she wasn't asleep. I assured her we would figure every-thing out in the morning.

She responded by nodding her head slowly, revealing her annoyance.

And how could it not be annoying? How would everything be figured out after all this time, all these years of uncertainty, in one morning? There are times when there is nothing to say and when saying nothing isn't good enough.

Ignoring my better angels, I watch her undress. She slips out of her jeans and pulls her sweat top over her head with the com-fort of familiarity. She seems not to care that I am sharing a room with her, a bed. After a day in which I have seen her stripped down to the bone, clothes, I gather, mean nothing. I know she is angry about me keeping the file and my grandfather's identity from her. But she helps herself to my t-shirt, pulling it out of my overnight bag without hesitation, knowing she still never has to ask.

Yes, I want to make love to her. I am a guy, after all, but I draw the line at just staring. They say people often have sex after funerals. The thought crossed my mind that once we got in here, she might be interested, just to shake off the stress.

She uses the washroom and gets into bed and I pretend-busy myself for twenty minutes, arranging our wallets and keys, charging our phones. Once I shower and exhaust any other possible procrastinations, I have no choice but to climb into bed beside her.

She didn't instruct me to sleep on the sofa and gearing down in front of me might be an invitation. Then again, as I stand over the bed awkwardly, I see she has both pillows, one holding her perfect head, the other between her legs where I should be. I find another in the closet.

The night is restless.

Jill speaks first at around three. It starts as a few unintelligible murmurs and aggressive thrashing. After the third time she whipped the blankets from me, I stumble into the bathroom to pee in the dark.

Jill screams, "The baby, the baby …" Over and over.

But by the time I put myself together and get back in the room, she is quiet, fast asleep, and there isn't as much as a ripple of movement.

After the day we had, I can't say sleep-talking is unexpected.

It's what happens at four that worries me. I thought Jill hold-ing conversations with herself was the most unsettling thing I'd ever wake up to.

This, however, is worse.

I open my eyes just in time to see her crawl off the end of the bed. It is almost like she drags herself onto the floor by her arms, her legs dead weight behind her.

It wasn't until her body thudded onto the floor and my own voice shouted "Oh, my God!" that I really woke up. By the time I got to her, she had positioned herself behind the thick black-out curtain, her legs coiled into her body, her arms wrapped tightly around her chest. When I reach for her, she flinches, her eyes fixed on whatever is directly behind me. From experience, I know not to wake her, but the state she is in doesn't feel safe. I can't imagine that the shock of being woken up would be worse.

I start with the lights, the bathroom first. I crack open a five-dollar bottle of water and bring it over to her, half expecting her to be shaken from whatever state she was in. She wasn't.

I pull the curtain back to let the light find her and then I kneel down to her.

Her expression has changed. It is no longer empty, though this isn't an expression I've seen on her before. It was as childlike as she'd ever looked. She puts her hand on my knee, her touch gentle but shocking nonetheless.

"The baby is back," she says with a smile, emanating child-ish innocence.

"Okay, Jill," I reassured, hoping to sooth her.

"Go see the baby, Dad," she said, tilting her head to the side, pointing to the other side of the room.

"I will, sweetie, but let's get you in bed first."

She takes my hand trustingly and I guide her across the room. She gets into bed with no resistance. I pull the comforter up and she nestles in.

Now she radiates peacefulness. Her lips curve upward in a serene smile as she closes her eyes.

My own breathing has slowed to match hers, but I can tell that any loud noise or sudden movement would send me scurrying.

Part of me feels triumphant, like a first-time dad successfully caring for his baby alone.

As I stand to go to my side of the bed, her eyes flash open and she clenches my hand firmly in hers.

She whispers, "The baby is crying."

CHAPTER THIRTY | *Jillian*

There is something so freeing about waking up in a new bed, like you might be someone new altogether.

It makes me think about when I moved in with Will—it took a good six months to get used to his muffled snores, the way he buries his head face down into his pillow like he is suffocating himself, his always cold feet finding mine under the covers.

More than that, it was getting used to waking up to a different ceiling, a different pattern of light on the walls. Today there is something about the light in the room that reminds me we are by the lake, and it makes me smile and reach for Will.

I must have slept hard. I can't recall waking up once. At the same time, I feel heavy and weary even before I try to move. I'm lying on my side; my hip has found a niche that feels fifty feet deep. There is a bottle of water on the night table. The cap is missing. I don't remember opening it, but I wouldn't put it past Will. He's thoughtful, always. Even now.

There is tightness in my chest, and I recognize it immediately as part panic and part embarrassment. It would take a miracle for Will to look at me the same way he did before all this happened.

We didn't talk much about what I told him. He didn't press the way someone who believed me would: "Holy shit! Tell me everything." Instead, once the subject changed, my disclosed secret lay like something dead between us.

Now I try to find the sound of his breath or a subtle movement in the quiet. I close my eyes to focus on the bed, trying to block out the world waking up outside the window, the dawn winds pushing water up against the boats.

It's too quiet in here. My swallowing is amplified, and I can hear my heart beating in the ear that is pressed against the pillow.

Before I finally bring myself to roll over, I know he is gone.

I turn my head toward his side of the bed, where I hope he slept. As suspected, it's empty and cold.

He isn't in the washroom.

I find my phone plugged in next to a vacant charger. It's six, too early for breakfast. His sneakers are tucked under the desk, so he didn't go for a run. Normally I wouldn't worry, but given everything that has happened, I'm anxious.

He didn't try to kiss me goodnight. And I don't blame him. Not for anything he's done, or anything he hasn't been able to bring himself to do.

I hear someone in the hallway: slow steps, a hushed voice. I tiptoe toward the door. It's Will. I glance at my phone; yep, six o'clock. Who is he talking to? Probably his mom—she seems to have suddenly become very needy. He's whispering to be polite; he doesn't want to wake me. That's all it is.

I should freshen up, get ready so we can leave and get back to the city. I have some calls I'd like to make alone: the Ravenscliff police department (an accident report), my aunt, my dad, and maybe even my mother. Something about Cedar's death report has rattled me—not so much that it is ridiculous, but more that, suddenly, it isn't. And how could that be?

I turn to abandon my eavesdropping, but something stops me. It's not so much the words Will is saying, but how he is saying them. He's arguing, whisper-yelling. I get as close as possible and lean into the space beside the door hinges. I press my ear to the wall and just like that, Will's voice is clear:

"Why would I take her to that doctor?"

He's talking about me, he's saying these very personal, very serious things about ME—to who? More than mad, I'm scared. It reminds me too much of the phone calls my mom and dad had with Dr. X. Once again something in me cries out: "Why aren't you talking to *me*?"

He is quiet for a moment. When it's his turn to talk again, I can hear the defeat in his voice.

"How do I get her there?"

My hands tremble to the point I drop my phone. I watch it fall in slow motion, dropping an inch at a time, before I jet my foot out to cushion the blow. It feels like a brick as it crashes into the boney top of my foot before bouncing onto the floor. I'm going to explode from anger, from pain.

I breathe a forceful exhalation through my nose that temporarily grounds me enough to hold steady.

"She needs to know everything, Dad …"

Dad? Jesus, Will, what have you done?

I cup my hand over my mouth and stand frozen, scared to hear anything else.

My nerves have had it—I'm going to throw up or worse. I

run for the bathroom and close the door firmly with both hands. I rest my forehead on its cool surface while my fingers find the lock on the knob and press it in securely.

I need a plan, I know that. I have to leave, alone and fast. I flip around and slide down the door until I'm seated on the cold tile. It's as if I can't find the language to think—everything is jumbled and nothing makes any sense. I feel like I'm having a heart attack. I loosen Will's shirt by pulling it roughly at the neck, stretching it until I hear threads tear. The room is spinning.

Breathe, Jill, breathe. In and out, in … and … out. It's too much. The cognitive therapy stuff isn't working. I've tried too hard for too long. I can't handle this. I. Can't. Handle. It. My head is swirling, I'm seasick and I'm heartbroken.

My vision is blurring and there are two toilets swallowed up by a dark aura, cinching in the borders of the picture like the end of an old movie.

I hear the door close and Will says my name. I hold my breath, wishing I had started the shower.

He's knocking on the door and panic races through my body as if he is an armed home invader rather than the man I love. My body is stressed from too much air and not enough. The dark aura grows bigger and bigger, eating everything like Pac-Man. I can feel it happening but there is nothing I can do—everything goes black.

My mom is crying again. Dad has shut their bedroom door, but I can hear her long sobs followed by quick breaths.

Aunt Jen is making spaghetti. The smell of her homemade sauce, the sautéing garlic and onion, the sizzle of ground beef, has made its way up to my room and is nearly enough to distract me. She left for a long while; went back to her life as a nurse. Curling up on her sofa without us, not watching cartoons, she joked. She left because we were happy again, the four of us. Dad was singing in the morning like he used to and Mom was playful and vibrant and filling out her beauty to the brim.

Sometimes when she held Cedar, it overflowed, spilling from her; enough for Cedar and for me.

But my aunt is back now, downstairs making spaghetti again, wearing Mom's apron.

I pray like I was taught in Sunday school. Dear God, please make Momma stop crying. Please make Momma stop crying.

"Get her out of here," she'd scream. And then Dad would shut the door. My feet in my navy-blue socks made their way down the stairs, one careful step at a time.

My father is in the kitchen now with Aunt Jen. They're hugging; dad's nose is sniffly and I almost get him a tissue to be helpful, but I don't. I can tell they don't want me to be in there. I sit on the bottom step and see Cedar's soother under the table, dust and hair clinging to the gummy part she puts in her mouth. I crouch down on all fours and snatch it. Like Dad, I wipe it on my shirt and then put it in my mouth to clean it. Then I slide it deep into my pocket because Mom won't want to see it.

Cedar's door is locked. They won't let me in there, and I don't know why. No one is talking to me. They call me sweetie, they usher me left and then right, but no one is paying any attention to me.

Where is the baby? Why has she stopped crying and cooing and doing her funny one-legged crawl? I left my doll in her room, but Aunt Jen says I'll get it back later when everything settles down.

The baby died. That's what Aunt Jen said to our neighbor, Mrs. Baxter. What baby died?

They're making me go to bed early.

Aunt Jen is taking my mom to see a doctor first thing in the morning. I hope he gives her something to stop her crying. I'm starting to miss my sister and even though my mom is here, I'm really starting to miss her too.

My sister died. Cedar. She died in her crib instead of just sleeping. Dad sat me down this morning and told me. The other babies died too. I pray to God that Cedar didn't die.

The doctor didn't help. Mom doesn't look any better. I gave her a biggggg hug like she always asks for, but she didn't hug me back. That's okay, because she is so sad. I draw her a picture, give her a rock I painted with a red heart. I tidy my room and bring my plate to the kitchen.

I'm so mad at Cedar for dying. I'm mad at God and Aunt Jen for letting Cedar die. Aunt Jen usually fixes everything. Not this time. If Cedar didn't die, Mom wouldn't be crying or taking the pills that make her so sleepy. She walked into the wall yesterday. I giggled and Dad got mad. I don't think we're supposed to laugh anymore.

I pray to God to make Cedar not be dead and I promise to be the best girl for Mom.

When I wake up, I hear Cedar crying. I tiptoe down the hall to her room. Mom is asleep in the rocking chair again, gripping Winnie the Pooh. The room is too happy to be so sad. I stretch up tall and lean over the wooden spindles.

"Mom, wake up!" I yell. I'm so excited I forget that people don't like to wake up like that.

She opens her eyes sleepily and looks at me as if she's forgotten something.

"Mom, come! Look Mom!" I pull her arm and she finally stands up.

I lead her to the crib, expecting her to scream with happiness like I did. But she doesn't. Instead, she just stares at me.

"Pick her up, Mom, she's crying."

Mom yanks her arm away from me, really hard. She tells me to stop, to just stop.

Dad is putting me to sleep tonight. Every time I tell him Cedar is back, he tells me she died. I try to explain how I know she died but that she is alive again and Mom is going to be so happy. Dad finally believes me and promises to tell Mom.

Cedar is magic. She talks to me now; just her and me in my head. Every time I tell Momma, she cries and then Dad gets mad.

The doctor comes by to see Cedar; he knows she is back. He's the only one who pays attention to her.

I think Mom is scared Cedar is going to die again. But she won't. She told me so.

The voices come first, quiet and distant, vibrating as if from the bottom of a well. My head is throbbing, a dull ache heavy above my brows. Then there's the light—the last thing I remember is the blackness overtaking everything, and now there's a blinding light. I can't squint it away. Through the glare I see an outline of Will standing above me. I realize there is a hand on my face, holding up my eyelid, one and then the other. The blaze makes my eyes water.

A stranger is calling my name. The floor is hard and cool and someone has laid a lush hotel towel across my legs. I can feel Will's t-shirt tangled up on my stomach. Something sticky is running down the side of my head and I bring my hand up to touch it—someone takes my hand and places it gently by my side. It's blood, I can smell the iron. The throbbing is now accompanied by an unmistakable sting.

"She's conscious," the voice says, talking to Will as if I'm not in the room.

Will sits down on the floor, lifts my head gently and rests it on his lap.

"Babe," he says, "you're okay."

I force my eyes open to meet his gaze.

Without thinking, I blurt, "I heard you, Will, talking to your dad. I heard everything you said."

It wasn't my intention to tell him. I intended to run, to get away from him and his plans. But then I fainted, and now he's beside me and the way he smells clouds my judgment.

"You need to rest for just a few more minutes," he says.

"I'm okay," I say, though I am not. I pull myself into a sitting position and the memories rush into my mind. Blood thrashes to the top of my head. The blackness threatens again, and I lie back down.

"Easy," he warns. I close my eyes and hope that what I'm remembering vanishes the way dreams do.

I surrender to the mandatory stillness and melt into myself.

My mind rests as Will holds my head, providing traction for my tense muscles, making room for fresh blood and clarity. It feels the way I've thought being hospitalized would feel, an excuse to quit fighting. The lightness allows me to float and daydream.

Then fear returns as I play the dream over in my mind. It's as if I'm teetering on the edge of an abyss. If I look down, I will fall.

The images are too vivid. I see the words, "Your baby sister died," come out of my father's mouth. It's as real as when I hear myself say, "She's back."

"Are you ready to try to sit up?" the paramedic asks.

I open my eyes and realize he has bandaged my cut. I can feel the pull on my skin where the tape clings to it. I need more time.

I'm afraid that I will be plunged back into the dream if I move.

It's too fucking much to think about while two giant men hover over me in a bathroom.

Though my legs are unstable, I somehow stand. Will braces me at the waist and elbow.

"I'm fine," I tell him. "This used to happen to me when I was a kid. It's just stress.

The paramedic seems relieved that this is just a spell and not a graver mystery to solve, like, did the boyfriend have something to do with the fall?

After a quick examination, he is comfortable leaving on the condition I agree to see my family doctor the next day. I sit in the armchair in front of the huge window facing the marina and the white-tipped mountains.

As instructed, Will elevates my feet onto an ottoman and

covers me with a blanket. He puts the bottle of water next to me and says he has to fill out an accident report for the hotel and will be right back.

I'm too shaky to do anything but sit and think. I hear the elevator door chime in the hallway and all the voices disappear.

The flight is as expected: Will caters to my every need and I scrutinize his behavior. I rub my temples and rest my head on his shoulder, occasionally moaning in pain.

As soon as we are in the car, I ask for Cedar's file. Will hesitates, as if he'd rather do anything else, but then reaches under his seat and hands it to me. The trip to Coal Harbour feels like it takes seconds as I look through Dr. X's notes.

My whole childhood becomes a blur and for the first time ever, the memories of Cedar and me all feel like a dream. I'm scanning through my mind quickly, attempting to sort real from fiction, as new memories tear through like a runaway train through a station.

My mother screaming, "Make her stop, goddammit!"

She was screaming about me. Cedar wasn't talking through me the way I believed—Cedar died.

Sickness floods my body. Confusion and a dizzying horror about what must have happened to me. There is too much to process.

Yet, suddenly, the fact that nothing has ever made sense, makes sense. The trauma of my mother's depression—the grief and shock of the baby's death—must have triggered a psychosis, my imaginary little sister.

It can't be real. Yet I see for the first time that my telepathic sister Cedar also couldn't have been real. The jagged lines of my past are somehow easier to follow than the ones I insisted be straight.

It's devastating and enlightening all the same, but I can't shake my mother from my mind. My insistence that Cedar was with us all the time must have made it impossible for my mother to love me. The torture I subjected her to: carrying her dead baby around on my back, insisting she was real; growing up with her and celebrating her first steps and our telepathic conversations.

Dr. X knew. Of course. There is a reason Cedar wasn't in the photo with him, that she disappeared from behind the tree and our family photos. She was never there.

I realize that the fact that she was vivid before and is now gone could mean I am getting better.

Without the medication, without my doctor, it seems that I am waking up, finally shaking off the psychosis that followed my sister's death and allowed me to cope with my mom's grief.

The idea of being so delusional is horrifying. I feel the way a person with Alzheimer's must when they regain clarity only to sink into confusion again.

I try to remember Cedar and me. I picture us playing tag, reading in our chair, her talking to me from the safety of her crib—

Now there is only me, a traumatized little girl trying desperately to make her mother happy again and somehow losing her way. I shudder as I am faced with the horrifying image of a solo child playing Ring Around the Rosie, giggling under the covers.

I am shattered by the dawning awareness of a wasted life, by all that could've been and should've been different.

When I open my eyes this time, everything is brighter.

I have a puzzle to solve. Even as I come to terms with the unreliability of my child-mind, the present comes into focus so quickly I'm overwhelmed by the questions. Cedar died at eleven months, so who is adult Cedar? Why is she after me? And what does Will's family have to do with it?

Will's near-silence is suspicious. Other than asking how I feel ("Awful.") he says nothing. We're barely in the front door when his cell phone rings. He checks it quickly and then replaces it deep in his jacket pocket.

"Who was that?" I ask, somehow knowing he will lie.

"Work. It's not important."

I nod, insist he return the call and feel the aching frustration of looking at the face of a liar you love. I need to get rid of him. I scan quickly and realize there are dozens of hiding places in our apartment: behind the books on the shelves, under the couch, the spaces I can't reach, his side of our room.

I fake hunger and send a too-eager Will out for food. Let him go conspire in peace while I attempt to uncover whatever it is he keeps hidden.

He is one step into the hallway when I lock the door. It's startling what you can put your mind to when your mind is your own.

I start with the obvious places first. The underwear drawer is just underwear. I rummage through his t-shirts and the sweaters on his shelf, folded like a Gap display. His sock drawer is so full I almost can't open it. Dress, gym and singletons all mashed together—his only concession to chaos.

I plunge my hand in and feel it right away. There is a stack of papers and envelopes buried deep under the mess. Ignoring the sock avalanche it causes, I pull it all out and head to our bed.

I leaf through nothing that cries espionage but stop at a photograph of his grandparents. Why had he kept this photo hidden? Had he known of the connection all along? Either way, the photograph makes me smile because, although the man may have cost me most of the first three decades of my life, he did so with such care. I place it down gently and open an envelope containing what looks like a year's worth of uncashed checks from Will's father. I can't imagine what money like this must feel like. I gather they're some sort of trust fund dividends. I carefully stash them back under the socks.

Moving along, I devour the hidden places in the apartment like I'm ravenous, which I am. I've wasted too much time.

I don't find anything about Will that I didn't already know. Then it dawns on me that he might stash his secrets in his car, like the cheating spouse who keeps an extra cell phone in his trunk.

Shoot. He took his keys.

I'm about to give up when I spot his MacBook. It's an invasion of privacy, true. But what kind of privacy is warranted at this point? He let me check movie times a couple of months ago when my phone was dead, so I know his password, unless he changed it. Luongo1, for the goalie he is obsessed with. I'm entering it before I've given any thought to what I might find. Other than his phone, I imagine this is as close to peering into

Will's brain as I will ever get.

His emails are open, as are his work files and bank accounts. Where to draw the line? I peruse his most recent mail, concentrating on any correspondence with his father. I read a few that don't scream betrayal, but by the third I see a trend. His father consistently requests a weekly report. Initially, it would seem a perfectly legitimate request. But the term BEHAVIOR ANALYSIS is not one I have seen used in the two years at the firm or my five years at university, other than in the single psychology course I took. Immediately, I close the window and start opening documents.

I figure that if there is anything to find, it would be inconspicuously filed. Instead, my stomach plummets as I see a batch of files saved as Jillian.

She has worked diligently to complete tasks at work …

I start opening documents wildly, one after another.

Took on two new clients …
Only consumed two glasses of wine at work dinner …
Withdrew $500 for an undisclosed purchase …
Runs seawall …
Sleepwalks into kitchen …
Calls out for Cedar again …
Throws her voice in her sleep, somehow …
Is more nervous lately …

The sound of the lock in the foyer snaps me from the screen.

I carefully click the small x at the top of each doc, then shut the laptop quietly.

"Jill," he calls as he closes the door behind him. The idea of the two of us alone in here is suddenly unsettling. I am able to get to our room without being seen.

Oh my fucking God! The cheques! Is he being paid to keep tabs on me?

Why?

I quickly cross the hall and duck into our washroom. I lock the door and start the shower. I pace in front of the mirror, gazing at myself in disbelief. That son of a bitch! That lying, manipulative bastard. Hovering just below my anger is the sensation of falling, the awareness that I've wasted two years of my life on a relationship that has always been a lie.

His electric razor stands beside his sink, a few bits of trimmed hair on the counter. This reminder of our intimacy, of my vulnerability in this game, ripples up my spine.

Is Will being paid to sleep with me?

Confronting him before I know everything is a bad play. I rule out the possibility that I could be in physical danger; Will is not a violent man. He is gentle. He is patient to a fault.

I'll need to extract more information from him and the easiest way to do that is to continue to convince him I am losing my shit. For whatever reason, to me, this means a quick shower, a French braid in my hair the way I wore it as a child, and mismatched pajamas.

I hear him come into our room. Lunch is here. I don't know how I can think about food, but I realize I'm actually hungry. I suppose I need to keep my strength up.

It's impossible to articulate the wild swings I'm feeling right now. On one hand, I'm crushed and bewildered. On the other, I feel alive and free—I understand my childhood for the first time, and it gives me a sense of power.

I stare at my reflection and find a stronger woman looking back at me. I will not lose her again.

But for now, I must keep her hidden.

"Cedar," I say, intentionally louder than the bathroom fan. "Where have you been?"

I cover my mouth and hear Will stop dead in his tracks. It feels good to be the hunter and not the hunted, or at least to be alert, aware of my stalker and calculating each move. I've got his attention, I'm certain of it, as he has not made a peep. I can picture him standing there, scared to breathe. I give him what he came for and continue: "I knew you would come back. I knew I would see you again."

As I say the words, though, I am swamped by searing pain—I loved this asshole. I can hardly stay on my feet as I think about how messed up I was, about how messed up this is.

And if I'm honest, the former Jillian was still living for the idea that Cedar was still alive. Without her—and now without Will—I am completely alone in the world. To some degree, falling in love with Will kept the need for Cedar at bay.

Hindsight is awful.

Love is blind, is blind, is blind.

"Jillian?" he calls. I recognize the tremor in his voice. Poor, weak Will.

"I'll be right out," I say, pretending to be startled. I pinch my cheeks until my eyes water. There, I look certifiable enough. When I open the door, he is standing within arm's reach.

"Who were you—"

I catch him looking behind me. I ignore him completely.

"Ever notice how our names rhyme? Jill—Will?" I stretch up and kiss his cheek. "Funny, right? What's for dinner?"

I leave the room ahead of him. He's dumbfounded. It serves him right. By the time he meets me in the kitchen I have successfully employed "the switch" he accused me of making so regularly.

"I'm going to call the police in Ravenscliff. They'll have the accident report—I know it! And that reception woman at the hospital was definitely up to something. Do you think she saw my sister? Maybe she knows her!"

I spit out questions as fast as I can without letting him talk. He is quiet, but fidgets more than I'm used to—is there something you'd like to say, Will?

Finally, he caves. "I found a doctor, babe."

"Oh?" I shove a piece of chili chicken in my mouth. "Why?"

"You said you would go." He clears his plate. He's hardly touched his food, which is a shame because Earls is his favorite.

"Could you just see him, Jill? It would be good for you to talk to someone, to talk to a doctor."

"Do you think he'd be able to help me track down Cedar's files?"

He slams the garbage shut and then apologizes for it.

"I'm sure he could but I think you should concentrate on yourself. On your sleepwalking, your fainting—"

"They're not a big deal, Will. Cedar has come back. You saw

the note she left me!"

Even though I'm acting, a small part of me realizes something big, something bigger than finding out that Cedar is dead.

I realize that if she came back once, she can come back anytime. No one has the power to stop her except me. And why would I? Who except Cedar has ever been there for me in the way I needed? The way everyone needs: wholehearted, accepting love.

Cedar doesn't have to be my dark secret—she could be my secret power.

Will excuses himself to shower. I shout to him to set up a consultation.

"Maybe it will help," I add, shrugging in pretend defeat, setting up the kill.

My surrender puts new energy in his steps. It's all I can do not to run after him and push his skeezy face into the floor.

CHAPTER THIRTY-ONE | *Will*

I hung up with my dad overcome by feelings of twisted pride and gut-churning guilt. Despite his attempt to mask his excitement, I could hear the sound of winning in his voice, the annoying forced monotone he uses when preying on the weak.

"Good job, son," he'd commended. "It's for her own good."

The appointment is set for tomorrow. Given Jill's recent behavior, I'm convinced she should see someone, but why this doctor? And I'm still no closer to knowing why my father is looking out for her. If he's interested, it's because he expects a big return on his investment.

Taking on a beautiful wife and having a son were just my father's way of ensuring his legacy, guaranteeing his inheritance, accessories in his "got it all" portfolio. I've always felt he hates my mom for being more emotionally demanding than his Rolex.

I know all this, know that he is not looking out for Jill's best anything, and yet here I am smirking at myself in the mirror, proud to have temporarily won his fair-weather approval.

Something has changed in Jillian since our trip. It's as if she has become someone else altogether. She's flighty where she was once strong, unguarded to the point of plainly exhibiting her hallucinations, talking to her sister in the bathroom like two girls giggling at a party.

I wavered before, the whole trip home really. How could I trust my father with this fragile woman I love?

When I had the chance, however, I didn't ask him why he has someone following Jill, or why he has her file. I didn't ask why he spent all of my mother's money.

It's my way of staying innocent in all of this. If I don't know for certain, then how can I be blamed?

Since we've been back in the condo, Jill has made it so clear she needs help, and my father is offering it to her. It can be that simple. He said so himself. All I have to do is make sure she gets to the appointment and tell the doctor she has been talking to her dead sister, to Cedar.

I'm nervous that he will sell me out to her. That at some point during the appointment, my father will storm in and tell Jill I've been reporting on her behavior for our entire relationship. When I think of it in those terms, I know it's hopeless. But there is still something in me that hopes to bury that secret so deep Jill will never know, so our kids will never know.

But like Cedar, secrets don't stay buried long. It's a matter of time before everything I've done is revealed.

Once upon a time there was a girl named Jill. She was loved dearly, but not enough to be kept safe. Her parents crushed her with lies and loss and sent her away but still she grew up strong. One day she fell in love, but sadly, her lover sold her secrets to the highest bidder.

Whatever happens, though, I won't leave her alone. If she'll have me, I'll sit right next to her and make sure no one hurts her. My grandfather's love for Grandma was so obvious people knew instantly they were a team, not the type of couple you could tease, no ole ball and chain jokes permitted. They had each other's backs. My father hated this, claimed there was no point talking to either of them separately because you'd never get an answer unless they were together. I always thought I would be more like my grandfather, not only in his kindness but in his commitment to the people he loved.

But it seems I am not like him at all. I've failed the very first person who chose to love me.

I hear the front door slam louder than normal, which suggests Jill is in a hurry or purposely slammed it. Either way it makes me run. I catch her just as the elevator is about to close.

"I need some air. I'll be on the sea …"

The doors come together as if they're protecting her, like a bouncer turning me away from a club. The elevator knows best. She didn't fumble for the button to hold the door—she didn't want me to join her. She needs to think and truthfully, I'm exhausted.

Can I trust her out there? That she won't do something … stupid?

I walk through the apartment on autopilot. I catch myself at the sink filling the kettle, not remembering when I decided tea would help. My mind is preoccupied with worry and guilt and a parade of intrusive what-ifs. I turn the burner on; it clicks twice and ignites. Step one, two, three. Things can be that easy. But not if I stay with Jill. There will always be this worry, this unnerving sense that anything can happen, that I will be found out, that she will really lose it.

Thanks to my mom, I'm comfortable with a drunk. Tucking her in and learning how to enjoy the moments between slurs and outbursts. I don't know how to handle whatever this is.

My cup burns the palms of my hands, but I only grip it harder. For some reason the harder I hold on, the more it scalds, the clearer my thoughts are. I carry it to the window and peer out into the darkness of the water. I picture Jill seated on the floor in our apartment, surrounded by pastel toys and stuffed animals, our child, barely able to sit, beside her. The thought makes me unimaginably happy. My family. My wife. She will get better. I will make sure she does. The thought of turning my back on her, on the cruelty of debating the pros and cons of her …

Then I see her. She's directly below our building, sitting on a bench beneath a lamppost. It lights her up like a spotlight. It's a black and white musical, as if she'll jump up and start a rendition of *Singing in the Rain* at any moment. She doesn't. I interpret her body language as sad—she is slumped, gazing out into the night just as I am. She's alone. I'm ashamed she is out there in the cold, that I have driven her to that spot on the damp bench instead of here beside me, her hands wrapped around her own mug, mine around hers.

If only I were inside the coffee shop behind her as she waits for my return with treats. But I am up here.

I am nearly out the door—in my mind I am already running to her—when I pause and see that she isn't sad at all. She's leaning forward on the bench, as if she is talking intently with someone beside her. She throws her head back as if in laughter;

her hands move like they're telling a story. I can't see her lips moving but I know immediately she is speaking to Cedar. I hold my fist in front of my mouth, looking down at the scene in disbelief. This isn't happening. To overhear it, to suspect it is happening, is a lot less disturbing than seeing someone you love talking to someone who isn't there.

She stands and I'm relieved it's over, but then she brings her arms up in a mime's embrace. If I concentrate enough, through the drops of rain on the window, I can almost see the faint outline of her ghostly sister hugging her back.

This is what my father was waiting for. This is the behavior he scanned my reports for glimpses of. Evidence that Jill is psychotic. And she is.

CHAPTER THIRTY-TWO | *Aaron*

I couldn't be prouder of William. I hated to put the kid in this situation, I really did, but my father left me no choice.

Sure, I made some investments that didn't work out—not entirely unheard of in my line of work. Disappointing, yes of course. Devastating? No. No one of my experience takes risks without a back-up plan.

A few regrettable decisions were made after a lifetime of conservatively moving money, of buying and selling at the right times, of continuing to build the Sutherby fortune. For this, I should be punished? I should face financial ruin? No way!

So yes, I was disappointed in the outcome of some recent investments, but it was our money, my problem to fix. It wasn't like I'd taken risks with clients' money.

My contingency plan, my father's estate, has been ticking along conservatively since his death. It was only when I tried to unwind the various trusts that his lawyer handed over the documents that put this latest mess in motion.

I'm guilty of nothing except misjudging my father. The key to every good back-up plan is access to more money—how could

I guess that my father thought leaving the bulk of his estate to a handful of mentally ill patients was noble?

I'm a money manager. I realize I should've asked more questions as soon as my father died, invited his lawyer for a drink at the club. But I didn't. I trusted my father's judgment and his love for his family. For his grandson. We'd set up everything in trusts so nothing would have to be done when my father died.

But when I needed the capital, I realized what he had done only a page or two into the trust documents.

These were not just tax shelters, they were completely separate accounts—as in, not ours. The biggest one—the account I had intentions of collapsing first, the one I carried around under my cap as a fallback plan, now holds five million dollars. That five million made it possible for me to invest aggressively with my wife's money and the money I had set aside for Will.

But as I would learn, it turns out this account only becomes mine if his longest-term patient, a woman named Jillian Gannon, is not mentally well. If she is, if the Sutherby Method treatment worked over the long term, she inherits five million dollars when his team's final research project is published. According to my father, he felt obliged to cover the cost of a comfortable life that will let her stay out of the way of any journalists trying to track down Patient No. 1.

If she demonstrates any symptoms of psychosis in the two years prior to publication, the research is not to be published, and she and his other patients in the project receive a few hundred thousand dollars each for their participation.

My fingers tingled and I sat holding my chest, not knowing if I should fear death or welcome it.

I've since learned more about the Sutherby Method. It's of potentially miraculous benefit to children who exhibit symptoms of treatment-resistant Dissociative Personality Disorder and other trauma-related psychoses. If cognitive behavioral treatments are ineffective, the patient is subjected to a carefully supervised trauma that mimics the initial trauma that led to the development of their disorder. In the case of Jillian [Cedar] Gannon, her DID was successfully eliminated following the constructed traumatic event. With continued therapy following the guidelines detailed in the Sutherby Method, Gannon was supposedly cured of her formerly crippling DID. She went on to successfully attend university and become something of a financial analyst prodigy. Although Gannon was only one of multiple patients to recover with the Sutherby Method, she was the first, and underwent the greatest degree of risk.

If she remains healthy until my father's research team is ready to publish their work, now just months away, she will become the beneficiary of the five-million-dollar trust after the other patients each receive a hundred thousand dollars.

My father never failed to pull the rug out from under me when I needed him, so I find all this out only when I need that money to save my family from financial ruin. Because who would fucking dream that their parent would give their family's money to *his patients*.

After recovering from the shock and rage, I eventually realize my work is cut out for me. He's given me an out, and I tell myself he did it because, on some level, he knew what he was doing was stupid and cruel.

All I have to do is prove that Jillian Gannon continues to

suffer from a dissociative disorder and most of the trust reverts to our family. My father's work with the Forksdale research team will never be published.

I do feel for her. Any my son. They seem to care for each other, but they'll both recover.

The truth remains—this is not her money.

As much as she meant to my father, whatever her recovery might contribute to other patients and my father's legacy—the money is rightfully ours.

Finding a woman who looked like her wasn't hard. All beautiful women look more or less the same, with variations of hair, eye and skin color. I called a modeling agency and sent over a photo I took over dinner at our house; they sent me profiles of women who could absolutely look like her sister.

I had people strategically placed to whisper Jillian's name, to break into her apartment, to go through her storage. And who could have predicted hitting the jackpot with those socks full of pills?

It was not without commitment and excellent research that this has all come together.

CHAPTER THIRTY-THREE | *Jillian & Cedar*

I make sure to wake up before Will. Surprisingly, I slept fine—great even.

Sleeping with the enemy is easier when you become the enemy yourself. This whole ordeal is not funny, it's not ideal and it certainly is not romantic. It may even be cruel. However, I have no choice but to see how this unfolds, to see why Will would do this to me. And so, I begin the day with little changes, more for me than Will, to help set the mood. I wear my hair up, tight. A sleek ponytail and red lipstick in lieu of loose and light. Instead of seeing Cedar, of carrying on the charade of speaking to Cedar, of hearing her, today I will be Cedar.

I wait until I hear him get out of bed, planting his feet heavily on the hardwood like he's woken with a sense of urgency. It's my cue.

Trancelike, I cross the room with my eyes focused on the window and run my fingers over the linen drapes as he says my name. I ignore him until he puts his hand on my waist, then turn to him, look in his eyes and tell him how lovely it is to see him again.

"A lot has changed since the last time we were together," I say.

He's puzzled. His mouth rolls into a half smile; he thinks I am joking, playing at something.

I push past him and leave him to imagine whatever he will. He stays in place, dumbfounded.

I want so badly to be out of this apartment. I thought about packing while he slept, sneaking out and leaving him as far behind me as possible within this small city—because leaving Vancouver and everything I have worked so hard to accomplish is not an option.

But I can't imagine leaving him without answers. This whole thing is a sickening déjà vu.

He does his best to move through the morning like everything is as it always was, which only proves my plan is working. If he were worried, he would have been asking questions, following me around and catering to my fragility. Those days are over, I guess.

I make sure to ask and then re-ask him where we are going, but I don't give him the satisfaction of objecting or questioning him, regardless of how fun it might be to watch him try and explain it.

In the car, we both become unnaturally quiet. I am still but Will's knee shakes, an irritating vibration. I try to silence it with my hand, but it only transfers the motion to the other leg.

Is it worry that makes you so nervous, dear?

Or is it guilt?

I long to dig my nails into the sensitive skin on his inner thigh.

It hasn't occurred to me to be nervous. It's not as though he could have me committed; I pose no danger to others or myself, nor have I behaved in any way that would cause anyone other than Will to worry about me. Basically, other than my five-minute mishap at my office, it's his word against mine, and no one at the office would risk negative attention.

As we pull up to what looks more like a law firm than a medical office, I see Aaron standing on the curb with another man. They're both dressed in business attire; the fellow I haven't seen before is holding a briefcase.

It dawns on me how unlike Dr. X Will's father is—opposites, really. Aaron is intimidating and calculating. Right down to the way he stands, one step above the mystery man. I don't know why, but I focus on the briefcase. It's unexpected, and it worries me. I have a plan and I shouldn't deviate from it, even if it looks like I might have underestimated the whole situation.

I'm guessing Will and his father have somehow decided to trap me into saying something to support Dr. X's work. Or maybe this is all part of the work, tying up loose research ends. All I know for sure is that I'm here because they want something from me.

My plan is to give the people what they want, find out what their motivation is and then get the hell out, as far away from this family as possible.

But I didn't anticipate that briefcase. Suddenly this feels like much more than a simple psychiatric meet and greet.

Will pulls up and parks illegally in front of the building, squarely at his father's feet.

My outfit is so out of character I realize I don't know how to wear it: the jeans are too tight, and the turtleneck is strangling me. I remind myself it's okay, because everything is foreign.

My boyfriend is a stranger, and my future is a blank slate.

A little discomfort is okay—because I'm not Jillian right now.

He opens the door and her legs make an appearance first. She slides them gracefully from the car, her knees pressed together and angled to the side like a lady. She places her heels firmly on the sidewalk before reaching for Will's hand.

She allows him to escort her up the stairs, not as the broken girl they are expecting but rather as a queen entering her court. She isn't nervous, the way Jill would be.

She introduces herself to the man with the briefcase: "Hi, I'm Cedar Gannon." Cleverly, she winks.

Will and his father exchange glances, and she notices the slightest smirk, a sparkle of triumph, in Aaron Sutherby's eyes. She buries the sting of betrayal down deep; she can't allow Jillian to think about that right now. The man she loved, and the man she thought she would call Dad someday, her children's grandpa. She turns to him and offers her hand.

"Lovely to meet you too," she says, her handshake is firm.

"Jillian … or is it Cedar, you said?" Aaron coyly makes the correction and looks to Will for affirmation. She says nothing. She does her best Cedar and stares into their souls.

Aaron clears his throat uncomfortably, "This is Mr. Barnes. He does some work for us—he is just here to make sure there are no hiccups with insurance and such."

And such? Liar! Jillian wants to scream but is silenced by her sister. As Cedar, she smiles politely but adds firmly that she has her own insurance.

Aaron doesn't press, but steps aside and offers a chivalrous, "After you."

If she is worried about blindly crossing the threshold to the next step, you wouldn't know it.

The reception area is empty when she confidently enters the room, save a woman behind a beautiful mahogany desk. A stylishly costumed Cedar sits before she is greeted and allows the men to do the talking, the paperwork.

Will must feel somewhat blindsided by all this, she thinks, as she observes him faltering in the shadow of his smooth-talking father.

But she can't worry about his feelings—she doesn't know him, after all, and neither does Jillian. A Dr. Miller introduces himself. Something about the slump in his shoulders, the lack of douchebag vibe, tells her he isn't part of the gang. His smile turns from tight and cordial to softly concerned when his eyes meet hers.

"Hello," he says, sitting in the chair beside her. He has a clip-board and asks her to sign a document, a disclosure agreement—he encourages her to read it first, seems to almost plead for her to pay attention. She finds Will's eyes, gives him a chance to stop all of this, to cease fire, to end this incredible invasion of privacy. But he looks away. He stands still, his tall stature now small in every regard. She wonders why Jillian ever found him attractive. Against the doctor's advice, she signs the form, making sure to shield her writing but emphasizing the J in Jillian.

Will, his father and the man that seems to be Aaron's lawyer seat themselves outside of the doctor's office like security. The doctor holds the door and Cedar enters the room to become Jillian again.

It's a cozy room with a lit fireplace that neutralizes the dampness of the city. I immediately feel like myself again. The doctor offers the couch, but I sit in one of the two chairs across from his desk. This feels more like a business meeting than a therapy appointment.

"Your family is worried you have begun to see your sister Cedar again?" He pauses briefly, without giving me time to reply.

"I have your file here." He looks up and offers a kind smile. "You spent some time in Forksdale Hospital when you were younger?"

I adjust my posture and free my hair from its tight binding, sensing the beginning of a ponytail headache. I inhale deeply before I answer.

"Do you mean Will and Aaron Sutherby? They are not my family. But yes, I have spent time in a hospital. I was traumatized by my younger sister's crib death and created a relationship with her in my mind—at the time, I must have really needed someone, her."

The doctor leans back in his chair without saying anything, though he nods his head, encouraging me to continue.

"It took a long time, and I'd be lying if I said I understood it all, or even remembered when I got better, but I do know my sister died when she was a baby. And no, I have not been seeing my sister again."

He straightens, frowns slightly and leafs quickly through the file on his desk. "Why do you think you are here, then?"

"Honestly, I don't know. I have only recently found out that my boyfriend, William Sutherby, is the grandson of my doctor from Forksdale—and I suspect that he and his father hired a woman who resembles me to follow me around, appearing on my route home from work, at my office and even in my home-town, trying to convince me she was my adult sister."

I shrug my shoulders, careful not to fidget because I know this all sounds ridiculous too.

His expression is flat. "Do you know anything about the treatment you received at the Forksdale Hospital for Children?"

"Umm—well, not the particulars. But I do remember an event, a hoax I guess, that may have contributed to my recovery."

He nods again. "Yes. That event you remember is actually an important element of a treatment your doctor, Xavier Sutherby, developed. Because of its success rate with formerly untreatable cases, including yours, his team's research is about to be pub-lished."

"Is that why I am here?" I interject.

"You're here because I've been appointed to examine you by the trustees of a fund that Xavier Sutherby set up before his death for some of his patients. I'll explain more in a moment, but first I want to talk more about Cedar.

"You say that you understand that Cedar died as a baby. But Will and Aaron Sutherby told me that you regularly talk to Cedar, have seen her at least three times recently and are obsessed with finding her. Are you telling me the Sutherbys hired someone who could be Cedar, and that is who you've seen?"

Without waiting for an answer, he goes back to pages of the file in front of him.

"Were you ever treated for paranoid delusions, Jillian?"

"Dr. Miller, honestly, I understand that this sounds paranoid." I reach into my tote bag. "That's why I brought Will's computer, where I found emails between him and Aaron and a file of many reports Will sent Aaron about me over the two years of our relationship. As you can imagine, I'm devastated."

I clicked on the file labelled Jillian, and then on one of Will's emails to his dad, swiveling the laptop to show Dr. Miller the screen.

I clear my throat and let tears well into my eyes. "I started to suspect Will was lying to me and that it had something to do with his dad, so I checked his computer to see if I could find out more. I played along because it seemed like the best way to find out why he would do this to me."

He stands to hand me a glass of water and then sits on the corner of his desk while I take a long sip.

"I think we should call the police," he says as I lower the glass.

"The police? Why would we—"

"There may be more involved in this than you and I know. I don't know how the Sutherbys will handle it when I tell them I've found you to be of completely sound mind. There will have to be an investigation, of course, but it sounds to me as if they may have tried to subvert the terms of the trust."

"What do you mean? What more could be involved?" I feel a sense of doom. I should never have stayed once I realized what was going on.

"When I attest to your continued recovery, Jillian, you stand to receive a trust worth millions of dollars." His face is serious, sincere.

"What? Why?" I'm unable to comprehend if this is real or yet another Sutherby mind-fuck.

"Well, to be frank, I had been led to believe you were experiencing regular delusions, so I was focused more on getting you the help you needed rather than on the agreement. What I do know is that Dr. Sutherby wanted to protect you from any unwanted attention when his work was published. I mean, your name wouldn't be released, of course, but we know the press has a way of tracking these things down and he didn't want you to feel vulnerable to that type of exposure.

"He left you enough to do whatever you want, to go somewhere else, for the rest of your life.

"But if it turned out that you weren't well, that the remission didn't last, then the work won't be published. And you can continue your life without any risk of becoming known as the first Sutherby Method patient. After some much smaller payouts to the study participants, the trust reverts to the Sutherby family."

For a minute, I'm stunned silent. I don't know how to respond. I'm so angry at Dr. X, I'm tempted to undo this entire appointment, to wake up Cedar for a surprise appearance to sabotage his study. But I quickly remind myself it's not him I am angry with. Dr. X cared about his work, yes, but he also cared about me. Why else would he do this?

Finally, the why in all of this becomes clear. Will and his father want the money. The two of them were willing to discredit their father and grandfather's work, to ruin my life and my career. For money.

"Yes. Call the police, please," I finally say.

CHAPTER THIRTY-FOUR | *Will*

They come into the office like a high-school football team hitting the field, confident, cocky, focused. We take them in, from their uniforms to their hardened, closed faces.

I assumed what I imagined to be the worst cast scenario, that Jillian had done something in that office, something Dr. Miller saw as harmful— perhaps to herself, perhaps to him.

My palms grew so sticky I had to run them down the sides of my jeans every few minutes. I thought of Jill carefully hanging my jeans to dry for me so they didn't shrink, and I felt the pressure of tears welling up behind my eyes.

There were no sounds of distress, no screams or toppled chairs. The doctor didn't stick his head out the door to give us an explanation. No one spoke. We held our breaths and tried harder to hear what was going on in the other room, what the youngest police officer was very quietly saying to the receptionist.

How could I have allowed this to happen? I saw the look she flashed me before she signed that form, a look that asked for help, for me to intervene. I did nothing but stand there, clenching my fists into sweaty balls of betrayal.

Father didn't prepare me for anything like this. He didn't say there would be lawyers and doctors and police. And like the shitty partner I am, I let Jill sign something without offering to read it first.

Instead, I watched. Now it looks like they have come to take her away to a hospital she shouldn't be in, to a hold that will undermine her accomplishments and haunt her future.

I can feel the acid sloshing wildly in my empty stomach, stirred with anxiety. I fight the urge to throw up and swallow air like water. For some reason, my father looks just as nervous. His face is white and beads of sweat are forming above his brows. This uncertainty makes everything so much worse, particularly when he stands abruptly, and demands, "What's going on?"

The young policeman tells him to sit and says that they'll deal with us later. Jesus. My father offers me an open-mouthed shrug. He looks like a little boy caught with his father's booze. Something in the way the officer looks at us shakes me—instead of looking at us like traumatized family members, I see disgust.

What have we done?

They disappear into the office, through the same doorway that Jill walked through without looking back after giving me every opportunity to help her.

When the door closes behind them, the lawyer Dad introduced as an insurance guy stands to leave. "I'm sorry, Aaron, I can't be involved in this," he says.

"Simon—"my father begins, but then halts, as if he thinks better of it. "Yes, you should go."

"What the hell is going on, Dad?"

"I'll explain it to you later, Will. Everything will be fine—just sit down for Christ's sake!"

Just then the door reopens and the officers escort Jill past us. One is in front of her and the other is close behind, but she is leaving with them willingly.

"Jill," I call out, attempting to rush to her side. But it's too late. They won't let me anywhere near her, and she won't look at me.

The doctor is speaking to my father but all I can hear is the sound of Jill's name rolling off my tongue the way it has thousands of times before. Just before they leave, she throws me a look, the first real look I've seen from her in maybe days. It is cold, ice cold—and worse, it's indifferent.

I know instantly what she has done.

The moments that come after are even more terrible. I am told that Jill, in the company of her police escort, is removing all of her belonging from our shared condo, from our home.

I am given the choice of waiting in the office or in a jail cell. I dial her number as soon as I am able to, but I'm not surprised when it goes right to voicemail. I plead with her machine, tell her I don't know what is going on, beg her to forgive me, to give me a chance to explain …

Even before the beep puts an end to my whining, I know it is hopeless—there is no way Jill would or should ever forgive me.

I don't want to hear my father's explanations in the same way Jill won't hear mine.

He leaves me messages that are more desperate than I expected. He's angry about Jill's refusal to let us scam her, he is sorry about how things shook out, but, he says, she wasn't for me.

He has a plan to get the money back …

It's my mother's reaction to it all that has proven the most shocking. Almost as soon as Jill left, she came to stay with me, with Mae tagging along. It wasn't the money, she'd said. It was the realization, finally, that the man she married was never coming back, and in his place was a man so lost in greed and ego he would never understand what he'd done to his family. To his wife, his father, his son and the woman his son loves.

What baffles me now is how I find myself pitying him—how lost he is without my mother despite ignoring and tormenting her for all those years. I think of him late at night, lying in bed, an old man left alone to remember to take his heart medicine, missing his family.

I feel an overwhelming need to reach out, to check in. But then I roll over in my own bed and her side is empty, as is her closet, her bathroom drawer and the way my heart feels each time I catch a glimpse of myself.

Most nights, after I rehash everything he has done, I'm able to whisper a chilly, "Fuck you, Dad," and then fall asleep.

CHAPTER THIRTY-FIVE | *Cedar*

Jill needed a break. Her hands trembled like she was freezing as she shook the hands of the men who got her safely tucked into the Georgia Hotel.

I can't blame her for her lethargy, sitting on the foot of the luxury bed, staring into space for hours, staying in the safety of the room for days.

At some point, she must have realized how much she needed a rest, to just go away for a little while the way people do after breakups or losing a job. She'd taken the lead for so long, kept her face forward and accomplished more than anyone could have expected. But Jill had to try to be strong and what doesn't come naturally is exhausting.

One morning, I woke up and she kept sleeping.

The money Dr. X left us appeared in my account two months later, but it didn't impress me as much as you would think. Still, I was able to resign from Jillybean's job and put a sizable down payment on a new condo, a nice two bedroom with a view of the ocean on the other side of the Lion's Gate Bridge. It seemed a fitting change, crossing the bridge. I don't know if I'll ever work again, or if I'll just live off the dividends of our now wisely invested inheritance. I'll decide later.

The switch came easily, like everything else was a dress rehearsal and this is the real show.

I called my parents and apologized for everything we put them through—told them of my epiphany.

I'll go see them soon. They'll be so proud, so relieved by their daughter's stability. They will be able to sleep easier, with lighter hearts and peaceful dreams.

As for William, I've seen him a few times around town. He looks awful as he takes his afternoon strolls through the rain, in this city full of people on their phones.

Yet I am drawn to him, unable to drown out Jill's feelings for him entirely. They must have been powerful, even though he is clearly such a weak man.

Who knows? I might give Will another chance one day. Jillian needed someone stronger, someone who knew whose side he was on.

Me?

I just need someone who takes direction well and doesn't bore me in bed.

Will might do.

ABOUT THE AUTHOR

KATIE BIEKSA grew up in Ontario, Canada. She graduated from Brock University with degrees in English Literature and Women's Studies. She lives in Newport Beach, California with her husband, Kevin, and children, Cole and Reese.

Award Winning Author of Newport Jane